LARGE PRINT BLO
Block, Lawrence.
Tanner on ice : an Evan
Tanner

LARGE PRINT BLO
Block, Lawrence
Tanner on ice

M
82

DATE		ISSUED TO	
	AP 1 1/06		1/06
	AP 2 2/06		
FEB 0 9 2009		F Colton	

Tanner on Ice

Lawrence Block

Tanner on Ice

An Evan Tanner Novel

WHEELER
PUBLISHING, INC.
ROCKLAND, MA

★ AN AMERICAN COMPANY ★

Published in Large Print by arrangement with Dutton, an imprint of Dutton
NAL, a member of Penguin Putnam Inc., in the United States and Canada.

Wheeler Large Print Book Series.

Set in 16 pt Plantin.

Library of Congress Cataloging-in-Publication Data

Block, Lawrence.
    Tanner on ice: an Evan Tanner novel / Lawrence Block.
      p. (large print) cm.(Wheeler large print book series)
    ISBN 1-56895-701-7 (hardcover)
    1. Tanner, Evan (Fictitious character)—Fiction. 2. Smuggling—
Burma—Fiction. 3. Rangoon (Burma)—Fiction. 4. Large type books.
I. Title. II. Series
[PS3552.L63T36 1999]
813'.54—dc21

99-19133
CIP

This one's for
Brett Pouliot

ACKNOWLEDGMENTS

The author is pleased to acknowledge the Listowel Arms Hotel, in Listowel, County Kerry, where this book was written. He is grateful, too, to Miriam Balmuth, Beverly Barsook, Ellen Benjamin, Ingeborg and Cody Engle, Jo Harberson, Lee and Wilson Harwood, Julia and Howard Klee, Margaret Milledge, Paul Smith, and Davida Tussman, brave travelers on the Burma Road, to Bob Schulte, and to Maren Rae and U Myint Oo.

Tanner's return owes something, too, to the unflagging enthusiasm of those who knew him when, and who begged for a reappearance. Thanks to all of you, and especially to George Fowler.

And thanks to Sharon Nettles.

Chapter One

I flew from New York to Los Angeles, then nonstop to Seoul. I had a few hours before my flight to Bangkok, and I rode a shuttle bus into downtown Seoul, walked around, snacked on fried shrimp, drank a beer, and caught a bus back to the airport. Nothing looked remotely familiar, but then it had been quite a while since I'd been in Korea. I hadn't spent much time in Seoul, but this time around it was noisy and bustling and furiously modern, a far cry from the Korean cities and villages I remembered.

This time around, too, nobody was shooting at me. There were no Chinese soldiers blowing bugles, no artillery rounds whistling overhead.

I have to say it makes a change.

I'd reset my watch in L.A. and in Seoul, and I reset it again a few hours later in Bangkok. By then I'd lost track of what time it was in New York, and, since there was nobody I wanted to phone, I didn't much care. It was three in the afternoon in Bangkok, and that was all I had to know. It was a half hour earlier in Rangoon, if I remembered correctly, but I would cross that time zone when I came to it.

1

My only luggage was the day pack I'd carried aboard the plane with me, and all it held was a clean shirt and a change of socks and underwear. My toothbrush and razor and such rode in the Kangaroo pouch clasped around my waist, along with my Swiss Army knife. I had some cash in a money belt under my Gap khakis, and once I'd cleared Customs and Immigration I ducked into a men's room and slipped my passport in there as well. Then I ran a gauntlet of overeager cab drivers, took a train to a spot where I could catch a water taxi, and floated on into Bangkok.

I'd been there before, and more recently than I'd been to Seoul. Late sixties, say. Thirty years ago, according to the calendar. Less than a fifth as long by the clock in my head.

Overhead, the sun burned in the afternoon sky. I welcomed it. A breeze off the water had a cooling effect, and of course I had the deep internal chill that was always with me. The sun might give me a burn—I really should have put on sunscreen—but in the meantime it felt good.

Other boats kept pulling up alongside my water taxi, full of people who wanted to sell me something. They all spoke some sort of English, though not one of them was ready to hire on as an announcer for the BBC. I got tired of saying no—to opium weights and ivory carvings, to pictures on rice paper, to rubies that were probably cut glass and lapis that was probably dyed, to bright-eyed offers of male and female companionship. "Very young," I was assured. "Very clean."

2

"No," I kept saying, in English. "No, thank you. I am not interested. No, thanks all the same, but no."

"Maybe you like better to watch," one thoughtful young man suggested, leaning forward and gripping the side of my water taxi. "Two girls together? Boy and girl? Two boys?"

"No, thank you, but—"

"Girl and a dog together. Very popular show, all the tourists like very much. Japanese businessmen, very wealthy, they all love this show."

"Good for them," I said.

"Oh, yes," he said. "Is very good for them. Is good for you, too. Girl is seven, eight years old, has never been with a man."

"Just with dogs."

"You like, after show is over, you can have the girl."

"Suppose I'd rather have the dog?"

"Girl, dog, whatever you want. Both, if you want."

In Thai I said, "All I want is for you to fuck off and leave me alone."

His eyes widened. My Thai is reasonably fluent, although I have a little trouble with the written language, which comes with an alphabet that makes my eyes cross. Thais never expect you to speak their language. (Nobody does, really, except the French, who expect you to speak it badly.) More to the point, they don't expect you to *understand* their language, and I have often acquired useful information as a result. I've thus learned to keep my linguistic ability a secret, and here I'd gone and tipped my hand to a floating pimp.

No harm in that, I decided. Who was he going to tell? He drifted off to plague someone else, and an old woman selling horoscopes and teak carvings took his place, and I defended myself once more in English. "No," I said. "Not today. I don't want any. Thank you. No."

The teahouse was where it was supposed to be, just across the street from the Swan Hotel and a stone's throw from the Grand Palace. There was a skanky-looking tobbo shop to its right, a store overflowing with electronic gear to its left.

I walked into the teahouse, and at first I thought it was empty save for the tired waitress leaning against the counter. Then my eyes adjusted to the dim lighting, and I saw the sole customer seated at a table against the back wall. He was smoking a cigarette and drinking a Kloster beer, and he raised his eyes at my approach but kept his seat.

I said, "Mr. Sukhumvit?"

"Yes?"

In Thai I said, "Today the Chao Phraya swarms with crocodiles."

In Thai he replied, "Elephants on the highway, crocodiles in the river."

We both smiled, and he got to his feet. He was on the tall side for a Thai, around five-nine, and lean as a sapling. He wore black pants and a shortsleeve khaki shirt, and his forearms were wiry and muscular. He had a mustache and goatee, the latter consisting of a half-inch band running down the center of his chin.

"Tanner," he said. "Welcome to Bangkok." We shook hands. "Recognition signals are ridiculous, aren't they? Crocodiles and elephants. Schoolboy nonsense."

"My sentiments exactly."

"And inadequate in the bargain. Suppose you show me your passport so that I can be confident you are truly yourself."

I went to the men's room, retrieved the passport from my money belt. When I got back to Sukhumvit's table there were two fresh bottles of beer on it, and a bowl of peanuts. I gave him my passport and poured myself some beer while he squinted at it, looking at my photo and at me, reading everything the passport had to say about me. Then, with a quick smile, he folded it and handed it back to me.

"You are enjoying Bangkok, Tanner?"

"I just got here."

"You speak the language well."

"Thank you," I said. "I'm pretty good with languages."

"How's your Burmese?"

"Not as good as my Thai."

"You've been to Burma?"

"No."

"Fascinating country. Cut off from the world all these years. You'll find Rangoon very different from Bangkok."

5

"I can imagine."

"Of course, it's Yangon now. And the whole country is Myanmar. But no one outside the government calls it that."

"So I understand."

He helped himself to a handful of peanuts, chewed thoughtfully, drank beer. He said, "You've been to Bangkok before."

"Not recently."

"No, not since that passport was issued. Do you find it changed much?"

"A lot of new construction, from the looks of things."

"Yes."

"And it seems to me the traffic is worse."

"It is worse each year than the year before."

"And there was a war going on the last time I was here," I said, "and *that's* over with."

"Not a war in Thailand."

"No, of course not."

"In Vietnam, you must mean."

"Yes."

He frowned. "But how can that be? It says on your passport that you were born in 1958. Americans were not drafted until the age of eighteen, is that not so? And the last American troops left Vietnam well before your eighteenth birthday."

"I lied about my age," I said.

"Ah. And volunteered for service."

"Yes."

"And fought boys younger than yourself," he said. "In the Vietcong, an eighteen-year-old was a grizzled veteran. If he was still alive. And in the hill tribes of Burma, the children fight alongside their parents. The Shan, the Kachins. The Kareni."

"Yes."

"But childhood itself is a Western invention, don't you think? Childhood as a time of innocence. Only the fortunate get to have such a childhood in this part of the world. The rest are not so innocent." He lit a cigarette, pursed his lips, blew smoke at the ceiling. "You know how a Thai girl celebrates her eighteenth birthday?"

"How?"

"She puts her daughter on the street."

I drank some more beer. I'd had Thai beer in New York, a brand called Singha, but I'd never even heard of Kloster, which tasted like a German beer—Beck's, say—but lighter. It wasn't bad.

I said, "On the river I was offered the opportunity to watch a seven-year-old girl have sex with a dog."

"And you passed it up, eh?"

"So that I could meet with you."

"I am honored," he said. "But it is upsetting to many people, this business of child prostitution. For myself, I would not want a partner of such an age. I prefer a woman who knows what to do. Although some of these children learn quickly."

"I imagine they do."

"But for most of their customers they are best advised to appear ignorant and

7

inexperienced. We get whole planeloads of men on organized sex tours, you know. Americans and Europeans and Japanese. Some want boys and some want girls and some don't seem to care. It is curious, isn't it?"

"Yes."

"Of course, the U.N. wants to put a stop to it. And now I suppose the SPCA will stick its nose in as well, saying it is cruel to the dogs. You want another beer?"

"Not just now."

"You go to Rangoon first thing in the morning, don't you? Do you have a hotel yet?"

I didn't have one because I wouldn't need one, but he didn't have to know that. "Out at the airport," I said.

"The Amari? A good choice. Will you want to have an early night? Bangkok's twelve hours different from New York, so I don't know how you stand on jet lag."

"I'm all right."

"You were able to sleep on the plane?"

"Off and on," I said.

He stroked his vertical stripe of a beard. "Forgive me for saying so," he said, "but you look a little peaked."

"Probably jet lag."

"You feel all right?"

"Well, I'm a little chilled," I said, "but other than that—"

"Chilled?"

"A little, but—"

"But it's a hot afternoon. The tempera-

8

ture is well over thirty degrees. That would make it close to ninety degrees Fahrenheit."

"That sounds about right."

"As a matter of fact," he said, "you're perspiring. So how can you be feeling a chill?"

"I'm sure it's part of the jet lag," I said. "And you're right, it does feel warm in here, and I am perspiring. It's more an internal sort of a chill."

"Internal."

"And it's no big deal," I said. "I can live with it."

"What you need," he said, "is spicy food. That is exactly what you need."

"You're probably right."

"We will go to a place I know," he said, "and we will drink beer and eat dog. How does that sound?"

"Uh," I said.

"And then we will drink whiskey," he said, "and then we will have some girls. But not children!"

"Certainly not," I said.

"I know just the place," he said. "The girls are twelve years old, possibly as much as fourteen. We won't be robbing the cradle, and we won't have the U.N. on our backs."

"What about the SPCA?"

He laughed, got to his feet, left some baht on the table to cover the bill. "An inner chill," he said. "My friend, after a plate of dog, a glass of scotch, and an hour with a pretty girl, you'll be as warm inside as out."

I wouldn't bet on it.

Chapter Two

It all started...well, who knows when it started? When I was born, maybe, or when I was conceived, or somewhere in the dim dark past when my great-great-grandfather met my great-great-grandmother and decided he liked the way she combed her hair. Maybe it started on a numbered hill in Korea, where a shard of shrapnel from an incoming artillery round embedded itself in my skull, forever relieving me of the need to sleep. (No one knows exactly how the sleep center works, or why we need to sleep, but mine doesn't, and I don't.)

Maybe it started when I got home from Korea and started to make a life for myself. I found a way to earn a living, supplementing the monthly disability check I got from the government. And I found a way to fill up twenty-four wide-awake hours a day, and learned, too, to live out the fantasies other people use up in dreams. I studied languages, and I joined political movements, and I supported lost causes. I had adventures. Somewhere along the way I stonewalled my jailers in Washington by insisting I worked for a government agency and refusing to tell them which one. Then a guy showed up to claim me, evidently believing I worked for him. And, as the years went by, maybe I did. It's not always easy to tell.

Enough. It all started on a Tuesday afternoon in October, in the pine-paneled basement recreation room of a house in Union City, New Jersey, where a man named Harald Engstrom poured me a glass of brandy.

"The trouble with Scandinavia," Harald Engstrom said, "is we're too bloody civilized. We used to be Vikings, for God's sake! We were the scourge of Europe, more to be feared than the Black Death. We'd raid your coastal villages. We'd butcher your cattle and rape your daughters—or was it the other way around?"

"Well, either way," I said.

"Exactly. We were a dangerous lot, Evan. And now we never go to war. We are peaceable and prosperous. All our citizens get medical care and education and a government that takes care of them from the cradle to the grave. Even the downtrodden, even those of us in southern Sweden, live a life the rest of the world would envy."

We were speaking Danish. Harald was from Lund, in southern Sweden, but he did not consider himself a Swede, nor did he consider his homeland to be a part of Sweden. It had once been Danish—most of each of the Scandinavian countries had once belonged to or been a part of one or more of the others— and, as far as Harald was concerned, he and his neighbors and kinsmen were Danes still, and all that remained was for them to wrest control of their benighted province from the

11

damnable (if benevolent) Stockholm government.

"It is difficult to stir up a rebellion against a welfare state," he said with a sigh. "If we are successful, what happens to our pensions? Evan, I ask you. Would a Viking ask such a question?"

"It's a problem," I agreed. "You've got to get people to realize they're oppressed before you can get them to revolt."

"But you have some ideas."

I did, and I began to run through them for him. For several years I'd been a member of SKOAL, an acronymic organization committed to restoring lost areas of Sweden and Norway to Danish control. (A fraction of SKOAL claimed Danish hegemony for *all* of Sweden and Norway, and for part of Finland as well, but I felt their claims were unjustified, and not terribly realistic.) I'd had some correspondence with members in Denmark and Sweden, but Harald was the first SKOALer I'd met face to face.

He nodded as I spoke. "You are truly committed," he said.

"Absolutely."

"And you believe you can get assistance from these other groups? The Internal Macedonian Revolutionary Organization? The League for the Restoration of Cilician Armenia? The Pan-Hellenic Friendship Society?"

He named some other outfits of which I'm proud to be a member, including one or two I couldn't recall having mentioned to him. That might have made me suspicious, but who would be suspicious of a Danish Swede (or a Swedish Dane) in the basement of a suburban house in Union City, New Jersey?

"Evan," he said, "there's some better brandy, and I insist you try a glass."

I'd had enough for that hour of the day, but it would have been impolite to refuse. Harald, a blond giant with guileless blue eyes, lumbered into the other room and came back with two glasses of a liquid a little darker than amber. He very deliberately set one in front of me and raised the other in a toast.

"To necessity," he said.

"Necessity?"

He nodded. "To it we must always bend our will. Skoal!"

"Skoal," I agreed, although I wasn't all that sure about the rest of it. But I drank, all the same.

We talked of other things, though I can't say I remember what they were. What I do remember is that a curious drowsiness began to come over me. My mind wandered. I yawned, and apologized for it.

"You must be tired," Harald said. "Would you care to lie down for a few minutes, Evan?"

"No, thank you. It's not necessary."

"Just for a little while. A nap, eh? I think it's a good idea. Look at you, you can't keep your eyes open!"

He was right. I couldn't keep my eyes open. But that didn't make sense. If there was one thing I could always do, it was keep my eyes open. I did close them now and then—to rest them, to go into a yogic relaxation mode—but it was always entirely voluntary. I closed them because I decided to, not because they decided to close of their own accord.

But that's what they were doing. Closing, all by themselves. And I couldn't seem to do anything about it. I couldn't even remember to try....

The next thing I knew, I was lying flat on my back. I had the sense of coming up from some cold dark place far beneath the earth's surface. That was true, I realized, only in a symbolic sense. I hadn't actually gone anywhere, let alone some dungeon in the bowels of the earth. I was still in Harald Engstrom's house in Union City. I might be in the basement, which was technically below the earth's surface, though probably not below sea level. And I might not be in the basement after all, because I seemed to be lying on a bed, and I didn't recall seeing any beds in his basement.

I'd evidently passed out, I thought, and maybe Harald had carried me upstairs to a bedroom. The brandy, I thought—and at once it occurred to me (as it will long since have occurred to you) that there was something in that brandy more to be reckoned with than mere ethyl alcohol.

For God's sake, he'd slipped me a mickey! I'd been drugged!

14

"Coming out of it," someone was saying. Not in Danish, or Swedish either. In English.

"He almost surfaced the last time," a second voice said, this one female. I noted this, and noted in retrospect that the first voice had been a man's. "Maybe he'll make it this time," she said.

"Don't say any more," the man said. "He can hear you."

Indeed I could, but from that point on there was nothing more to hear.

No words, anyway. I could hear them breathing, if I put my mind to it, and distantly I could hear the hum of machinery and the muted sounds of human activity. I was beginning to get the feeling that I was not in Harald Engstrom's house after all, but I couldn't think how or where I might have been moved. I certainly didn't remember any movement, though I probably wouldn't if I'd been deeply comatose as a result of whatever had been in that last glass of brandy.

How long had I been out? I was lying on my back with my arms at my sides, and I hadn't moved a muscle except to breathe, but I moved now, lifting a hand and bringing it to my face.

A sharp intake of breath from one or both of them greeted this move of mine. So they were watching me closely, whoever they were. And they were impressed that I could move.

What was going on here?

I touched my chin, ran my hand up along my cheek. I had shaved that morning, I remem-

15

bered. Sometimes I skip a day, if all I'm going to do is stay home and write somebody's thesis and answer my mail, but I'd definitely shaved before my visit to Harald's house, and my beard had scarcely grown since then. There was a little stubble against the grain, but at worst I'd look like Richard Nixon ten minutes after he left the barber's chair. So I couldn't have been unconscious for more than a dozen hours, a whole day at the absolute outside.

They still hadn't said anything. They'd seen me move, and they'd since watched me trying to tell time by my five o'clock shadow, but they hadn't been willing to comment.

Up to me, evidently.

First I took a quick inventory. I wiggled my toes to make sure I still had them. I tensed muscles here and there, just to assure myself that everything still worked.

Then I opened my eyes.

There were two of them, the man a stocky fellow about my age, the woman a sallow blonde a good deal younger. They were both dressed in white, and the room I was in looked to be a hospital room, and what the hell was I doing there?

I decided to ask them. "Where am I?" I said. "And what am I doing here?"

They exchanged glances. The man—the doctor, I suppose—ignored my question and asked one of his own. What was my name?

I hesitated, not because I didn't know it but because I wondered if there was any reason to

16

keep it to myself. None I could think of, I decided.

"Evan Tanner," I said.

"Good," he said. Not that my name was Evan Tanner, I gathered, but that I was able to supply it. For God's sake, what did they think was wrong with me?

"How do you feel, Mr. Tanner?"

"I feel fine," I said.

"Any pain? Dizziness? Anything of the sort?"

"No, I'm fine," I said. I was still lying flat on my back, and it somehow had not occurred to me to sit up. It did now. I sat up a little creakily—you'd have thought I'd been lying down forever—and the woman's eyes widened. I'm just sitting up in bed, I wanted to tell her. Don't act like I'm Lazarus, takething up his bed and walkething.

"Still no dizziness, Mr. Tanner?"

"No."

"That's good."

"Yeah, it's great," I agreed. "But I've got a few questions of my own, and if you don't mind—"

"I'm sure you do," he said. "But let's take mine first, shall we?" He brandished a clipboard. "Forms to fill out, you know. And once that's out of the way I'll be better able to answer your questions."

I nodded.

"Can you tell me the date?"

"Today's date?"

"Yes."

"Well," I said. "The last I knew it was Tuesday, October fifth. I drank a glass of brandy. It wasn't enough to get me drunk, so my guess is there was something in it to knock me out. And it *feels* as though it all happened an hour or two ago, but in that case I wouldn't be here and you wouldn't be making a fuss over me. I'd have to guess that I've been unconscious for several days, so...do you want me to take a wild guess? I'm going to say it's Friday, Friday the eighth of October."

"And the year?"

"The year?"

"If you don't mind."

"That's the sort of thing they ask people who've been hit over the head, to find out just how scrambled their brains are. Mine aren't scrambled at all, or even shirred or poached, as far as I can tell. It's 1972."

"1972."

"Uh-huh. Next I suppose you're going to ask me who's president."

"And what would your answer be?"

"The trickster himself," I said.

The woman looked puzzled. "The trickster?"

God, were they Republicans? But even a Republican would have had to have heard that sobriquet applied to our Gallant Leader. "Tricky Dick," I said. "Richard M. Nixon. Only...wait a minute."

"Yes, Mr. Tanner?"

"There's an election coming up next month," I said, "although the result looks like a fore-

18

gone conclusion. But have I been out of it for a full month?"

"Does that seem possible to you?"

"No," I said, "but neither does having a quiet drink with a friend"—I almost said comrade, but how would that go over with a pair of Republicans?—"and waking up here. Did they have the election already? And did McGovern somehow put it all together and come out on top?"

They looked at each other again.

"Just a few more questions," the doctor began, but I wasn't having any.

"No," I said, "you answer a question for a change. Did they have the election?"

"Yes."

"Jesus God. Did McGovern win?"

"No. Nixon carried every state but one."

"Which one?"

"Massachusetts."

"God bless Massachusetts," I said.

The woman said, "Do you feel all right, Mr. Tanner?"

"You people keep asking me that. I feel fine."

"You're holding yourself," she said, "as if something's wrong."

I hadn't noticed, but she was right. I had my arms folded, with each hand fastened on the opposite upper arm. For warmth, I realized.

"Now that you mention it," I said, "I'm a little chilly."

"The room's quite warm," she said.

"The room's warm," I allowed, "but I'm not. I feel chilled on the inside."

"On the inside?"

"My bones feel cold," I said. "The rest of me feels warm enough."

"Have you ever felt like that before?"

"Not that I remember," I said, "but then I don't remember the presidential election, so who's to say what else might have slipped my mind? He's still president, is he? Dick Nixon?"

They hesitated, and that was answer enough. "My God," I said, "he's not, is he? Don't tell me there's been another assassination."

"No."

"Then what happened to Nixon?"

"He resigned."

"He *resigned*? Presidents don't resign. Ohmigod. If he resigned, that means Spiro T. Agnew is the president of the United States."

They exchanged significant glances again. I was really beginning to wish they wouldn't do that.

"Agnew resigned as well," the doctor told me.

"They both resigned? Hand in hand, they kicked up their heels and quit?"

"Actually, Agnew resigned first. Gerald Ford was appointed to replace him."

"The congressman from Michigan?"

"That's right. Then Nixon resigned, and Ford took over, and he pardoned Nixon."

"Pardoned him?"

"Yes."

"For what?"

"For Watergate."

"Watergate," I said. "You mean that burglary? That blew up into something big enough to make Nixon and Agnew resign?"

"Agnew resigned because of something else. Some scandal, payoffs and kickbacks while he was governor of Maryland. Nixon resigned because he was about to be impeached, and that *was* because of Watergate."

"I don't know how you can remember all that," the nurse said admiringly. "They taught us all that, but I can never keep it straight."

"They *taught* you?" I said. "Who taught you?"

"You know. In school."

But why would they have had to teach her? Wouldn't she have lived through it?

Wait a minute....

"Wait a minute," I said. "Ford's not still the president, is he?"

"No, I'm afraid he's not."

"Who came after Ford?"

"Carter."

Carter? Who was that? Aside from the fact that he was now president of the United States—

"And Reagan followed Carter, and—"

"Reagan? You don't mean Ronald Reagan."

"Yes, that's right."

"The actor? He's the president?"

"He was."

"Was? Who's president now?"

"Clinton."

"Clinton? DeWitt Clinton was governor of New York State back in the nineteenth century. He dug the Erie Canal. Well, not personally, but you know what I mean." They were exchanging glances again, and I began to wonder if this place was in fact a mental hospital. If so, maybe it was where I belonged.

"And there was a George Clinton," I said. "I think he was a vice-president, but I can't remember who he served under. Has this Clinton got a first name?"

"Bill."

"Bill Clinton," I said. "Never heard of him."

"He was governor of Arkansas," the woman said, "before he was elected president."

"And he succeeded Reagan?"

"First there was Bush," the man said.

"Bush?"

"George Bush."

The name was familiar, though I couldn't think why.

"Bush followed Reagan," I said, "and Clinton followed Bush."

"Yes."

"And Clinton's in there now."

"That's correct."

Nixon, Ford, Carter, Reagan, Bush, and Clinton. What did that add up to, twenty years? And any or all of them could have had more than a single four-year term, and—

I looked at the backs of my hands. They looked just as I remembered them. No liver spots, no signs of age since I had looked at them last. I looked down at the rest of me and saw that I was wearing a hospital gown. I had somehow failed to notice this until now, but it didn't come as a great shock. I was, by the looks of things, in a hospital. What else should I be wearing?

I said, "I want a mirror."

"Mr. Tanner, if you'll just—"

"No, dammit, I won't just. Bring me a mirror." They looked at each other again, damn them. "The hell with it," I said, and swung my legs over the side of the bed. The doctor moved to support me if I fell, but I waved him aside. There was a bathroom, and I walked to it, and there was a mirror over the sink, and, not without trepidation, I looked into it.

And there was my own face staring back at me, looking none the worse for wear. No older, and certainly no wiser.

"No dizziness," the doctor was saying, "even in an upright position. No problem with motor skills."

"We noticed his muscle tone was excellent."

"True," he said. "Still and all, it's quite miraculous. Theory is one thing, but when you see it right before your eyes—"

I turned on him. "All right," I said savagely, "who's the president?"

"Mr. Tanner, I believe I told you—"

"I know what you told me, and I know what the mirror's telling me, and the two don't go together."

"No," he said. "I don't suppose they do."

"Who's the president?"

"William Jefferson Clinton."

"And what's the date?"

"March fourteenth."

"Well, that's good. I haven't missed St. Patrick's Day. What year?"

"Mr. Tanner—"

"What year?"

"1997," he said.

"1997."

"Yes."

"March 14, 1997."

"Yes. It's a Friday."

"I drank a glass of brandy on Tuesday and woke up on a Friday. That would be remarkable enough, but this particular Friday happens to be twenty-five years later. Well, twenty-four and a half, anyway. It's like Rip Van Winkle, isn't it?"

"Sort of," he said. She looked puzzled, and I wondered if she knew who Rip Van Winkle was. She was young enough to have trouble remembering who Nixon and Agnew were, so how could you expect her to cope with Washington Irving?

"Except it's not," I said. "He slept for twenty years, and he woke up with a long white beard. I don't even need a shave. Or have you people been shaving me?"

"No, we haven't."

"So presidents have come and gone, and my beard hasn't grown at all. That's hard to believe. As far as I can tell, I'm not a day older than I was when I drank that brandy. I gather there must have been a drug in it, but

24

was there also an eyedropper's worth of water from the fountain of youth?"

"Not exactly."

"Not exactly," I echoed. "Is this all some mind-control experiment? It's not really 1997, is it?"

"I'm afraid it is."

"I was born in 1933," I said, "so if it's really 1997, I ought to be sixty-four years old. Do I look sixty-four years old?"

"No," he said without hesitation. "You look about thirty-nine."

"I *am* about thirty-nine. And it's 1972, isn't it?"

"No, it's 1997."

"It's 1997 and I'm thirty-nine."

"According to the calendar, you're sixty-four. But yes, I'm going to agree with your last statement. It is indeed 1997, and you are indeed thirty-nine years old."

I looked at him. He looked at me. I said, "I give up. How can that be possible?"

"Mr. Tanner," he said, "have you ever heard of cryonics?"

Well, of course I had. Based on the notion that biological processes ground to a halt at a lower temperature, cryonics postulated that dead people might be frozen for years on end, then thawed when science had advanced to the point of finding a cure for whatever it was that had killed them. Today's incurable illness might be a mere nuisance twenty or fifty or a hundred years from now, when a pill or a shot or a surgical procedure could make you fit as a fiddle again.

There had been rumors, I remembered, that various prominent persons had had themselves frozen after death. It seemed to me I'd heard it said about Walt Disney, though I couldn't be sure whether he was ultimately going to be thawed or simply animated.

It sounded nice in theory. It was a new wrinkle in the hopeless war against mortality, and while it might not extend the normal life span, it might serve as a weapon against early death. If your heart failed, well, we'll just freeze you until artificial hearts have been perfected. Same with the liver and lungs. Whatever's wrong with you, sooner or later medical science will work out a way to fix it, and when that happens we'll warm you up and set you straight.

The trouble was that it was still highly theoretical. While various cryonic facilities around the country had various deceased citizens as clients—"Many are cold and a few are frozen" was the phrase which leapt unbidden to mind—no one had as yet been thawed out to see if it was possible to restart his engine. (Some of the frozen ones were disembodied brains, the doctor told me. It seemed that it was considerably less expensive to have your brain frozen than to have them do your whole body. It struck me as a false economy. How could you go about reviving a frozen brain, and what on earth would you do with it? You needed a body for it, and where would you go for a volunteer? I suppose you could transplant it into the body of a horse, say, but would you really want to return to life as Mister Ed?)

And it was still as theoretical as ever, the fact notwithstanding that I had a pulse once again after a quarter-century in the deep freeze. All my pulse proved was that you could successfully freeze and thaw the living, something they'd long since established through experiments with fish, frogs, and the occasional mammal, including at least a few human volunteers. Such volunteers had never spent more than a day or two frozen stiff, but, if time essentially stopped for one when the body temperature got low enough, then a few days and a couple of dozen years were all one.

That was the theory, anyway, and I looked to be the living proof of it. Dramatic proof at that, if I said so myself. Twenty-five years at zero degrees—I'm guessing at that, nobody was ever able to tell me the precise temperature at which I was maintained—twenty-five years, by God, and I didn't even need a shave.

How had this happened to me? That's what I wanted to know, and Dr. Fischbinder wasn't much help on that point. (That was his name, Warner Fischbinder, and he was an M.D. and a specialist in heroic procedures. At first I thought that meant he saved people trapped in burning buildings, but it turned out his specialty involved treating patients brought back from the very brink of death. His associate, the sallow blonde, was Laura Westerley, and she was a doctor as well, specializing in internal medicine, which, if you think about it, ought to take in just about everything but dermatology. I'd assumed she was a nurse, because most women in white had been nurses when I was frozen. That was just one of the things that were not the same anymore.)

"You were found," Fischbinder told me, "in a frozen-food locker in the sub-basement of a house in Union City, New Jersey."

"At 673 Parkside Avenue," I said.

"You remember the address after all these years?"

"As if it were yesterday. As far as I'm concerned, it *was* yesterday."

"Yes, of course. For years the house was owned and occupied by a family named Akesson."

"Swedish Danes," I said. "Or Danish Swedes."

"You know them?"

I shook my head. "I knew a man named Harald Engstrom, and the last thing I remember was drinking a drink he poured for me. He was staying at a friend's house, and Akesson must have been the friend. And I wound up in the family freezer, next to the cans of Birdseye frozen orange juice."

"Not the family freezer."

"Well, I didn't exactly mean—"

"I doubt the family could have known about it," he explained, "This was a special hi-tech unit, state-of-the-art in 1972 and still impressive all these years later. And it was installed in a sub-basement of the Akesson house, a small one-room affair reached through a trapdoor in the floor of the furnace room. Someone had run an electrical line to the chamber, and that supplied the power to keep the thing running and you well frozen. And there was also a backup system, a battery-operated generator that would kick in and power the chamber if the power lines were down in a storm. Whoever did this wasn't taking any chances that you would thaw prematurely."

"Then how come I'm not still there?"

"The family sold the house," he said. "It changed hands a couple of times, as a matter of fact. The most recent tenant was doing some remodeling, and had reason to take up the tile floor in the basement instead of just laying new tile on top of it. And in the course of it they discovered the trapdoor, and went to see where it led."

"They were probably expecting buried treasure," I said, "and found me instead. But how did they know to call someone who would know what to do?"

"There was a notice posted," he said. "Hand lettered in block capitals. I don't recall the wording, but the point of it was that the unit contained a living human being in a frozen state, and that it should not be opened or the power shut off except under the supervision of qualified medical personnel."

"And that's where the two of you come in."

"Not immediately, but soon enough."

"And you brought me here, or someone did, anyway. Where's here, anyway? Where are we?"

"New York University Medical Center."

"On First Avenue?"

"Yes."

"And you thawed me out. I suppose it took awhile."

"It was a very gradual process."

"When you asked me my name," I said, "it was the same as asking me who was the president. You already knew the answer."

"Your name is Evan Michael Tanner. And there is a government file on you. I've seen parts of it, but only parts of it."

"How was I identified? Fingerprints?"

He shook his head. "There was a small suitcase found next to the chamber in which you were frozen. In it were clothes, which I presume were yours."

"I was wearing a striped shirt with a button-down collar," I said, "and a pair of khaki pants, and a tweed jacket with elbow patches. And don't look so surprised, Doctor. Can't you remember what you were wearing yesterday?"

"I can't," he said, "but I know that most people can. Those are in fact the clothes that were in the suitcase, along with shoes and socks and underwear. There were also a watch and wallet, and the wallet held identification, along with membership cards in a variety of organizations. Are you really a member of the Flat Earth Society?"

"Well, I was for many years," I said, "but if I haven't paid my dues in twenty-five years they may have dropped me from the rolls."

"Then there really is such an organization?"

"There was," I said. "I can only hope there still is."

"And they believe...."

"That man should trust the evidence of his senses," I said, "which make it very clear that the earth is flat."

"How can you possibly believe that?"

"And how can you possibly believe otherwise? Oh, I know how entrenched the globularist heresy has become, but—"

"But to believe as you do now, after men have walked on the moon. Or was that...."

"After my time?" I shook my head. "The moon walk happened three years ago. Well, more like twenty-eight years ago, come to think of it. I could explain it in Planoterrestrial terms, but I don't expect it would convince you. Anyway, the real point of the Flat Earthers hasn't got that much to do with the shape of the planet. It's philosophical, and it's about trusting one's own interpretation of evidence and not...."

"And not what?"

"And not swallowing everything the Establishment tells you. The only reason you believe the world is round—or spherical, really—is that's what they told you in school. And the only reason I believe I spent twenty-five years colder than a welldigger's ass in the Klondike

31

is because *you* told me so. Now I can't imagine why you'd want to lie to me, and I don't think that's what's happening, but I'd feel a lot more in tune with my Flat Earth principles if you could show me some supporting evidence."

He started to say something, then decided to humor me and slipped out of the room. The woman asked if I really thought they were making this up to fool me. I didn't, and told her so. "But if I see something concrete," I said, "it'll help me believe it."

Fischbinder came back with a copy of the *New York Times*. The date was right—March 14, 1997—and there was a front-page story about the president, who did indeed seem to be named Clinton. There was turmoil in the Middle East, for a change, and there was trouble as well in Zaire and Bosnia. There was a map, and Bosnia seemed to be a country, and not just a province of Yugoslavia. In fact they all seemed to be countries, Bosnia and Croatia and Macedonia and Serbia and Slovenia.

Could I be dreaming? Because I had dreamed of the day when all the parts of Yugoslavia would be sovereign nations, I and my brothers in a handful of disparate groups. If the newspaper was to be believed, the day had come while I lay frozen and unknowing. And now, from the looks of things, the citizens of all these new republics were busy killing one another. Not quite the heaven on earth I'd had in mind, but still....

"I don't suppose it would be that difficult," I said, "to have a newspaper printed."

They exchanged glances again. Neither of them actually said the word *paranoia*, but I could almost hear it just the same. And I guess I knew I was being unrealistic. They might have dummied up the front page of a newspaper, with some imaginative headlines over blocks of jumbled type. They do that all the time in the movies. But this was a whole copy of the *New York Times*, pages and pages of it, with ads and photos and stories all the way through.

And it cost sixty cents, I noticed. The last time I bought it, all it set me back was a quarter.

"I'm being silly," I admitted. "I think I believed you from the beginning, and the paper's a convincer, even if it does raise two questions for every one it answers. But, see, I look the same. You both probably look a lot older than you did in 1972, but I didn't know you then, so you couldn't prove it to me. You know what they say, seeing is believing, and if I could just see something that would cut through this inner skepticism of mine...."

Wordless, Fischbinder took me by the arm and led me to a window. We were evidently on a high floor, facing south and west, and we had a good view of the city. And it was New York, of course, and there were buildings I recognized—the Chrysler building, the Empire State—but there were also plenty of buildings that had not been there the last I looked.

I took it all in in silence, my mind racing yet standing still. I could feel myself struggling to adjust to this new reality. Because that's what it was—reality. Seeing isn't necessarily believing, not all the time, but I was seeing and I was believing. It was 1997—for God's sake, just three years short of the millennium—and Yugoslavia was five different countries, and I was sixty-four years old. I'd lived a mere thirty-nine years, but I was sixty-four all the same.

I said, "Why?"

"Why?"

"Why me? Well, why anybody, but I'm the person it happened to, and I can't figure out why. Why did someone think it was a good idea to freeze me like a package of breaded shrimp and hide me away from the world for all these years?"

"Nobody knows."

"Somebody has to," I said.

"There was a letter," he said, "but no one could read it. Then a man from Washington came to collect it. I suppose they found somebody there who could make it out, but they haven't sent us word as to what it said, and somehow I don't think they will."

"Not unless things have changed a lot in the past twenty-five years," I said.

"But I kept a copy."

"They let you do that?"

"I'd already made a copy," he said, "before they turned up, and I kept it. It seems to be some Germanic language, but it's definitely not German."

It was Old Norse, and I could see why they'd have had to take it to an expert to get it translated. I missed a few words here and there myself, but I got enough to make sense out of it, if you want to call it that.

"Harald Engstrom was not the man he pretended to be," I said.

"Harald Engstrom? Was he the man—"

"Who gave me the brandy? Uh-huh. And he was supposed to be an activist in SKOAL, working to bring about the independence of Southern Sweden. But actually he was an agent provocateur of the Stockholm government."

"Oh?"

"He wanted to learn just how committed I was to the cause," I went on, "and evidently I convinced him of the depth of my feelings, and that meant I was a dangerous man. He saw it as his patriotic duty to nullify me." I read some more, shook my head. "But he couldn't just slit my throat and leave it at that," I said. "He was too Scandinavian."

"Too Scandinavian?"

I nodded. "Too civilized. Too highly evolved. Too humane. No more death penalty, not even for enemies of the state. He couldn't kill me, but he had to neutralize me, and that meant putting me on ice."

"For twenty-five years?"

"Forever, if the folks in Union City hadn't taken up the basement floor. But I don't think it was supposed to go on that long. As soon as SKOAL was eliminated as a political force, he'd have had me thawed and returned to society. But I think something must have happened to him. Maybe he got hit by a bus. Or maybe some players on the other side decided that *he* was dangerous, and he's tucked away in a meat locker somewhere, hovering at zero degrees. That would be poetic justice, wouldn't it?"

"And the people who owned the house?"

"Engstrom's friends?" I tapped the letter. "He mentions them. They didn't even know about his little excavation project beneath the furnace room, let alone that they were harboring a low-temperature guest. So if anything happened to Engstrom, I would just stay there until hell froze over." I frowned. "That's the wrong metaphor, but you get the idea."

"What I don't get," Laura Westerly said, "is why he was afraid of you. Something about Swedes and Danes?"

I gave her a very brief rundown of the aims of SKOAL and the grievances of the southern Swedes, and she seemed understandably incredulous. "It was never a movement with a whole lot of political credibility," I said, "but neither was Slovenian separatism, for God's sake, and they've got their own country now. My God, it just occurred to me. There wasn't anything in the paper, not that I noticed, but it could have happened anytime in the past twenty-five years. But did it?"

"What?"

"Was there an armed revolt in Sweden? Did the Danish Swedes break away?"

"It's been pretty peaceful there," Fischbinder said.

36

"Well, maybe it'll stay that way," I said forcefully, "and maybe it won't. We'll have to see. Where are my clothes?"

"Your clothes?"

"My clothes. My striped shirt and khaki pants and whatever else I was wearing. I'm going home."

Chapter Three

They weren't crazy about the idea. They'd have liked to keep me a few days for observation, and tried to talk me into staying overnight at least. But I wasn't having any. I had a lot of new reality to adjust to, and I didn't even know what most of it was. Twenty-five years! I wanted to go home and start catching up.

So I had my first shower in twenty-five years, standing a long while in the hot spray and hoping it would warm my bones. Then I got dressed—the clothes still fit me, as why shouldn't they?—and signed myself out of the hospital. That's an expression—in actual fact there was nothing to sign, and no bill to pay. And there wouldn't be anything in the papers, either, about Rip Van Tanner's emergence from Time's magical icebox. One of the good things about being a known security risk is that the government can ring down a curtain of secrecy when it wants to. This time around, I have to say I appreciated it.

Outside, Fischbinder slipped me a twenty-dollar bill. "Cabs cost more than they used to," he said. "But then so does everything else. If you have any medical problems, call me. For other problems, I can recommend someone for you to talk to."

"Other problems?"

"It's quite an emotional adjustment you've got to make. Some therapy might not be a bad idea. But the first thing you will want to do is eat a meal and get a good night's sleep. But you don't, do you?"

"Don't?"

"Don't sleep, according to what I read in your file. You get government disability for it, if I remember correctly."

"A hundred and twelve dollars a month."

"That won't go too far these days, I'm afraid."

"It never did," I said. "I wonder. Do you suppose I'll be able to sleep as a result of all this?"

"Of being frozen, you mean? I can't think why. No proof that freezing restores the sleep center, not that I'm aware of. Still, there's an irony there, wouldn't you say?"

"Irony?"

"For years you couldn't sleep at all," he said. "And then for all those years that's all you did. Ironic."

The cab cost more than it would have in 1972, but I still had change from Fischbinder's

38

twenty dollars, even after a good tip for the driver. He was from East Pakistan, which now seemed to be called Bangladesh, and he was evidently not the only one of his countrymen to have reached New York. There were plenty of Indo-Pak restaurants on the way home, and the streets were full of Asian and Latin American faces as they had never been before.

And that was the least of it.

The city was changed utterly. Whole blocks of buildings I'd been seeing my whole life, and which had still been there a few days ago in my personal time scheme, had been replaced by other buildings out of a science-fiction movie. And some places looked somehow the same while managing to be entirely different. Times Square, for instance. All the old wonderful signs were gone, but they'd been replaced by other more wonderful signs, and the result was still unmistakably Times Square.

I'm going to leave it at that. What's the point in noting every change that caught my eye? The city had done what all cities do— although, being New York, it had done it faster and more dramatically than most. It had changed, it had evolved. And, from my particular vantage point (or disadvantage point, if you prefer) it had done it overnight.

My cab headed north on Broadway, past Lincoln Center (which was still there, thank God!) and across Seventy-second Street. As the blocks passed and the meter clicked away and Hassan Ali chattered away about the

39

adventure of driving a taxi in this extraordi-
nary city, I felt my anxiety level starting to climb.
Because every turn of the wheels and every click
of the meter brought me closer to home.

And what was I going to find there?

I had lived for years in four and a half rent-
controlled rooms on the fifth floor of a tenement on 107th Street west of Broadway.
And, freshly defrosted and out of the hospital,
I was blithely returning to my home, as I had
always returned to it after each adventure in
foreign lands. I had always come home, and
it was always there waiting for me.

But what made me think it would be there
now?

I stopped the cab at Ninety-sixth Street, paid
the driver, and walked the rest of the way.
Eleven blocks, just over a half a mile. I passed
some familiar stores and some unfamiliar
ones. I didn't spot any familiar faces.

Would my building still be standing?

No reason to assume so. There were new
buildings strewn all along Broadway, and
whatever had been there before was gone forever. From what I could see there had been
less change on the side streets, but that was
no guarantee that I wouldn't find an empty lot
where I used to live, or a thirty-story high-rise.

Even if the building remained, that didn't
mean I still lived there. After all, I'd been away
for twenty-five years. Sooner or later even
the most patient and understanding of land-
lords would tire of waiting for the rent. God
knows who would be living in the apartment

that used to be mine. God knows what had become of my books, my correspondence, of everything I owned.

And what about Minna?

I stopped dead in my tracks. I hadn't thought of Minna in—well, in twenty-five years, of course, but, more to the point, in the couple of hours since I'd returned to consciousness. And now, having thought of her, I could think of nothing else.

Minna had been six years old when I first encountered her in the basement of a house in Vilna, the capital of the Lithuanian Soviet Socialist Republic. She was at the time the idolized captive of two dotty old ladies, who believed her to be the sole living descendant of Mindaugas, who had been in his turn the sole king of an independent Lithuania for a little while back in the thirteenth century. Minna's captors saw her as a monarch in training, the logical choice as queen when Lithuania achieved her independence. Meanwhile, they kept her hidden away so no harm could come to her.

I got her the hell out of there and installed her temporarily in my place on 107th Street, fully intending to find a home for her, but Minna made it very clear that 107th Street was home and she didn't want to leave it. I took her to Canada one time and almost lost her forever in the Cuban pavilion at the Montreal Expo, but aside from that she's been happily ensconced in my apartment ever since, picking up languages from the building's polyglot tenants, tricking my occasional female companions into taking her to the Central Park Zoo, and picking up a fair education without ever crossing the threshold of an actual school.

She was not quite eleven when I let Harald Engstrom pour me that glass of brandy, so that made her what? Thirty-five, thirty-six in November.

That was now. But back then she'd been a little golden-haired child waiting for...well, not her father and not her uncle, because we'd never entirely defined our roles. Her father figure, anyway. The guy who made a home for her, and put food on the table, and tucked her in at night. That was the guy she'd have been waiting for, and the son of a bitch never turned up.

So what happened to her?

Best-case scenario, I thought, some friend of mine took her in. A couple of times when I'd had to travel I left her with Kitty Bazerian, and maybe she'd called Kitty when I failed to reappear, and maybe Kitty gave her a home. Or maybe she wound up in an orphanage, or in a foster home, or on her own somewhere in the city.

Impossible to guess what had become of her, and each guess was more disturbing than the last. I quickened my pace and tried to concentrate on the changes in the neighborhood. Better to focus on the superficial, I decided. The important stuff was too unsettling.

My house was still there.

No one had knocked it down, I saw. Nor had it collapsed of its own accord, although I suppose it was a quarter of a century closer to doing so. But it looked the same as ever from the outside. Built sometime in the late nineteenth century, it had achieved a state of decrepitude by the time I moved in that it had been able to maintain without apparent effort ever since.

I went into the vestibule and checked the double row of buzzers. About a third of the slots lacked names—tenements generally house a few folks with a passion for anonymity—and the names I saw were not the names that had been there the last time I looked. What had become of E. GOLDSTEIN and M. VELASQUEZ and MARKOV FAMILY? And who were T. D. SHIRRA and PATEL and R. BESOYAN?

And then I saw a name I recognized. 5-D—E. TANNER.

Oh?

My front-door key didn't fit the lock. No surprise there, not after so much time. Even a lethargic landlord changes the locks every few years. I used to be able to slip the old one with a credit card, but this one seemed to be made of sterner stuff. I rang a couple of bells—Patel, for one, and someone named Gilbey—and somebody buzzed me in and I climbed four flights of stairs. That wasn't any easier than it had ever been, but it wasn't noticeably harder, either, and I suppose that was something to be thankful for.

My name was still on the bell. I pondered that fact as I climbed the stairs. I still lived here, but how could that be?

A doppelganger, I thought. A sixty-four-year-old Evan Tanner, padding around in a moth-eaten cardigan and carpet slippers, writing cranky letters to cranks all over the world, making coffee in my kitchen and sleeping in my bed. And what would happen if we crossed paths? Would one of us vanish in a puff of smoke? If so, which one would it be? Or would we cancel each other out like positive and negative charges, both simultaneously ceasing to exist?

I know it sounds far-fetched. But the whole day had been far-fetched from the moment I opened my eyes, and it wasn't growing ever more plausible with the passage of time. It was only the persistent chill deep in my bones that let me believe I really had been in the deep freeze. If I could swallow that particular camel, why strain at a doppelganger?

I mounted the last step, walked the length of the hallway, and stood in front of my own door. The nameplate beside the doorbell held my name, but I didn't ring the bell, nor did I knock on the door. I just stood there for a long moment, listening but not hearing anything, and then I tried my key in the lock, and it turned. I pushed the door open and walked on in.

It was still my apartment.

Oh, it was different. The walls had been painted—probably more than once—and there were different pictures hanging on them. Some of the furniture was new, but some of it was the same as it had been when I left it. And the floor-to-ceiling bookshelves which I'd installed in every room were there still, and I recognized my books on the shelves.

Could time have somehow stopped in here even as it had gone on outside? But it hadn't stopped in here. There were new things—a matte black radio and record player, from the looks of it, and an entire carousel of what were evidently miniature records, smaller than 45s, and holding entire symphonies. And, on what had been my desk, there was some strange sort of television set all tricked out with a typewriter keyboard. There was a test pattern playing on the screen, winged toasters flying hither and yon to no discernible purpose.

I looked closer and tapped one of the typewriter keys to see what would happen. Incredibly, the pop-up toasters popped away, wings and all, and the screen brightened, with different rectangles of print and pictures appearing here and there on it. It couldn't be an ordinary television set. It was something else, and I had evidently done something to it, and I hoped it wasn't disastrous.

"Who's there? Did someone come in?"

I looked up. A tall blond woman, quite beautiful and entirely elegant, had emerged from within the apartment. My doppelganger's paramour? The son of a bitch had good taste, I had to give him that. Long golden hair, high cheekbones, a full-lipped mouth, a pointed but not severe chin. Full breasts, a trim waist, long legs. I wasn't sure what she was doing here, but I was perfectly willing for her to keep on doing it.

"I'm sorry," I said. "I touched a key, and something happened to your toasters."

"My toasters? Oh, the screen saver. That's nothing." She'd been looking at the screen, and now she looked at me. "My God," she said. "It's you. Evan, it's really you!"

"It's really me," I agreed, mystified. But who the hell was she? She hadn't been here when I left. She was the sort of thing I'd remember.

"Evan," she said, "don't you know me? Have I changed so much? Because you have hardly changed at all."

But she didn't say any of that in English. She said it in Lithuanian.

"Minna," I said. "Minna, is it really you?"

"Of course it is," she said. "Who else would it be? And it is really you, Evan. I thought you were dead. All these years, Evan, I thought you were dead."

"Well," I said, "I'm not."

"I know that, Evan. And in my heart I always knew it. For years and years I waited for that door to open and for you to walk in. And then I stopped waiting, or at least I stopped thinking about it. And then the door opened. And then you walked in."

"Good thing you didn't change the lock."

"Oh, Evan," she said, and threw her arms around me.

It was very strange. She missed me, of course, after all those years. And I didn't exactly miss her, because it seemed to me I'd last seen her just two days ago when we had breakfast together. If I missed anyone, it was the eleven-year-old girl I'd scrambled a couple of eggs for, and that little girl was gone, and this, this goddess had taken her place. I'd been a sort of father to that little girl, albeit an unorthodox one. I didn't know what I was going to be to this grown woman, and I was a little leery of finding out.

"You kept the apartment," I said. "How did you manage that?"

"I just paid the rent each month, Evan. I bought a money order at the post office, filled it out in your name, and sent it in."

"How did you get the money?"

"There was some in the apartment. You showed me where you kept cash for emergencies."

"That couldn't have lasted very long."

"And there was your check every month from the government."

"My disability check, $112 a month."

"They kept raising it over the years."

"Really?"

"Cost-of-living increases, I think they called it. Anyway, it's up to $428 now."

"That's a respectable sum," I said. "Or at least it would have been back in 1972. But if the cost of living has increased proportionally, then I suppose it's still a pittance."

"It's useful," she said. "It's gone up more than the rent has. It pays the rent now, as a matter of fact."

"That's great."

"I had to cash your checks," she said, "or they would know you were dead, and then I would lose the apartment. Besides, I couldn't believe you were dead. If you were dead I would know, I would feel something here inside me. But if you were alive, surely you would not stay away for so many years. Evan, where were you? What happened to you?"

I went over to the bookcase. "There used to be a bottle of scotch here," I said, "but I suppose it's long gone."

"There's liquor in the kitchen. Scotch? Or would you like some brandy?"

"Not brandy," I said with a shudder. "Scotch will be fine."

"You stay here," she said. "I'll get it."

She came back with two glasses. I was about to ask her just when she started drinking whisky when two things occurred to me. One—it was none of my business what she did, and two—she was seventeen years past the legal drinking age. (I later found out they raised the drinking age to twenty-one while I was chilling out in Union City. She was really only fourteen years past it.)

"Little Minna," I said, taking a glass. "Did you live here alone all the time?"

"Except when I was married."

I almost dropped my drink. "You were married?"

"For two years, and we lived together for a year before that. At his apartment, in the East Village. But I kept this place, Evan, and when the marriage broke up I moved back."

"You were divorced? What happened?"

"Things just didn't work out."

I took a long drink of scotch. I wondered how it would sit after all those years, but it went down just fine. I felt the glow spreading in my body, rich and warm. But the warmth didn't seem to be reaching the bone-deep chill.

"Did they make you go to school, Minna?"

She shook her head. "I stayed home," she said, "and I read the books, and I think I learned more that way than I would have learned in school. And of course I had jobs, because the monthly check wasn't enough to live on."

"What kind of jobs could you get?"

"In the neighborhood. Helping out in the shops, delivering for the liquor store, working at the newsstand when the *Sunday Times* comes out."

"Assembling the sections."

"That's right. I was always available to work, because I didn't have to go to school."

"Handy," I said.

"Yes. And then when I was seventeen I took tests and got my general equivalency diploma so that I could go to college."

"You went to college?"

"At Columbia. I took some tests, and I guess my scores were good, because they gave me a scholarship. I majored in history, and then

49

I got a master's in comparative linguistics, and then went back to history for my doctorate."

"You're a doctor," I said.

"Yes."

"What did you choose for a thesis topic?"

"The reign of Mindaugas in Lithuania."

"Your ancestor."

"So they tell me."

"If I'd been here," I said, "I could have written your thesis for you. But I guess you did a good job of writing it yourself. And why shouldn't you pick Lithuanian history as an area of expertise? You grew up speaking the language, and you're going to be queen if the place ever gets its independence."

"That's what we always said, Evan. But now that Lithuania *is* independent, nobody has come knocking on the door to offer me a crown."

Lithuania was independent? What was she talking about? The Soviets would never allow it.

"Little Minna," I said again, for lack of anything better to say. "Little Minna the Doctor. Only you're not so little anymore."

"I grew," she said. "Evan, I'm thirty-five years old. And you must be—" She broke off, frowning in puzzlement. "How old are you, Evan? Because you don't look any older than the last time I saw you."

"Oh," I said, and tossed off the last of the scotch. "Well, it's a long story."

I told her all of it, or as much of it as I'd pieced together from my own knowledge and what I'd learned from Fischbinder and Westerley. Minna asked questions and made comments, and when I reached the end she gave me a long and thoughtful look.

"I asked how old you were," she said, "and you didn't answer, and now I understand why. Because it is a question without an answer, isn't it, Evan? You were born sixty-four years ago, but it is more accurate to say that you are thirty-nine."

"Like Jack Benny," I said.

"I am thirty-five," she said, "and you are thirty-nine. That is going to be very difficult to get used to."

"You're telling me."

"When you are a child, adults are so much older that they inhabit a different universe. Then you grow up and the age difference is not so great, not so important. I have friends now who are fifteen or twenty years older than I. They were grown-ups when I was a child, but now we are all grown-ups and it is possible for us to be friends."

"Yes."

"But this is different. There really is hardly any age difference between us, Evan."

"That's true."

"I always thought...promise you won't laugh."

"I promise."

"I always thought you would marry me when I grew up. I believe it's a natural fantasy for a child under such circumstances. But now I have grown up and you have returned and you are still a young man. It is very confusing."

"I know."

"In a few days," she said, "I will find my own apartment."

"Don't be ridiculous. This is your apartment. You've been living here for the past thirty years."

"But it's your apartment, Evan. I kept it for you, with all your books and files. Everything is here for you."

"And it's a large apartment," I said. "Lots of rooms, anyway, even if they're not very big rooms. Certainly enough space for two people."

"I suppose we can see how it works out."

"It'll work out fine," I said, "and if it doesn't work out, then I'll be the one to move."

"No, I'll move."

"No," I said, "I will. It's my apartment, so I get to decide who moves out of it. Except I really don't see why either of us has to move. I think we'll do fine here."

"You can have your bed back," she said. "I'll be comfortable on the couch."

"I think the bed should go to somebody who sleeps," I pointed out, "and I don't. When I need to stretch out and do my yogic relaxation, the couch is fine."

"You still don't sleep?"

"Not as long as my body temperature stays in the plus column. At least I don't think I do. I've only been on my feet a couple of hours, so I wouldn't be sleepy yet in any case." I had a sudden image of Minna getting ready for bed—this new Minna, not the child I remembered—and I tried to blink it away. I turned aside, and there was the television set with its curious keyboard, and I snatched at it as a topic of conversation and asked her what the hell it was.

"It's a Mac," she said.

"A Mac?"

"Yes, a Macintosh."

"A Macintosh. Isn't that a kind of apple?"

"Yes, it's an Apple Macintosh."

"Don't you mean to say it the other way around? A Macintosh apple."

"Apple is the company," she said, pointing to the corporate logo on the metal box that supported the TV set. "And Macintosh is the name of the product line. And this particular model is a Power Mac 6600." And she went on to tell me a lot about it in a string of sentences that made no sense at all to me, using words like "modem" and "megahertz" and "hard drive" and "gigabyte." That last got mixed up in my mind with the trilobite, the not uncommon fossil of a triform prehistoric creature, and I was trying to work that out when she said, "Evan, you don't know anything about computers, do you? I guess they didn't have them when you got frozen."

"Companies had them," I seemed to

53

remember, "and there were these punch cards that you weren't supposed to fold, mutilate, or spindle."

"This is a personal computer," she said. "And it doesn't use punch cards. It uses software, but you just install it and forget about it. Unless it's Windows 95, in which case you have problems with it."

"Oh."

"And you don't know what I'm talking about, do you?"

"No," I said, "but it's just another language, and I have a good head for languages. What do you do with this thing, Minna?"

"Anything you want."

I gave her a look.

"I'm sorry, Evan. It's just that everybody takes computers for granted, and of course there's no way for you to know what they are. You can do almost anything with them. You can create a document, you can maintain a database—"

"Create a document," I said. "You mean like forging a passport?"

But that wasn't what she meant. She explained, and I found the explanation reassuring. "In other words," I said, "you do what you used to do on a typewriter, except you can edit it before you print it out. But it's basically the same thing. So what's involved really is a matter of learning a new language. It's like the difference between driving an automobile and flying an airplane. You really do need a new vocabulary, but what you're doing isn't all that different."

"I guess so."

"And the other thing you said? A database?"

"I suppose you could say it's not much more than a glorified card file."

"See? Language. Vocabulary. What else can you do with this thing?"

Then she started talking about E-mail and the Internet and the World Wide Web, and it wasn't just a new language, it was a whole new world. I realized this, and I guess it showed in my face, because she stopped herself in the middle of an incomprehensible sentence and reached to take my hand.

"Evan," she said gently, "I think you've got a lot of catching up to do."

Chapter Four

It took me six months.

I don't know if you'd call that a long or a short time for the task at hand. All I know is that's how long it took, and it was an intensive six months. I was at it twenty-four hours a day, seven days a week, with time out for meals and not much else. Even the exercise I got, which consisted of walks around the city, was a sort of busman's holiday; I tried to take a different route each time and acquaint myself with changes in the neighborhoods.

Mostly I read. Every week I went through a solid year of newsmagazines—*Time* or

Newsweek, I alternated between them, plus the "Week in Review" section of the *Sunday Times*. I maintained that approximate ration—one week to one year—and supplemented the news with the books and magazine articles my reading led me to.

For example, the news coverage could give me a sense of the increasing role of computers, but I had to read books to find out what they really amounted to. The newsmagazines provided a good idea of the way the AIDS plague had impacted on America and the rest of the world, but I had to read *And the Band Played On* for a fuller report and an overview. And so on.

I just read all the time. And, while I was taking the years one by one in the same order Time had dealt them out, there was no way to avoid skipping around some. The daily paper kept throwing things at me that I hadn't yet encountered in my reading, and I couldn't really pretend I didn't notice.

Like, for example, the dissolution of the Soviet Union and the collapse of world communism. How, when you come face to face with a fact of such magnitude, could you put off paying attention to it? A system that had looked for all the world like the inescapable future for all the world had overnight wound up on the dust heap of history, along with Prohibition and feudalism and the Stanley Steamer. The Red Chinese (except no one called them that) had a stock market now, and the Brits had given Hong Kong back to them. The only place communism survived at all, as far as I could make out, was in Cuba, which in turn was the only place where the United States had strenuously opposed it. (There was a lesson there of a sort which probably wouldn't be lost on a master of the Asian martial arts, but I wasn't sure exactly what it was.)

For my part, I went right on reading. Years ago (obviously!) I'd taken a course in speed-reading. I hadn't used it all that often—sometimes you want to take your time with a book—but I hadn't forgotten the technique, and I made good use of it now.

Meanwhile, Minna taught me how to use the computer. At first we spent an hour a day at it, and early on I was convinced that I was hopeless, that I would never catch on, that merely learning what to call things was hard enough but actually using the thing was impossible. I reminded myself that some languages were like that—I'd had a perfect hell of a time learning Chinese—and that all I had to do was stay with it. And then I began to get the hang of it.

Once that clicked in, Minna had me using the thing to study the past quarter-century. It was amazing the access it gave a person. I could sift through the world's libraries without leaving my apartment. I could also go off on tangents without realizing it, too, and could waste whole hours playing Tetris and computer solitaire, but eventually they lost their curious charm and I managed to get back to work.

So much to find out! So much to catch up on!

A lot of it was exciting. It had been evident even back in the early seventies that Europe was in the process of becoming one nation, and that process had continued, but so had its opposite. Yugoslavia was a prime example, having during those same years become five nations, but it was by no means an isolated example. The bad old USSR had become more than a dozen nations, and even Czechoslovakia had somehow found it incumbent upon itself to bifurcate into Slovakia and the Czech Republic. Four short years before my personal Ice Age began, Russian tanks had rolled through the streets of Prague. Now Vaclav Havel, whom I'd met once in a garret in Montparnasse, was president of the country. I remembered him as a chain-smoking young playwright, a gentle idealistic dreamer, and now the son of a gun was a head of state.

Quebec, where I'd spiked a plot against the life of the queen of England, had moved far closer to secession from the rest of Canada. Basque separatism flourished, and so, it now appeared, did separatist movements in Galicia and Cantalonia. There were strong pushes for autonomy for the Flemings in Belgium, and both Scottish and Welsh nationalism had heated up some, although the Cornish separatists seemed disappointingly docile.

On the other hand, some things hadn't changed a bit. The United States, doing no end of business with such traditional allies as Hanoi and Bejing, continued its blockade of Castro's Cuba. In Northern Ireland, Catholics and Protestants kept up their reprise of the Thirty Years' War, their version of which was outrunning the original.

And so on.

And then there were the deaths.

Well, hell. Twenty-five years. You have to expect a certain amount of mortality over that great a span of time. The bulk of the world's leaders had been well along in years, and it wasn't all that much of a surprise that they were no longer with us. Nixon was dead, and Agnew, and well, dozens of others. Jack Benny, that perennial thirty-nine-year-old, had left us not long after my body temperature plunged; George Burns, on the other hand, had lived to be a hundred. Francisco Franco was dead—evidently that had been taken up as a running gag on a television program. Evelyn Wood, inventor of speed-reading, was dead, too, and I wondered how long her funeral had taken. Two or three minutes, I thought, was how she would have wanted it.

The deaths of prominent persons struck me in a variety of ways. Many seemed both inevitable and appropriate. Some came as a shock, either because the person seemed far too young to die or because—like Franco, say—I'd somehow assumed he would live forever. But the sheer number of deaths was overwhelming. Over twenty-five years, one might have taken them in stride. When they came all at once, in a flood, they were enough to drown you.

Then there were the deaths I took personally. Friends, acquaintances. Fellow tenants and other people in the neighborhood. The owner of the deli at Broadway and 106th—I didn't know his name, but one day he'd made me a sandwich (corned beef and Russian dressing on rye) and the next thing I knew he was ten years dead.

So many of my gay friends, dead of a disease that hadn't even existed. Women I'd known, women I'd slept with, dead of breast cancer. The Grim Reaper, never less than up to date, had traded in his scythe for a power mower. He was cropping whole fields and cutting a wide swath through my world.

People I hadn't even heard of, people who'd barely been around, performers and politicians who hadn't yet stepped upon the stage twenty-five years ago, had left it forever. One day I'd learn their names in my relentless pilgrimage through *Time* and *Newsweek*, and a few days or weeks later I'd read that they had died. *Sic transit gloria mundi. Sic transit* everything.

It was, as Minna remarked, a real mind fuck. And those words, pronounced so trippingly on her tongue, were a mind fuck all by themselves. The eleven-year-old Minna I remembered would not have said them, but then again neither would a Minna grown to maturity in 1972. These days the nicest sort of woman said words formerly reserved for male company. They even said them in magazines and newspapers, and on television.

On the other hand, there were words you couldn't say anymore, like Oriental and girl. I could sort of understand why women didn't want to be called girls, although I didn't see why they wanted to make such a fuss about it. (And they seemed to be making less of a fuss now than they had ten years ago.) But how did Oriental get to be a bad word?

"It's a matter of political correctness," Minna explained. "I thought about doing a thesis on it, but I was afraid it wouldn't be politically correct itself. It's fascistic, a sort of fascism of the academic left, and it's all based on the idea that we need euphemisms to hide the fact that we know we're superior."

"Superior to whom?"

"To the people we use euphemisms for," she said. "Look how we keep changing what we call black people. First the polite thing to call them was colored people. Then it was Negro. Then that was an insult, and you had to call them Black."

"Right."

"And than *that* was wrong, or at least it wasn't right enough, and the proper term was people of color."

"What's the difference between that and colored people?"

"I don't know, Evan. I think people of color means anybody who isn't white."

"There's a word for that," I said, "assuming you absolutely require one."

"Non-white."

"That's the one."

"But then you're defining people by what they're not, and that's supposed to be demeaning. Anyway, the current name for black people is African-American."

"Not Afro-American?"

"No."

"Because that had its turn a while back, although it never did catch on in a big way. African-American? That's seven syllables."

"I know."

"Black is only one syllable. I have a hunch I know which one I'll be using."

"African-American might last," she said. "Because it's so cumbersome most people won't use it. As long as most people don't use it, it can remain politically correct."

"How's that?"

"The whole point," she said, "is to show that you're not like other European-Americans, and that you don't—"

"European-Americans? White folks?"

"Right, people of non-color. You're not like them, and you don't call black people by the same insulting term they do."

"Insulting because they use it."

"Exactly. Once all the rednecks start calling blacks African-Americans, the P.C. people will have to come up with something else. But that may not happen for a while, because African-American is such an awkward phrase to say."

"Especially for a redneck," I said. "Speaking of which, how do they feel about being called rednecks?"

"I don't think they give a fuck," Minna said, "but I don't think it's because they're more enlightened than everybody else. I don't think they're paying attention."

"Well, good for them," I said.

It's a damn good thing I didn't have to sleep. Twenty-four hours a day was little enough time for all I had to do. I don't know how the rest of the world makes do with sixteen.

It was all I could do to get through my cram course in the final quarter of the twentieth century, but that wasn't the only thing on my plate. I also had to play catch-up with my own life. That meant finding out what remained of the various political movements in which I had participated, and renewing my ties with whatever fellow members I could track down. (And, while I was at it, renewing the memberships themselves, after all those years during which I'd gone without paying a forint or a zloty or a dinar in dues.)

Here again, death had taken its toll. Some old comrades had gone gently, while others had been untimely ripped from this world and flung into the next. Many more had simply disappeared, nudged by time or fortune out of the political orbit in which I'd encountered them.

But some remained, and some were glad to hear from me, and responded by letter or fax

(fax!) or E-mail (EvnTanr@aol.com). And they referred me to other kindred spirits, and, bit by bit and person by person, I began to reconnect myself to the world.

At the same time, I had a living to make.

I've never really held a job, so I didn't lose one when I went into cold storage. Ever since my army days, I'd supported myself in the shadow world of ex-officio academia. A high school dropout myself, I had never been to college. But over the years, I'd got a lot of other people through.

I'd written term papers and theses. Early on I'd even take exams for students—finals at Columbia and NYU, LSAT's for people who inexplicably longed to be lawyers.

I gave that up when the march of time left me looking a bit advanced in years to be in an undergraduate exam room. The proctors were starting to look closely at me, and I decided I didn't need the pressure.

But I had a good business turning out term papers in virtually any area of the humanities. If your field was science I couldn't help you at all, but in literature or history or philosophy I was your man, and I'd deliver on schedule and guarantee a B. (No extra charge if the professor gave us an A, and your money cheerfully refunded if we got a C or less.)

It was a nice way to make a living. Sometimes I got to recycle my efforts—it was safe and ethically sound, say, to adapt for NYU a paper I'd done for Columbia—but most of what I did was one-time-only, so I was forever learning

64

and writing about something new. The research was a pleasure and the writing came easy, so it was the ideal situation for me.

But now it was 1997, and I felt like the messenger services must have felt after everybody in New York got a fax machine. Because my line of work was outmoded.

It wasn't that students had suddenly turned honest, and it wasn't that educators had finally figured out how to keep students from presenting others' work as their own. But what had once been a cottage industry for a handful of enterprising freelancers had become Big Business. A couple of outfits operated nationally, purporting to offer "term paper assistance," and in fact offering term papers, impure and simple, on an entire catalog of subjects. They would even give it to you on disk, so you could personalize it with a few awkward sentences of your own, reformat it in the style preferred by your particular institution of learning, and print it out and turn it in.

Since they could sell the same paper over and over, dozens upon dozens of times, they could offer their wares at attractively reasonable prices. It was, in fact, a wonder that any college student went to the trouble of doing his own work. It wasn't cost-effective, if you stopped to think about it. With what you had to pay to go to a decent college, why not pay a few dollars more to be sure of a good grade? And look at the time you'd save, and think what you could do with it.

I suppose I could have knocked out term

papers for the catalog outfits. They needed new work all the time. But my gorge rose at the very thought. It was like putting a man who did custom coachwork on the assembly line at the Ford plant. Thanks, but I don't think so.

But you couldn't ring an 800-number and order up a master's or doctoral thesis, and that was the sort of work I preferred, anyway. With a thesis you could dig in and buckle down and really produce something. I might fabricate some of the footnotes—one doesn't want to approach scholarship with too much in the way of reverence—but I did good work all the same. And, without any real effort on my part, I found myself back in business.

I got a phone call one afternoon from a young man named David Van Sumner. The name rang a bell, and I soon found out why.

"My father suggested I give you a ring," he said. "Bruce Van Sumner? You did some work for him in 1968 or 9. That was a while ago, I wouldn't expect you to remember, but—"

It wasn't that long ago, not to me. "Bruce Van Sumner," I said. "'Blake's Lamb and Tiger and Their Influence on Charles Dickens.'"

"You remember."

"It would be hard to forget," I said, "because he chose the topic, of course, and I've never been convinced that Blake's lamb and tiger *had* any influence on Dickens. But I guess I was persuasive enough. How's your father doing?"

"He's at Iowa State. He's tenured, and first in line to head the department when the top man retires."

"That's great."

"And I'm following in his footsteps. I've done all my course work for my doctorate at Columbia. And I've done plenty of research for my thesis, but I can't get the thing written."

"Like father," I said.

"You said it. And my dad told me how you'd helped him out, and said he didn't know if you were even alive, let alone still, uh, in the business. But he said you might know somebody, and—"

Young Van Sumner's thesis topic was ethnocentrism in the novels of Tobias Smollett. That meant I was going to have to read *Roderick Random* and *Humphrey Clinker* again, and thank God for Evelyn Wood. As he'd said, he'd done a good deal of reading and research himself, and taken abundant notes. That would make my job easier, and would be a big help to him when he had to defend his thesis at his orals. I met him at an Ethiopian restaurant on 125th Street—all sorts of ethnic groups, scarcely discernible in New York twenty-five years ago, have moved in and opened restaurants—and I looked over his notes and quoted him a price and a delivery date. He shook my hand and wrote out a check for half my fee.

"You're younger than I expected," he offered. "My dad looks good for his age, but you're amazing. What's your secret?"

"Good genes and clean living," I said. "And plenty of sleep."

So I was back in business. I knocked off his thesis, putting in a few hours a day as a break from my own studies, and I beat the deadline I'd set myself by a full week. I'd written the thing on Minna's computer, and I printed it out and admired the typeface I'd selected. It looked good, and the content was good, too. I could be proud of it, I told myself, and so could David Van Sumner.

I was in a mood to celebrate. If Minna had been around I'd have taken her out somewhere, but she'd gone out earlier with some friends her own age. (I still found myself thinking that way, although they were my age as well.)

So I went out for a walk, and a couple of blocks down Broadway I felt myself drawn to a tavern called the Pit Stop. There was nothing special about the place, but it was halfway between my apartment and the 103rd Street subway stop, and so I'd gotten in the habit of stopping in once or twice a week for a beer.

I hadn't been in since the Great Defrosting, but I went in now, and the place looked exactly the same. A little dimmer and dingier, maybe, but otherwise unchanged. Amazingly enough, the same bartender was behind the stick. His name was Charlie, and from the looks of things he was still drinking the same drink. It consisted of Drambuie, vodka, and prune juice, and he'd invented it for a contest sponsored by the cordial's U.S. importer. He called it a Rusty Can Opener, and never could understand why it hadn't won, and how come nobody in the place ever ordered one.

"Charlie," I said.

He looked at me. "Tanner," he said, and drew me a beer without asking. "You been out of town or something? Seems to me I ain't seen you in a while."

"I was away."

"Yeah, I figured," he said, and took a swig of his Rusty Can Opener. "Must be a few weeks since I seen you, maybe as much as a month."

"A long time," I agreed.

"Yeah, well," he said. "I'll tell you, you ain't missed a thing."

~

A couple of nights later Minna and I were having dinner. I'd worked up a new version of beef stroganoff using Portobello mushrooms. I generally cook kasha as an accompaniment, and at Minna's suggestion I'd combined the buckwheat groats with an equal amount of quinoa, an Andean grain only recently introduced to the U.S. market.

The results were a success. "You're right," I told her. "They complement one another. And the cooking times are the same, which simplifies things. I've combined kasha and bulgur, and that works, but I think I like this even better."

The phone rang. She went to answer it—it was generally for her these days—and came back a minute later wearing a frown.

"It was a wrong number," she said.

"I hate when that happens."

"It was the third time today, Evan. And it was the same wrong number each time, and I even think it was the same person calling."

"We used to do that when I was a kid," I remembered. "Call the same person five times running. 'Is Joe there?' Then your friend calls. 'Hi, this is Joe. Were there any calls for me?'"

"How amusing."

"Not if you're more than ten years old," I said. "Did it sound like a kid?"

"It sounded like an adult," she said. "Except...."

"Yes?"

"Well, whoever it was sounded Chinese."

"The two aren't mutually exclusive," I said. "There are loads of Chinese adults."

"I know, but—"

"Or adult Chinese," I said. "Whatever you want to call them. Whatever's politically correct."

"I think it was a fake Chinese accent."

"Oh? What did they say?"

"They wanted to know if this was the Blue Star Hand Laundry."

"The Blue Star Hand Laundry."

"Except it came out sounding like 'Brue Stah Hand Raundly.' You know, with the l's and r's all switched around in a very unconvincing way."

70

"Brue Stah Hand Raundly," I said.

"Yes, like that, in a sort of all-purpose fake Oriental accent."

"Asian, you mean."

"Whatever."

"Do you remember," I said, "how I used to go away now and then?"

"Of course. I would stay with someone, usually Kitty Bazerian. And you would be gone for a long time, and you would bring me a present when you came back. One time you brought me the little jade cat. I still have it."

"I know, I saw it the other day. The point is, those trips usually started with a phone call. And more often than not it was from someone trying to reach the Blue Star Hand Laundry, or pretending to *be* the Blue Star Hand Laundry."

"Hey, mistah, when you come pick up you shirts?"

"That's the idea. When they call back—"

"I'll give you the phone."

"Good idea."

At which point it rang.

She was reaching for it when she stopped herself, drew back, and nodded for me to take it. I picked it up and said, "Blue Star Hand Laundry," but didn't bother with the Charlie Chan accent.

There was the slightest of pauses. Then a man's voice, uninflected, said, "You should look in the mailbox."

He rang off.

"I should look in the mailbox," I told

Minna, and went down four flights of stairs only to climb back up again. I came back carrying a three-by-five index card. I suppose they must be obsolete now that people have databases.

I said, "Look what I found," and handed it to Minna.

There was an address and suite number on lower Fifth Avenue, along with "9:15."

"It's after nine already," she said. "Are you supposed to go there tonight?"

"It doesn't say a.m. or p.m.," I said.

"Maybe they're thinking in terms of a twenty-four-hour clock."

"He'd think that was European," I said. "and hopelessly effete. If a.m. and p.m. was good enough for Andrew Jackson and Teddy Roosevelt, it's damn well good enough for him."

"Him?"

"The Chief," I said. "Whatever this is, it can wait until tomorrow. I'll show up at nine-fifteen in the morning, and if that doesn't work I'll try again twelve hours later."

She thought about it. "Evan," she said, "are you sure this is from the same people who called the first time? The man who told you to look in the mailbox never said anything about the Blue Star Hand Laundry. You were the one who mentioned it."

"Turn it over," I said.

"Turn it over?"

"The index card. Look on the back."

And there it was, hand-stamped, the blue ink slightly smeared. A five-pointed star.

Chapter Five

"By God. Tanner. All these years I thought you were dead. Part of the game, of course. You get a man, and he's good, and you rely more and more heavily on him. And then one fine day you learn that he's dead. You remember Dallman?"

He thought Dallman had recruited me, and in a sense I suppose he had, handing off some documents to me in a pub in Dublin just before some players on the other side caught up with him and took him out of the game, wiped him right off the board. The Chief and I had raised a few glasses to Dallman's memory.

"The better a man is," he said, "the more he dares, and the greater the risk that he'll be killed. They tell me it's the same with hang gliding. When you become expert, you can fly much higher. But if the wind changes suddenly, all your skills don't help you a bit. And you have a longer way to fall." He ran a pipe cleaner through the stem of his briar, took it out, sniffed inquiringly at it. "Or so they tell me," he said. "I've steered clear of hang gliding myself."

"So have I."

"It's probably wise," he said. "We're neither of us getting any younger, Tanner. Although I have to say you look the same."

"So do you, sir."

"Ha! Decent of you to say so, Tanner, but that's an awful load of codwallop and we both know it."

It was codwallop, all right. He was an older man when I met him the first time, perhaps the same age as the calendar said I was now, and he hadn't had the benefit of a few decades in a frost-free Frigidaire. He had to be ninety, or close to it, and he looked about a hundred, with wispy white hair and a time-ravaged face. His tan suit looked expensive, but he'd lost weight since he bought it and it hung loosely on him. His shoes were freshly polished but down at the heels. His striped tie had been inexpertly tied, with the rear part longer than the front. His collar was frayed, and there were food stains on his shirt front.

But his mind was still as sharp as ever. I wasn't sure just how much of an endorsement that was, because I was never entirely certain how much the Chief had on the ball in the first place, but it was reassuring all the same to see that he hadn't lost it. Truth to tell, I was glad enough just to know he was alive.

"Where were you, Tanner? What the hell happened to you?"

"I was frozen," I said.

I hadn't planned on telling him. So far I'd only told Minna, and she'd kept it to herself. The Chief was hardly a confidant of mine—my reports over the years were sketchy at best, and often highly imaginative. But the words came out of their own accord, and before I knew it I'd filled him in completely.

"So that's how the Scandinavians deal with spies and secret agents," he said. "They put them on ice. Well, it's a cold climate, isn't it? I suppose ice is abundant in their part of the world."

"I was in New Jersey."

"Yes, and they didn't literally use ice either, I don't suppose. Still, you take my meaning." He made a clucking noise. "We're a pair, Tanner. They put you on ice and they stuck me in mothballs."

"Mothballs?"

"The mothballs are metaphorical, the same as the ice. They put me on the shelf, Tanner. Tied my hands. Took my box of toys away from me. Cashiered me, man. Relieved me of my duties."

"The bastards," I said.

"First it was age," he said. "Some nonsense about mandatory retirement. But I had them there. My whole operation was always unofficial, you know. Off the books, deep in the shadows. How do you strike someone off the books when he's never been on them?"

He took out a handkerchief, coughed into it, and examined the result. Evidently satisfied, he said, "But they kept cutting my appropriation. Slashed my budget. Reduced my staff. Still, I held on. My boys are like you, Tanner. No names, no pack drill. Make their own way, write their own tickets, employ and develop their own resources. And often as not turn a neat profit in the course of things, so they're not greatly troubled if there's no money coming their way from Washington."

What enabled them to ease him out, he went on, was success.

"The fucking Russians," he said with feeling. "Who ever expected the sons of bitches to quit on us? They were the enemy, along with the damned Chinese, and damned if they didn't plain fall apart. The whole Evil Empire collapsed like a pack of cards. Maybe we played a small part in it, and maybe we were entitled to a little bit of the credit, although I wouldn't care to sit on a hot stove waiting for it.

"Doesn't matter. The Soviet Union is gone and the Red Army's soldiers are begging for food on Moscow street corners, or enlisting in the Russian Mafia, or standing around with signs—'Will Work for Roubles.' Will work even harder for hard currency, I shouldn't wonder. Russia fell apart and China's become a bastion of State Capitalism. Still the same rotten lot running things, and still the same repressive government, the iron fist in the bamboo glove. We'll go up against them someday, mark my words, but just now they're our good friend and trading partner. So's Vietnam, for God's sake. Men who fought there are going back with tour groups, taking pictures, buying souvenirs. You believe that?"

"I believe everything."

"You might as well," he said, "because sooner or later everything comes true. Just a question of sitting it out. And that's what I had to do when the idiots at the top decided there was no threat to our security anywhere in the world. Except for Cuba, and if the refugees didn't own half of South Florida the government would have made peace with Castro ages ago. No threats, nothing but peace and love, so that was it for me. Out you go, old fellow, and be a good chap and don't slam the door." He sighed heavily. "What did I just say? About sitting it out? I sat and waited, and along came Rufus Crombie. Ever hear of him?"

"I don't think so."

"No surprise there. He's kept as low a profile in his area as we have in ours. Worth billions, but you won't even find him on the *Forbes* list. Business interests all over the world. Rubber plantations in Malaysia. Copper mines in Shaba province in Zaire. Oil tankers sailing the seas. Microchips, textiles, superconductors— you name it, he's got a finger in the pie. Unless he owns the whole pie outright. Been at it for years, Crombie has, and lately he's pretty much turned over the management duties to his four sons. Not because he wants to slow down, but so that he can concentrate on what really matters to him."

And what was that?

"He wants to do some good in the world," he said. "Not by giving to charity. Doesn't much believe in charity. Said as much to me the first time I met him. 'Give a man a fish,' he said, 'and you feed him for a day. Teach that man to fish, and for the rest of his life you can sell him rods and reels and hooks and leaders and flies and lures and God only knows what else.' I'd heard something like that before, but Crombie put a different spin on it. Shows you the kind of man he is."

"I guess it does."

"He wants to have an impact," the Chief said. "Stir the stew. Make waves. Wants to work behind the scenes, naturally. Not for commercial gain, although if a trading advantage comes along he won't turn his back on it. But that's not the main objective. Hell, the man's already got more money than God." He coughed again, used his handkerchief. "Where we come in. His eyes and ears, don't you know. Hands and feet as well, you might say. Stirring the stew for him. Pulling his chestnuts out of the fire. The metaphors are piling up, but you get the idea, don't you?"

"The general idea."

"Well, let me get more specific, then. Suit you, Tanner?"

"Of course."

"Burma," he said. "How's that for getting down to cases? What do you know about Burma, Tanner?"

"I know they don't call it that anymore."

"They call it Myanmar. Know what old Thoreau said about enterprises that require new clothes? Said to beware of them. Well, same goes for countries that feel the need to change their name. One thing when it's a colony that's gone independent. You can see why the Belgian Congo would want to call itself something else once it got rid of the Belgians. Still, most of those nations merit wary treatment. But when a country's been on its own for years, and all of a sudden decides out of the blue that the old name's not good enough anymore, that's cause for alarm, isn't it?"

"Anything the SLORC generals do is cause for alarm."

"I see you know about SLORC. You've been catching up since you got out of Sweden."

"New Jersey, actually."

"Well, six of one, eh? Point is you've been doing your homework. Nasty buggers, the chaps of SLORC. Between them and the bastards before them, they kept the country isolated from the rest of the world for thirty years. That's even longer than you were on ice, isn't it?"

"By five years or so."

"Well, what's five years in the mysterious East? 'Better twenty years of Europe than a cycle in Cathay.' I forget who said that but I suppose it must have been Kipling."

"It was Tennyson, actually."

"Same difference. Sweden, New Jersey. Kipling, Tennyson. Six of one."

Maybe it wasn't entirely accurate to say he hadn't lost a step. Maybe he was missing a whole staircase.

"For years," he said, "they wouldn't let anybody in. Tourist visas were for a maximum of seven days, and you could only go to a couple of the big cities. They changed the names of the cities, too. I forget what they call Rangoon these days."

"Yangon."

"That's it. Tried to change Mandalay while they were at it, but they gave up and changed it back. If you're lucky enough to have a city with a name like Mandalay, you'd have to be out of your mind to change it. Same goes for Rangoon, of course. I had a professor once, used to ask the class, 'What time does the noon balloon leave for Rangoon?' His version of 'Who's buried in Grant's Tomb?' but it's got a ring to it, doesn't it? 'What time does the noon balloon leave for Rangoon?' Try that with Yangon and it won't work at all."

"Won't get off the ground," I said.

"Ha! Very good!" He cleared his throat, filled his glass from the water carafe. We were in a bare office on the seventh floor of a commercial building on Fifth Avenue in the Twenties, sitting in chairs on opposite sides of an old metal desk. He said, "The names are the least of it. The regime's extremely repressive. Doesn't trust intellectuals, and you're considered an intellectual if you own more than three books, or write letters, or wear glasses. You run a risk of jail or a beating or worse. There have been massacres. They're not the Red Guards or the Khmer Rouge, not by a long shot, but they're a right bunch of bastards all the same. They've got statues all over the country to Aung San. He's the lad who got them free of the British. First he joined the Japs to fight the Brits, then he saw what swine the Japs were and took his ten-thousand-man army to the other side. Fought for the Brits, and managed to get the country independent in 1948.

So Aung San's the national hero, and one of the first things SLORC did was put his daughter under house arrest. Aung San Suu Kyi's her name, and she—"

"Chee," I said.

"How's that?"

"Aung San Soo Chee," I said. "That's how you pronounce it."

"Then why spell it with a KY?"

"Well," I said, "that's Burma for you."

"If you ask me," he said, "they should have let the Brits go on running the show. At least you had people speaking English and spelling things the way they sound. Any rate, 1988's when SLORC got in. They put Suu Kyi under house arrest and wouldn't let her participate in the national elections, which they figured they were in a good position to steal. Well, she won anyway. With all their fiddling, they still got voted out of office."

"But they stayed."

"Of course they did. Threw out the election results and held onto the power. Kept the lady under house arrest while they were at it, and of course that got her the prize from your friends in New Jersey."

"My friends in New Jersey?"

"Is that what I just said? Well, six of one. I meant Sweden, of course. Stockholm. Gave her the Nobel peace prize. Best way to get that is to be locked up by the government of a country nobody gives a shit about. You'd think they'd have given one to Salman Whatsit—"

"Rushdie."

"—after he got the death threats from What-sisname—"

"Khomeini."

"—but do that and you piss off the entire Islamic world. Give it to the Burmese girl and all you piss off is SLORC, and who cares?"

"Not me," I said recklessly.

"Or anybody else, either. So she's still under house arrest, and they've stopped letting journalists see her, and God knows how many other enemies of the state are rotting in jails in Rangoon and Mandalay. Meanwhile, they've made peace with some of the ethnic minorities, but they're still fighting with the Shan and the Kareni, and suppressing the others."

"The hill tribes," I said.

"They've got some exotic ones there," he said. "Women with necks like a giraffe. Ripley wrote about them in *Believe It or Not*."

"The Padaung," I said. "They put copper rings around a young girl's throat and keep adding more as she grows."

"Until she winds up with a neck a foot long."

"The neck isn't actually lengthened," I said. "The ribs and collarbone are pushed down. If you remove the rings, the woman can't hold her head up."

"Out of shame?"

"No, literally. The muscles haven't developed. Remove the rings and her head flops over and she suffocates."

"Women," he said heavily. "Who can figure them?"

"Uh."

"We can't live with them and we can't live without them, Tanner." That last sentence came out as a dry croak, and he drank some water. "This past year," he said, "SLORC decided to join the twentieth century while there's still time. Started issuing longer visas, making a pitch for tourism. Let the Chinese come in and build hotels all over the country. Forced the minority tribes to pay a heavy labor tax, with each family sending a member to work on the roads. They're getting good roads built, you have to give them that, but they're not scoring high marks in human rights."

"Are they getting tourists?"

"Not too many. Before they kept the reporters away from her, Suu Kyi was telling the world to stay away, that tourist dollars only helped SLORC. There's another side to it, the argument that opening up Burma to the outside world is the best way to press for a change of government. As to who's right, your guess is as good as mine. Mr. and Mrs. Tourist can stay home and read Kipling if they want. Far as I'm concerned, there's only one person who has to catch the noon balloon to Rangoon."

He didn't have to tell me who that person was.

"Passport," he said. "What kind of shape is yours in?"

It was rectangular, as I recalled, but that wasn't what he meant. "It's expired," I said, "and that's annoying, because it had a few years to go the last time I used it."

"You haven't renewed it?"

"I've been busy getting caught up," I said. "And I didn't know I'd be going anywhere."

"I'm not sure it's renewable at this point," he said. "It's probably too long out of date. You met young Cartwright, didn't you?"

"I don't think so."

"Well, you will. He'll have some forms for you to fill out, and he'll get your photo taken. We'll see to the passport and arrange a Burmese visa. That usually takes a while, but I still have strings I can pull. By the time you've had your shots and got started on your malaria pills, your papers should be in order. A few days, I'd say. A week at the outside. You'll get word as to where and when."

It was hard to know what shots I needed. A yellow-fever inoculation, for instance, is good for ten years, and I'd had one in 1969. That was either three or twenty-eight years ago, depending on how you counted. On the one hand, I couldn't explain to a public health official in a third world nation that I'd spent all that time in cold storage. He'd want to see the right numbers on my health certificate. But how would my system handle one shot three subjective years after the last one?

I got the shots the book said I needed and let it go at that. I had two days of muscle aches and low-grade fever, but it wasn't so bad. Truth to tell, I was too busy trying to learn Burmese to pay much attention to how I felt. It didn't come easy. A language is always more difficult for me when it has its own alphabet, and the Burmese alphabet was particularly elusive, with all the letters looking pretty much the same. They were made up of circles, with or without tails, and a page of written Burmese had the look of a colony of bacteria seen under high-power magnification. The letters didn't actually wiggle around the way germs would, but after a while they seemed to.

The spoken language was a little easier, but it gave me trouble, and I wasn't sure how much point there was in the little time I had. As far as I could tell, most Burmese had at least some English. The British had run the place long enough for their tongue to have had lasting impact, and what the empire had failed to accomplish in that regard was now seen to by CNN and SkyNews. If Burma was opening up to tourism, that meant they were opening up to English. In recent years it had become the whole planet's second language.

I wasn't sure how I felt about that. I'd always hated the whole idea of Esperanto, the simple tongue specifically created to tear down the language barriers between nations.

As a man who spoke so many languages, I *liked* those barriers; they kept out other people while I slipped right past them. But the mother tongue of Chaucer and Shakespeare was a little different from the artificial creation of L. L. Zamenhof. I still disapproved on principle, but I couldn't work up much in the way of righteous indignation.

I wasn't sure how well English would serve me in the tribal areas. I read a dozen books on the country, and navigated the Internet to half a dozen web sites, most of them passionately anti-SLORC. Among the many intriguing facts I learned was that 350,000 of the Chin people lived in Burma, and that they spoke forty-four mutually unintelligible dialects. There were barely enough of them to make up a city the size of Albany, and the odds on being able to ask your next-door neighbor for a cup of shrimp paste were 43-to-1 against. When you butted up against a fact like that, it was hard to say it would be such a bad thing if they all learned English.

I had ten days to study Burma and its languages before the phone rang and Minna handed it to me and that same uninflected voice said, "Hotel Maxfield, Room 314, half past two." A.m. or p.m., I wanted to ask, but he broke the connection before I could get the words out.

I'd never heard of the hotel, but I found it

in the yellow pages. It didn't even have a bold-face listing, and when I got to it, on Forty-eighth Street west of Broadway, I could see why.

The desk clerk eyed me suspiciously. I guess he wasn't used to customers unaccompanied by young women in hot pants and halters. His face changed when I gave the room number, and he pointed me toward the staircase and told me unapologetically that the elevator wasn't working.

The Chief was waiting for me. They'd had, he said, a little trouble with my passport. "It's your face," he said. "Dammit, you don't look like you were born in 1933. We thought of doing some computer aging of your photo, but then it wouldn't look like you, and where does that get us? Just look like you were using a stolen passport."

"Couldn't you get the passport and alter the date?"

"That would work fine for getting you into Burma," he said, "but you might have problems reentering the States. The data on the passport wouldn't jibe with what's in the computer in Washington. That could set off an alarm or two."

"I see."

"Same problem if we took the easy way out and forged a passport for you. We've got good forgers, but they've got scanners that are even better. Makes it almost impossible to get into the United States with a forged passport."

"Suppose it's not a U.S. passport?"

"We thought of that. Give you a forged American passport for getting into Burma and a forged Belgian passport, say, for getting back to the States. Too risky, too much of a juggling act. Best thing was for you to have a legitimate United States passport, with the right photo and the wrong birth date. Same day and month, so it's easy for you to remember, but 1958 instead of 1933."

"But if it's not a forgery and the date's not altered—"

"We forged a birth certificate for you, and let the government issue a bona fide passport with an erroneous date." He handed it over with a flourish. "Evan Michael Tanner, born 1958. Hang onto this, why don't you? Be a nuisance to go through that again."

I took the passport, flipped through it, winced a little at my photograph, found my visa for Burma.

"Tickets," he said, with another flourish. "A bit roundabout, I'm afraid. You have to change planes twice, in Seoul and in Bangkok. Coming back, well, you may have to sneak out of Burma, so you probably won't be able to use your return ticket out of Rangoon. But if you can get to Bangkok, there's an open return to New York."

I looked at the tickets. "Business class," I said.

"We're not working for Uncle Sam anymore, Tanner. And Rufus Crombie doesn't make his boys sit in the back of the plane." He passed me another envelope, a thick one. "Expense money," he said. "Spend it freely and keep whatever's left over."

I was beginning to like the sound of this.

"You leave the day after tomorrow," he said. "Not much advance warning, but the passport and visa took longer than planned. Sooner gone, sooner home, eh?"

"I suppose so," I said. "There's one thing, though."

"Oh?"

"Either I wasn't paying attention," I said, "or you haven't told me yet. But I'm not too clear on what I'm supposed to do once I get there."

"Ah. Well, the first thing you'll do is take a sounding. Put out some feelers, get the lay of the land. Then you'll want to go to ground so you don't have some SLORC lackeys following you around all the time."

"And then?"

"Then you want to look for the best way to destabilize the government, don't you? You've got the dissidents in the cities, and you've got the ethnic minorities in the outlying regions. From where I stand, Aung San Suu Kyi looks to be the key."

"So should I make contact?"

"In a manner of speaking," he said. "What the boys in the Company would call 'contact with extreme prejudice.'"

I looked at him.

"Kill her," he said. "What better way to make the balloon go up?"

He got a faraway look in his eyes. "The noon balloon to Rangoon," he said. "Sailing far overhead."

Chapter Six

"You Americans," Suk said. "Hopeless sentimentalists, and so illogical. You don't eat dogs, you don't eat cats, you don't eat monkeys, you don't eat horses—"

We don't plant taters, I thought. We don't plant cotton. But them that plants 'em....

"But you use monkeys for torturous laboratory experiments," he said, "and dogs and cats as well. And you slaughter no end of horses and feed them to your dogs and cats. And the surplus dogs and cats, the ones nobody wants as pets, you put to death at great trouble and expense. You kill them, but you don't eat them. You cremate them or bury them. What an absurd waste!"

"I suppose we could ship them over here," I said. "Dead dogs for the tables of Thailand."

He gave me a look. "You make a joke," he said, "to hide the fact that you are squeamish."

"Who says I'm squeamish?"

"Here comes our dinner," he said. "Let's see how squeamish you are. You speak like a Thai, but can you eat like a Thai?"

The plates arrived, little cubes of meat

broiled satay-style on small wooden skewers, with a mound of white rice alongside and a smaller mound of curried carrots. This once ran around and barked, I thought, and nuzzled people companionably with its cold nose.

Even so, I thought, how much cuter was a puppy than a bleating wooly lamb, or a bunny rabbit, or even a baby chick? All the animals available for our delectation are either endearing, like the dog and the sheep and the hare, or disgusting, like the snake and rat and the lizard. I'd eaten some strange things in strange places, and I'd had my share of mystery meat. More dishes have been called lamb than ever wore wool. In the present instance, I was fairly sure that what they served in this *klong*-side outdoor café was in fact dog and nothing else. And they brought it on a clean plate.

I unskewered my meat, picked up my fork, and took a bite. Chewed, considered, chewed some more, and swallowed. I'd been prepared for a gamy taste, but if anything it was on the sweet side.

"Not bad," I said.

"I should take another look at your passport," Suk said. "I never thought I would live to see an American eat dog."

"Americans were eating dog two hundred years ago," I told him. "Lewis and Clark would have starved to death otherwise. They kept trading with the Indians, taking dogs in exchange for blankets and meal and such. And the mountain men of the Old West ate anything that turned up in their traps. Beaver and muskrat, of course, but also weasel and otter and skunk."

He looked a little queasy himself, I was pleased to note.

"Some of those mountain men took Indian wives," I went on, "although they may not have felt wholly committed to the relationship, no doubt for lack of a proper church wedding. In any case, there were men who got through a bad winter by slaughtering their wives and roasting them a piece at a time. I don't suppose it happened terribly often, though you could argue that once was enough."

He was fairly dark-complected, was Mr. Sukhumvit, but all the same he was beginning to look a little green around the gills.

"I myself," I went on, "have never eaten human beings. Except in Africa, that is."

"In Africa...."

"In a place called Modonoland," I said. "There's never been any cannibalism there, so far as I know, but there was this one madwoman there who called herself Sheena, Queen of the Jungle, a white girl, as a matter of fact, and when her men massacred people they cut off certain portions of the male anatomy. Now I can't swear they went into the stew pot, but I can't think what else they did with them."

"And you...."

"I spent a few days with her merry little band," I said. "You might say it was eat or be eaten, and don't ask me what it tasted like because it's hard to remember." I took another bite of dog. "As a matter of fact...."

He held up a hand. "Please," he said.

"I was just going to say this isn't very spicy," I said innocently. "Do you suppose we could get some hot sauce?"

I'd told the truth about Lewis and Clark, and about the Rocky Mountain trappers, too. And Sheena, née Jane, and her version of missionary stew. The only time I'd stretched the truth was when I asked for hot sauce. Our satay aux chien was spicy enough the way they served it. So I was showboating, but what the hell. A little hot sauce never hurts.

And Suk was impressed. That's what he'd told me to call him, shortly after I asked for the hot sauce. I told him to call me Evan, but he seemed happier staying with Tanner. Between the plate of dog I put away and the stories I told, he evidently decided my macho credentials were authentic. I won more points when they put a bottle of Johnny Walker Black on the table between us. By the time we got up it was empty, and I'd knocked back my fair share of it.

In return, Suk told me what he could about Burma, and the hill tribes and the opium trade and the smuggling of rubies and antiquities and Buddha images. (A drug lord in the Shan state controlled the opium, and SLORC was offi-cially at war with him, but some of the generals seemed to be helping him launder his profits. The government controlled the ruby trade, and forbade the export of anything more than a hundred years old. You couldn't take Buddha statues out of the country, either, new or old, but unless they were old there was no reason to smuggle them. Unless you were a tourist who wanted one for a souvenir, in which case merchants throughout Burma would be delighted to sell you one, and the customs inspectors would be every bit as delighted to confiscate it on your way out of the country.

Why? I wondered.

"They are afraid," he said. "What use could a non-Buddhist possibly have for a statue of the Buddha? They might be used for a sacrilegious purpose."

"Like what? A ring-toss game?"

He spread his hands. "They are afraid of everything," he said. "Remember, they were afraid to have tourists, afraid to allow foreign investment. Now they see the money come in and they like that. One of these days someone will figure out that they can levy an export tax on antiques and Buddha images. 'You want that bronze statue of the Enlightened One? Very good, it will no doubt make a splendid ornament in your fish pond. That will be twenty dollars tax, please, payable in hard currency, not in kyat. Thank you very much.'"

"'And have a nice day.'"

"Ah, so," he said. "'Y'all come back.'"

I ate enough and drank enough so that I managed to get out of going to the brothel without looking like a wuss. Suk agreed that it was late, and that I had an early flight and needed to get what sleep I could. And then there was jet lag, always a factor to be taken into consideration.

But would I be able to sleep without having a woman? For his part, after a night of dog and whiskey, sleep would be unattainable without sexual release.

"In my younger days," I said, "that was true of me as well. But as the years pass, so does the urgency."

He seemed pleased to hear this, not at the prospect of diminished virility but at learning I had reached the downward slope before him.

"And then there was the leg of the flight from Seoul to Bangkok," I added.

"Oh?"

"I was in business class," I said, as if that explained everything.

"But that should make you better rested, not more tired. It is more comfortable, is it not? Seats that recline. More room for your long American legs."

"Very true," I said. "But the stewardesses are more attractive than in the rear of the plane. And more attentive as well."

"Oh?"

"The stewardess I had could not have been more attentive."

Was she a Thai girl? A mixture, I replied. My guess was that her mother was Vietnamese and her father a black American. Whatever the combination, the result had been a beautiful woman. And, I added, a talented one.

"So you will understand why I'd prefer to get some rest before my flight to Rangoon," I said.

He nodded. He understood.

~

It was a lie, of course. The stewardess, who did not appear to be of mixed ancestry, had indeed been extremely attentive, bringing me an unending stream of drinks and snacks and hot towels and peppermint candies and cups of strong coffee. But if sexual services were part of her repertoire, you couldn't prove it by me.

I figured Suk would believe me. It was the sort of thing a man would want to believe, because if it could happen to me, then someday it could happen to him, and the possibility, however slight, would make him approach every flight from now on with a feeling of anticipation. It might even move him to shell out big bucks and fly business class.

In the meantime, it would give him a fantasy to enliven his own visit to some over-the-hill twelve-year-old hooker. And it would make him feel a lot better about life in general—and Evan Tanner in particular—than the truth of the matter.

Which was that I hadn't been to bed with a woman in twenty-five years.

～

Now that's the sort of statement relatively few men can make, aside from those who are otherwise inclined to begin with. There are Catholic priests who might equal or surpass my record—though perhaps fewer of them than we used to think—and the Buddhist world has no end of monks whose vows forbid them to touch or speak with a woman, let alone have it off with her.

I would argue, though, that the first twenty-four and half years of celibacy were none of my doing, and didn't really count. Take any man, freeze him into suspended animation, and tuck him away in a sub-basement in Union City (or anywhere else, come to think of it) and the guy's not going to get a lot of action. I don't care if he's Errol Flynn. I don't care if he's Warren Beatty. I don't care if he's a former governor of Arkansas. The guy's going to have a very easy time keeping it in his pants.

The last six months are a little tougher to explain.

For openers, I was incredibly busy. I had a whole lot of current events to catch up on, and the computer age to enter into. That really did occupy me night and day, and it kept me almost too busy to think about sex, let alone get out and go after some.

And when I did think about it, I didn't even know where to start looking.

For one thing, I didn't know anybody. Before the Great Ice Age, I'd been slightly involved with a couple of women. I'd had a long on-again-off-again affair with Kitty Bazerian, but that wasn't really going anywhere, and the other women I saw from time to time were just casual friends and equally casual bedmates.

Remember, this was 1972. This was before herpes, never mind AIDS. People slept around without having to devote a whole lot of thought and advance planning to the matter. If you picked up something, well, it was no worse than a bad cold, and, unlike a cold, a shot of penicillin could cure it.

Sex was wonderful, and sometimes it was a big deal, but the thing was it didn't have to be. There were girls who stayed over at my place because it was late and they didn't want to take the subway at that hour, or squander ten bucks on a cab all the way out to Forest Hills. There were girls I made a pass at because I didn't want to hurt their feelings, and girls who went along because they didn't want to hurt mine. And why not? It didn't cost anything, it didn't hurt anybody, and it felt good and was good for you. Why keep it in your pants when there were so many better places to put it?

By the time they thawed me out, the world had become a very different place. All changed, changed utterly, all right.

I didn't go out looking to meet women, I was really too busy for that, but when I circulated for other purposes women occasionally appeared, and I wasn't too brain dead to notice them. One Sunday afternoon in a church basement in the Bronx I joined a dozen Albanian monarchists to discuss the prospects of King Leka, son and rightful heir of the legendary King Zog. (Zog had ruled the Balkan kingdom for eleven years before fleeing Mussolini's invading army in 1939. The communists took over when the war ended, and Zog died in Paris in 1961, although he lives on to this day in crossword puzzles.)

The meeting was a good one, and the movement's prospects were pleasing—Leka, every inch a king at six-eight, had drawn enthusiastic crowds on a recent visit to his homeland. I left in the company of a woman who was no more Albanian than I. Her name was Marina Boyadjieva, and she was Bulgarian, and an enthusiastic supporter of the Bulgarian pretender, Simeon I. We went to a bar in the neighborhood for slivovitz, and then we took the subway into Manhattan and ate at a restaurant in the Village. (The owners were Albanians, with monarchist sympathies; the menu, like that of most Albanian-owned establishments in New York, was Italian.)

We hit it off. She was a few years younger than I, having been born two months before JFK's assassination. This made her the right age biologically, but it didn't give us much of a common frame of reference. She was, after all, only nine years old when I got frozen. She hadn't been born during most of my life, and I hadn't been around during most of hers.

But that was only a problem for two people planning to spend their lives together. It didn't matter if you had short-term goals, like taking her back to her apartment, getting her clothes off, and screwing her brains out.

The first part was easy enough. She lived alone in an L-shaped studio in the east Twenties, where she made a pot of coffee and turned the radio to a golden oldies station. (Oldies for Marina; I was hearing most of them for the first time.) We sat side by side on her sofa, and I kissed her, and things were off to a nice start.

But that was as far as they went. After some pleasant moments she disengaged herself and said it was a shame we had to stop. And she told me that we would have to go slow, and take plenty of time to get to know each other, and eventually, if we were serious about our relationship, we would go together for blood tests. And then, after we got the results, we could go to bed together. But in the meantime it was good to know that we were indeed physically attracted to one another.

Cold comfort, I'd call it. "I'll call you," I assured her, and, riding home on the subway, I decided I wouldn't. Because I didn't want to go to bed with this woman if I had to court her for six months first and then pass a blood test. Why not go whole hog and get our DNA comparison-tested so we'd know how our children would do in school?

If that was what dating in the nineties amounted to, I figured the hell with it. Still, a man has needs, whether he's thirty-nine or sixty-four, and it occurred to me that there were ways to satisfy them that didn't involve months of chatting up some sweet young thing who didn't have a clue who Hubert Humphrey was. There were, after all, women who did that sort of thing for a living. The ones on the street were about as inviting as the town pump during a cholera epidemic, but there were others, higher up on the food chain, who ran ads and took credit cards.

For some reason I didn't seem to be interested. If love seemed like too much trouble, a commercial transaction was too cut and dried. It just didn't seem as though it would be any fun.

And then, just to complicate things, there was Minna.

There we were, sharing the same apartment, taking turns using the bathroom, eating meals together, and just sitting around talking. She was out during business hours—she'd recently started working for a magazine publisher, in the advertising and sales promotion department, a natural choice for someone with a Ph.D. in Lithuanian history. But she was home the rest of the time, and I was aware of her presence even while she slept.

I didn't know what we were to each other. I was simultaneously a man her own age and a guy old enough to be her father, and I'd actually *been* her father, or the closest thing to it, for a bunch of years.

And yet I wasn't her father, and never had

been. I was a guy who had rescued her from stultifying captivity and brought her home to a real childhood, and she'd spent it having fantasies of growing up to marry the handsome prince.

And what kind of fantasies had I been having? Was I unconsciously waiting for Minna to grow up so I could put the moves on her? How would I have felt when she began to blossom as a teenager? How would I have reacted when she started going out with boys? Would I have been calm and cool about it? Or overprotective? Or downright jealous?

No way to know. I wasn't around for those years.

But I was around now. How did I feel about her?

Well, I loved her, of course. She was the only person left in my life and, until my meeting with the Chief, the only person I'd told about my personal Ice Age. And you could make the case that she'd awaited my homecoming with devotion not seen since Penelope sat around waiting for Ulysses. True, she'd gone through a marriage and divorce in my absence, which Penelope hadn't done in the version I read. But she'd kept my apartment there with my books on the shelves and my clothes still hanging in the closets, and that's devotion enough in this day and age.

I was attracted to her, I knew that much. And it was pretty clear the attraction wasn't a one-way street.

But was it a dead end?

Suppose I made a pass at her. If she deflected it, however gently, things would be forever changed between us. We might be able to go on living together, although I wasn't too sure about that. But we would never be as easy with one another as we were now.

And if she didn't turn me down? If this was indeed what she'd been waiting for since I walked in the door? Then what?

You could, in Lorenz Hart's words, make two lovers of friends, although it didn't always work out as well as you might have hoped. But what happened when you tried to make two lovers of relatives?

Because we were family, Minna and I. Our roles might have changed, and what had been an ersatz father-daughter relationship may have been transformed into an ersatz brother-sister relationship, but in either case we were related, we were family members, and how on earth could we be lovers as well?

We couldn't.

And we didn't. And most of the time I didn't even think about it. I was busy all the time, and she was out of the house a lot, and when we were together we had no end of things to talk about. So we never had to talk about this yen we had for each other, but it was always there, hanging in the air between us. It was, I suppose, the thing we didn't talk about.

I don't know how much it had to do with my continuing celibacy, and I doubt it had anything at all to do with resisting the allure of the pubescent professionals Suk would have introduced me to. Whatever age I was, they were too young to tempt me.

But I wouldn't be surprised if the situation at home had something to do with my going to Burma. I couldn't just hang around the house all day, lusting after my roommate. Why do that when I could travel halfway around the world and kill the last best hope of the Burmese people?

Chapter Seven

They were polite at the airport in Rangoon, but surprisingly thorough. The customs agent examined my passport, compared my face to my photograph, and assured himself that my visa had all the right things stamped on it. He went through my day pack, even uncapping my toothpaste and shaving cream. I don't know what he expected to find in there.

There was an Englishman who'd flown in on the same flight from Bangkok, and he went through the line just ahead of me. He studied a map while I had my turn, and refolded it while I zipped up my pack. "Next time through," he said to me, "I intend to pack one of those dummy cans they sell in novelty shops in Piccadilly. It looks like shaving soap, but when you open it out pops a great green snake."

"You'd give the fellow a heart attack," I said.

"What do you suppose he was looking for, anyway? I know there are all kinds of things you can't take out of Burma, but what is there that anyone would want to smuggle in?"

"Drugs," he said.

"Isn't that coals to Newcastle? I thought most of the world's opium came out of the Golden Triangle."

"I wouldn't say they were rational about it," he said. "I can't imagine why anyone would want to bring drugs in. The people here haven't any money, so what kind of market would they be? They can barely manage a couple of kyat a day for betel nut. My sense is they're fearful of moral corruption. That's why they sealed this place off all those years, and now that they want the tourists they're terrified of what we might bring in with our luggage. Well, it's Western ideas that they've every reason to fear, and there's no way to catch them up in a Customs queue. I say, do you want to share a taxi into town? I'm booked at the Strand, but I could drop you anywhere along the way."

The car was a blue Toyota, the driver a slim Burmese with an outgrown brush cut who seemed to understand English but didn't offer any of his own. He stowed us in the back seat and our bags in the trunk and bent over the wheel.

"Sun's out," my companion said, "and it'll be a scorcher in a couple of hours. First time in Burma? Business or pleasure?"

"Pleasure," I said. "Though if I happen to

run into any business opportunities—"

"You won't turn a blind eye to them. What's your line?"

"Import-export," I said. "It's my uncle's firm, and he told me to keep my eyes open. But I'm really here as a tourist."

"Rangoon, Mandalay, and the ancient city of Bagan, right?"

"The usual places, I suppose."

"Well, the natural sights to be seeing. And it's not as though they'll let you go anywhere you want. Certain regions are off-limits. They'll bend the rules for an organized tour group, but the man on his own who wants to stray from the beaten path won't find it easy."

At the roadside, an enormous billboard loomed, its Burmese legend helpfully rendered in English as well. LOVE YOUR MOTHERLAND, it counseled. RESPECT THE LAW.

"The gospel according to SLORC," he said. "Inspiring, don't you think?"

"It's longer in Burmese," I remarked. "I suppose English is a more concise language."

"It takes fewer words to get your point across than French or Spanish. I don't know how it compares with Burmese." He leaned forward, a barrel-chested man in his forties, his black hair gone snow white at the temples. "Of course," he said, "there might be more to the Burmese message."

"How do you mean?"

"They may not have translated all of it. It might say something like 'Love your motherland and respect the law or we'll lock you up and throw away the key.'" I chuckled, and he said, "I asked your line and didn't tell you mine. I'm an agronomist, trying to sell the Burmese on the idea of putting more into the soil so they can get more out of it. Human waste only goes so far."

"Is that what they use?"

"If you get close enough to the Irriwaddy, you'll swear it doesn't all go on the fields. Name's Harry Spurgeon."

"Evan Tanner."

"And you're an American. What part of the States?"

"New York."

"Never got there myself. Spent some time on the West Coast—Portland and Seattle. Vancouver, but that's not the States. And I got to Kansas City once. Now, there's a town. Ah, another uplifting homily from SLORC."

It was another of the same white letters on a red field, but the message was different, something about the duty of the citizen to reject influence from outsiders.

"I wonder who handles their public relations," Spurgeon said. "That's quite the thing for the tourists, and who else travels this road? 'Welcome to Myanmar, and keep your outlandish ideas to yourself.' But of course that's not what it means."

"What's it about?"

"Our Lady of Perpetual Indignation," he said. "Aung San Suu Kyi."

I was looking at the back of our driver's head when Spurgeon spoke the name, and it seemed to me his neck muscles went rigid at the sound of it. I nudged the Englishman's arm, nodded at the driver.

"No harm," he said. "You wouldn't want to engage a Burmese in conversation on the subject. Might be awkward for him. But it doesn't matter what he overhears, so long as he doesn't need to acknowledge it."

"But foreign influences," I said. "How—"

"Ah. Well, she lived abroad for a time, didn't she? Got an Oxford education and married a don. Came back to her homeland, which you or I would regard as an act of patriotism, and foolhardy in the bargain. SLORC's line is she's been tainted by her time and associations abroad."

"Are they serious?"

"No, they're just trying it on. The Japanese could take a stand like that and be sincere about it. Look at the lot who emigrated to Peru. When their sons and daughters tried to move back, they were regarded as *gaijin*. They'd lost their Japaneseness for having been raised overseas. But the Burmese aren't quite that xenophobic. This is just SLORC trying to get around the fact that her father is the greatest hero the place ever had. There's a street named after him and the city's major market, and there are statues and pictures of the man everywhere. So they've got to say she's not a true daughter—of her father or of Burma, either. She went abroad. She got corrupted by foreign ideas. I don't know if this fellow buys it"—he indicated the driver—"but if he does he's an exception. The people voted for her, and they'd vote for her again if they got the chance. But SLORC's got the guns and the soldiers, and they're not going to make the mistake of calling another election. Why embarrass themselves?"

"Why bother with the billboards?"

"Well, I wouldn't say the campaign's the work of a genius, Tanner. It's entirely wasted on visitors, unless the idea is to show who's in control. As far as the native populace is concerned, I daresay there's something in the Big Lie theory. Say it loud enough and often enough and people will believe it in spite of themselves."

"I suppose."

"And there's a 'Big Brother is watching' effect, a verbal equivalent of having an over-sized statue of Mao or Lenin forever glaring down at one. Now there's an importer's opportunity!"

"I beg your pardon?"

"The Lenin statues," he said. "They've pulled them down all over Russia, and nobody has any idea what to do with them. They've carted some of them to the smelter, but there are still plenty left. Here's what you do, Tanner. Get yourself over to Russia and find the largest and tackiest one you can. Then see if you can't peddle it to that town in Arizona that bought the London Bridge. Be a perfect companion piece, wouldn't you say?"

There were more SLORC billboards in

109

Rangoon, along with signs welcoming us to Yangon and a hideous multicolored statue of a child who was evidently the mascot of Myanmar tourism. She had her hair in pigtails and carried a little basket, and if she'd been a living breathing child you'd have wanted to smack her one. In comparison, the billboards looked pretty good.

Spurgeon asked me where I was staying. I hadn't booked a room, and didn't want one. I wouldn't be sleeping, and was traveling light enough that it would be no hardship to keep my pack with me—and a blessing if I had to leave in a hurry. And I wasn't sure how it worked in Burma, but in a lot of countries they wanted you to leave your passport at the hotel desk, reclaiming it when you left. I didn't much want to do that.

All I told Spurgeon was that I hadn't selected a hotel yet, and the look he gave me showed he thought I was daft. "We'll see if they can find room for you at the Strand," he said. "It's like Raffles in Singapore, one of the great old hotels, and they've kept it up well. You'll be happier there than at one of the sterile new hotels."

I didn't say anything, but when we pulled up in front of the Strand I shouldered my pack and told Spurgeon I thought I'd rather walk around first and see something of the city. "I might want to stay someplace a little more modest," I said. "This looks awfully grand. I'd feel a little too casually dressed for the lobby."

I was wearing khakis and a bush jacket, and he assured me my attire was perfectly acceptable. I said again that something smaller and more modest would suit me, and he caught on that the Strand was a little too rich for my blood.

"Smart man," he said. "Save your money for rubies. Mind you don't pay for a load of cut glass, now."

"I'm not sure I'll be buying any rubies. First I want to do a little sightseeing."

"I suppose your first stop will be Shwe Dagon Pagoda."

"Well, I don't want to miss it."

"No, and it's quite the experience to be there at sunrise, but you won't spoil it for yourself by trotting over there now. You know about shoes?"

"You can't wear them into the pagodas."

"Can't even wear them on the grounds of the pagodas. Have to leave them at the outer gates. Not that you'll have much chance of making a mistake on that score. There are plenty of signs to tell you to remove your shoes, and of course you'll see other people's discarded footwear. That should give you a clue."

"I guess they take it pretty seriously."

"The business of shoes? It's the one thing guaranteed to set them off. Buddhists in Thailand have the same passion for bare feet, but they're a little more relaxed about it. It's only the holy areas of a Thai pagoda where you can't wear shoes. Here it's the whole shooting match." He raised a hand, scratched the blaze of white hair at his temple. "That all you brought, that little backpack? Why, you can pop your shoes in there, carry them with you. Not that you have to worry about anyone walking off with them—or *in* them, eh? They're an honest lot, the Burmese. Just a little bit queer when it comes to feet. Never point your feet at anyone, shod or bare. I suppose you know that."

"It said something to that effect in one of the guidebooks."

"The feet are considered unclean," he said, "and small wonder after they've been traipsing through filthy pagodas all day. Never point them at a Buddha image either, although I can't imagine how you would avoid it. Wherever you aim them, they're odds-on to be pointing at a Buddha image, aren't they?"

He wouldn't let me split the cab fare with him, and after the poor-mouth act I'd pulled to get out of staying at the hotel, I couldn't very well argue with him. I walked a block, checked my map, and set out for Shwe Dagon.

There was no dearth of other pagodas en route. As far as I could make out, the Burmese felt about pagodas the way Imelda Marcos felt about shoes. You can't have too many of them. If you've got two fine pagodas standing side by side, why not build a third right across the road? And wouldn't it be a neat idea to put a fourth one right next door, and...Well, you get the idea.

Shwe Dagon dwarfed them all. I walked

barefoot down a long aisle lined on both sides with shops selling handcrafts and, yes, Buddha images, then rode up on an escalator, then walked some more and climbed some more to emerge into what has to be one of the wonders of the Eastern world.

There was a stupa in the central portion, of course, a sculpted upended cone, blindingly white and topped with a gold finial. Around it was an enormous marble courtyard, with shrines or chapels of one sort or another on either side. What you did, as far as I could make out, was walk around the courtyard circling the stupa. Every time you turned a corner another fantasy landscape struck your eye. It looked like the ultimate amusement park, but with no rides or food concessions and no lines to stand in.

It didn't seem to matter whether you walked clockwise or counterclockwise. The locals, including the monks with their shaven heads and red robes, walked in either direction, and so did the camera-toting Westerners. The latter made up about a third of the company, and were the only ones who got charged admission. The Burmese got in free.

They weren't there to worship. For all the innumerable Buddhas to be seen there—Buddhas made of every material, Buddhas painted or gilded or left unadorned, Buddhas sitting or standing or, yes, reclining—the Enlightened One was not adored or beseeched or asked to intervene. He was there in all his forms, as I understand it, to raise the level of one's thoughts and improve one's chances for a better life next time around. Meditating in a place of high spiritual power was, with alms giving and pagoda building, a way to make merit, and the more you made merit the higher you stood in the Reincarnation Sweepstakes.

You could also make merit by releasing captive animals, and while I was contemplating a seated Buddha strung with lights like a Christmas tree, a woman came into view carrying a small cage made of twigs. She found a spot she liked, smiled gloriously, and opened the cage to release a white dove, who looked around suspiciously before trying his wings and heading off for the wild blue yonder. The woman followed him with her eyes, then walked off in the other direction.

All well and good, I thought. She'd made merit, and the bird didn't even have to wait until his next life to have a better time of things. He was out of there, up up and away, free at last.

At least until some enterprising chap trapped him and caged him again, so that another seeker of merit could purchase him and let him loose.

Jesus, talk about the wheel of rebirth! There you had a bird's-eye view of it. And, if all the people who took turns ransoming and liberating the bird were making merit, what was being made by the people who kept trapping the poor little bastard? Did they pile up demerits? Was the whole deal another zero-sum game, with every bit of merit gained offset by merit that someone else lost?

I decided not to worry about it. Maybe the bird catchers were earning merit in their own way by making it possible for their customers to perform a righteous act. Then again, maybe not. If nothing else, they were earning a few kyat. It was an odd little dance they were all doing, and I didn't really get it, but these people didn't need my understanding or my approval.

Maybe it wasn't as crazy as it looked. In the West, most of us earned a living by taking in each other's washing. Here they took in each other's karma.

Same difference.

At four-thirty that afternoon I was sitting cross-legged in front of a sort of chapel immediately to the right of the western gate. I was pretty sure it was where I was supposed to be, but to my untrained eye one chapel looked rather like another.

Still, how hard should it be to find me? My fellow tourists were a busy lot, but the bulk of their activity consisted of either taking pictures or posing for them. When they weren't behind or in front of a camera, they were gazing rapturously at something and trying to decide if they had enough film to record it for the folks back home.

The Burmese, on the other hand, did almost everything imaginable *but* take or pose for pictures. Families walked around, the children clutching their parents' hands. Red-robed monks, ranging in age from small boys to old men, circled the central stupa in a solemn procession. And here a man howled and spat, and there a fellow puffed on a cheroot. Spitting and smoking were evidently okay, as long as you kept your shoes off.

I looked at my watch. 4:32. It was funny, I thought, how twenty-five years could pass in the wink of an eye, and two minutes could take forever. I wondered how long I should wait for my co-conspirator to make contact. I should wait a little while, I had been told, and then return at the same time the following day. But how long was a little while in this holy place? Five minutes? An hour and a half?

Mr. Sukhumvit in Bangkok was a contact the Chief had arranged for me, and he'd been helpful enough, though in one respect I'd have been better off with the Thai equivalent of Zagat's or Egon Ronay's Good Food Guide. The person who would meet me in Shwe Dagon was someone I'd located on my own, working what remained of my old network of activists and supplementing it with some contacts I'd made on the Internet. There were exiled Burmese dissidents all over the place, and especially in northern Thailand, and it was through them that this meeting had been arranged.

I had thought about skipping it, even as I'd considered passing up Sukhumvit even before I learned what was on the menu. But I felt so ill-equipped for the task at hand, so utterly unprepared, that I didn't dare. I needed all the help I could get.

I guess my eyes closed as I sat there, because I didn't notice the boy's approach. He coughed gently, no more than a quiet clearing of the throat, and I looked up and saw him. He was standing as straight as a little soldier and I was sitting cross-legged, but our eyes were on a level. He was a tiny fellow, his face a perfect oval, his eyes large and dark. With his shaved head he could have been a monk-in-training—I'd seen some no older and taller—but instead of a red robe he wore a longyi, the close-fitting wraparound skirt all Burmese men wore instead of trousers. His shirt was an ordinary American T-shirt showing Bugs Bunny chewing on a carrot.

He was holding a twig cage, and it was holding a dove just like the one I'd seen released. The same one, for all I knew, although I'd say the odds were against it.

"No, thank you," I said English. "No birds today."

He didn't seem to get it. He smiled, and extended the cage.

"Bah boo," I said, which means *No*. Unless I was giving it the wrong tonal quality, in which case it very likely meant something else. It certainly didn't seem to discourage him. "Jay zu bah boo," I said, which ought to mean *Thanks but no thanks*. This got me a smile, but it didn't get rid of him. He wanted to sell me that bird.

People were looking at us, too. Maybe the easiest thing was to buy it. "How much?" I

117

asked, and searched my memory for the Burmese phrase. I hadn't had nearly enough time to study it, I'd just managed to cram in a few words and phrases, and—

"Beh lout lay?" I said. I'd either asked the price or directions to the post office, I wasn't really sure which.

"Shit," he said.

I stared at him. His expression was curiously matter-of-fact. I said, "Shit?"

He nodded, pleased that we were communicating. "Shit." And he followed that with a string of words I didn't get at all.

"Na malay bah boo," I told him, which ought to mean *The guy from Singapore made a mistake,* but which actually means "I don't understand."

"Shit," he said.

"You said it," I agreed.

He put the cage on the marble floor between us and held up both hands, the thumbs tucked into the palms. When I didn't react he tried again, counting on his fingers: "Tit, nit, thone, lay, ngar, chak, kunnit, shit. Shit!"

Oh, right. Shit was eight in Burmese. But eight what? Eight dollars seemed ridiculously high, while eight kyat worked out to around a dime, and seemed ridiculously low. And I didn't have any kyat, I hadn't changed any money yet, and—

"Shit," he said. His face showed the beginnings of exasperation, and I wasn't sure whether the latest utterance was in Burmese or English.

"No shit," I said, and dug out my wallet. The smallest I had was a ten-dollar bill, and I handed it to him. His eyes widened and I gestured to indicate that he should keep it, which clearly delighted him. He tucked it into the waistband of his longyi and handed me the cage. I handed it back and indicated that he should keep it, and perhaps sell it to somebody else.

That didn't please him at all. "Taik, taik," he implored, and I was trying to guess what the word meant when I realized he was speaking English, insisting I take the thing.

"Oh," I said, taking it, and thanked him politely: "Amyah ee jay zu tin ba day."

He nodded and bowed and ran off.

Shit, I thought. I set the caged bird down beside me and looked at my watch. It was ten minutes to five, and I'd have given up on my contact, but suppose he'd waited while the kid gave me the bird? I ought to give him a few more minutes. And so I waited until five o'clock, not really expecting anything, and nobody came within five yards of me, or took any real notice of me at all.

I stood up, bent to work the cramps out of my legs, then straightened up again. I could come back same time tomorrow, I thought, or I could say the hell with it. The latter course seemed the most likely, but I had a whole day to make up my mind.

I started walking, then remembered the bird cage. I could leave it there and let someone else knock a few spokes out of the wheel of

119

rebirth, but maybe it was time I earned a little merit myself. It seemed to me that it had been a while since I'd done anything the least bit meritorious. Since I'd just paid one hundred and twenty times the asking price for this poor benighted white dove, the least I could do was let him loose.

I unlocked the cage door, reached in, got hold of the bird. He did what birds do, although they generally do it on statues, or women who've just had their hair done. "Shit," I said, and I wasn't talking about the price, either.

I lifted him out and let him go, and my spirit might have soared along with him but for the souvenir he'd left behind. I didn't have anything to wipe my hands on, and I was damned if I was going to part with another ten dollars. I wiped them on my pants.

Now what was I going to do with the cage? Just set it down, I thought, and let it be somebody else's problem. And I was in the process of doing just that when I saw the envelope.

Well, actually, I'd seen it earlier, but I'd just assumed it was a piece of scrap paper of the sort you'd use to, well, line the bottom of a bird cage. The bird had evidently made the same assumption, and had acted accordingly, and in abundance. Perhaps he'd assumed the little boy was speaking English when he recited the price, perhaps he'd regarded the word as an exhortation, a command. Or perhaps he'd merely had the benefit of a high-fiber diet.

Whatever the cause, his output had been prodigious, and he'd pretty much covered the cage's paper liner. But now I got a look at it and saw that it was in fact an envelope, and I took a closer look and saw that something was written on it.

"Eight," I said, in Burmese.

I reached in, gripped the thing carefully between thumb and forefinger, and drew it out. TANNER EVAN someone had penciled on the front of it, in block capitals. The flap was unsealed, just tucked in, and I untucked it and removed a single sheet of paper, folded twice. I unfolded it and read the message, in the same awkward capital letters as my name:

GET OUT OF BURMA OR YOU DIE.

Chapter Eight

Just about everybody wore the longyis. They looked entirely unremarkable on the women, just long tight skirts that would have been appropriate anywhere. One was less accustomed to seeing men in skirts, but you got used to it, at least among the Burmese. Here and there, though, I saw a male tourist gamely sporting a souvenir longyi, and they all looked embarrassed, and rightly so. When they got home to Frankfurt and Antwerp and Keokuk, I had a feeling those longyis would go straight into the closet and stay there.

But not every Burmese wore a longyi. The cops and the soldiers, I saw, were dressed like cops and soldiers anywhere. They had short-sleeved khaki shirts with epaulets, and they had square-toed brown half-boots, and they had squared-off peaked caps. And they were wearing pants, either black or khaki.

I guess a longyi wasn't sufficiently military. I guess they figured the blood wouldn't go gelid at the sight of a horde of men in skirts charging down a hill at you. I guess nobody ever told them about the Scottish Highlanders.

Still, I'm not sure it would work without bag-pipes, and I didn't even want to think what Burmese pipers might sound like. What I did know was that the fellow standing in front of me looked very military indeed, and efficient, and quietly intimidating.

"I am so sorry," he said, in excellent English. "You would not want to walk down this street."

"I wouldn't?"

"It is no street for sightseeing," he assured me. "There are many fine things to see in Yangon. Have you been to Shwe Dagon Pagoda?"

"I've just come from there."

"Then you must go to Sule Pagoda," he said. "Shwe Dagon is the soul of Yangon, and Sule is its heart. A hair from the Buddha is preserved there."

"I see."

"And Botatamy Pagoda. Also a hair of the Buddha!"

"He must have had a lot of hairs," I said.

"And the Bogyoke Aung San Market. So much to see there! So many things to buy! Perhaps you will have a longyi made for you, so that anyone who sees you will think you are a native of Myanmar."

He laughed, so I would know he was joking, and I laughed, so he would know I got it. He named other tourist attractions—he was a regular Insight Guide—and I just stood there and nodded and smiled.

"If you wish to go to any of these places," he said, "I will be most happy to provide directions."

"I have a map," I said.

"I could trace the route for you," he said.

I told him that was very kind of him, but actually I just wanted to walk down this one particular street.

"You would not like it," he said. "There is nothing to see, nothing to do. No shops! No pagodas!"

"Even so—"

"No restaurants! Perhaps you are hungry, you would enjoy a meal. There are many fine restaurants in Yangon. Most people like the Chinese restaurants the best, but there are also fine Myanmar restaurants. Do you like Myanmar food?"

"Very much, but—"

"Or there is Indian. Or other cuisines." He smiled broadly. "But there is not a single restaurant on this unimportant little street."

The trick, I could see, was to keep me out without quite saying so. I had read about this particular ethnic tic, and the Burmese even had a word for it. An-ah-deh, they called it, and it means never giving no for an answer by convincing you that what you want—and can't have—isn't worth having in the first place, and that you don't really want it. I'm not sure whether they do it to avoid losing face or to keep you from losing face, but this fellow was certainly doing it, and trying to win the argument with him was beginning to seem a lot like trying to blow out a lightbulb.

"I was told," I said, "that a certain woman lives on this street."

"If you would like to have a woman," he said, "this is not the street for it. You would not find a woman on a street like this, and if you did you would not care for her. She would not be clean." He leaned forward, lowered his voice. "I know where you can find a woman. Very young, very pretty, very exclusive."

"I don't want a woman. I—"

"You prefer a boy? I don't blame you. Of course there is no homosexuality in Myanmar, but for a man of refinement such as yourself, certain arrangements can be made. But you could never find a boy on this poor street."

"I don't want a boy."

"Then you are a normal man! I am delighted to hear it."

"I believe Aung San Suu Kyi lives on this street."

"Ah," he said. He looked disappointed in me.

"And I would like to see where she lives," I said.

"There is nothing to see," he said. "She is

all the time inside her house. Before, she would come to the front door and talk to people, but she no longer does this."

Because SLORC wouldn't let her, I knew.

"Because it is not safe for her," he said. "So many patriotic citizens of Myanmar wish to do her harm!"

"Why would they want to harm her? Her father—"

"A great hero," he said solemnly. "But she left Myanmar, you see. She brought back ideas that are not what the people of Myanmar wish. Thus she stays inside for her own protection."

"It would be interesting," I said, "just to walk by and look at the house."

"But it is not interesting," he said. "I have seen it, and it is a most uninteresting house. Here in Yangon, where there is so much of genuine architectural interest...."

Well, you get the picture, and so did I. The street was closed to traffic, and this fellow was on hand, a holstered automatic on his hip, to deny access to pedestrians. He seemed capable of inventing endless ways to say no without saying no, but I didn't want to test his commitment to an-ah-deh to the limit. Sooner or later he would run out of patience. Sooner or later he would haul out his gun and shoot me.

Years ago, before the big wave of federal civil rights legislation, before the sit-ins and the protest marches and the Mississippi summer, states in the American South had a variety of

125

ingenious ways to deny the vote to black citizens. The literacy test was a popular one, and
in one Georgia county, so the story goes, a black
man, recently graduated from a prestigious
Northern university, presented himself to
register to vote. "All you have to do," the
local official explained, "is read a paragraph
or two of this here newspaper and tell us
what it means."

And he handed him a Chinese newspaper.

The prospective voter looked it over. "Well,"
he said, "I can make out what it says, all
right. It says no nigger's gonna be voting in
Georgia this year."

The story ran through my mind as I smiled
at the officer. "It sounds," I said, "like a very
boring street with nothing to recommend it."

"It is precisely that," he said.

"I thank you," I said, "for saving me from
a pointless and unpleasant walk. I can much
better spend my time visiting a pagoda."

"An excellent idea," he said. "It is said
that there are three things a man must do
before he has fulfilled his purpose in life."

He paused, and I obligingly asked what
they were.

"He ought to take a wife," he said, "and father
a son. And then he must build a pagoda." He
smiled and bowed. "Visit as many pagodas as
you can," he said. "But remember—no shoes!"

There was another way around to Suu Kyi's

house, but I didn't even bother to check it out. They wouldn't seal off the street at one end and leave it open at the other. And, if by some miracle I did get through, how would I explain myself if I happened to run into my little an-ah-deh master? He would not be happy, not after all he'd gone through to save face for both of us, and I could see how I'd be hard put to explain myself.

I walked for a while, and wound up on Maka Bandoola Street, past Sule Pagoda (which really was at the heart of the city) and the city hall. A block or so beyond it I gave up waving away the moneychangers and let one of them lead me into a tea shop, where I drank tea and changed a hundred dollars' worth of FEC into kyat. (They make you change three hundred dollars a person on arrival at the airport, but the official exchange rate is robbery. However, you can take dollar-value Foreign Exchange Certificates instead, and later on you can change those quite openly on the black market, which is what I was doing.)

I knew I'd get a better rate with less chance of getting ripped off if I changed my FEC at any of the large hotels, but I had another reason for doing business with a street-level entrepreneur. I could ask him questions I couldn't try on a hotel clerk.

His English was serviceable. He had a limited vocabulary, and a sometimes challenging accent, so he was not in the same league conversationally as the fellow with the gun on his hip. On the plus side, he didn't have a gun on his hip. And he wanted to do a deal with me, not stop me in my tracks and shine me on.

We did our business, a process that was not made any easier by the curious denominations that kyat come in. In addition to the bills you expect them to have, they've also got a forty-five-kyat and a ninety-kyat note. This stems not from a disdain for the decimal system but because one of their Gallant Leaders believes forty-five or ninety (I forget which) to be his lucky number. So he had the treasury print currency accordingly.

I'll tell you, I kind of liked knowing that. It was the one thing I knew about any of the SLORC-heads that sounded even halfway human. I could picture the guy sitting around the house, playing a stack of 45's and knocking back shots of ninety-proof sour-mash whiskey. Just a regular fellow, I thought, with a regular fellow's quirks.

When I had all the kyat my friend was going to give me, I sat back and smiled, then motioned to the waitress for a fresh pot of tea. "Yangon is a beautiful city," I told my new friend.

"Ah, Rangoon," he said. "Beautiful."

Was he making a subtle political statement by using the city's pre-SLORC name? Or was it just his accent making his pronunciation an imperfect echo of mine?

Hard to say. I told him that I was from New York, and that it too was a beautiful city, and very large.

He knew about New York; he'd seen movies that took place there. "Buildings ver' tall," he said. "Much bright lights."

"That's New York, all right."

"Wor' Trade Center. Liberty statue. Empi— Empi—"

"Empire State Building," I supplied.

"Empi Stableding," he agreed. "Big, ver' big."

He was from the Shan state himself, he told me, from a small village near the hill-station town of Kalaw. It was up in the mountains, with a pleasing climate. "Not so much hot," he said.

I told him it sounded lovely.

"You travel Shan state?"

"I don't know," I said. "It's possible."

"Sometimes possible. Sometimes they say no."

"The government?"

"Gov'ment," he said, and looked sidelong at me, as if to assess my feelings about the government.

"You are very fortunate," I said evenly, "to have such a strong government to care for your country." And I leaned over and spat on the floor.

His eyes lit up. "For'nate," he said, and spat. "Gov'ment ver' strong. Care for Shan people." And he hawked and spat again.

"The generals must be great men," I said. And spat.

"Great men," he agreed. And spat.

We looked at each other and smiled.

"I wonder," I said. "Is Shan food as good

as Burmese food?"

"Ha," he said. "Is better!"

"Where would I get some true Shan food in Rangoon? Is there such a place?"

Grinning, he leaned over and clapped me on the shoulder. "You come," he said. "You come. We eat good."

~

There was a Shan noodle shop just a few blocks away. I couldn't have said if what I had was better than Burmese food, since I hadn't had any Burmese food yet, but it was very good indeed. The main dish was a bowl of chicken soup with rice noodles, and it was accompanied by a dish of sour rice salad, the rice colored a deep orange-yellow with turmeric.

The local beer was Mandalay, but Ku Min wouldn't let me order it.

"Costs more," he said. "Tastes like water." It sounded like a Miller Lite commercial to me, with one contingent of ex-jocks shouting "Costs more!" while the others countered with "Tastes like water!" He ordered us bottles of San Miguel, which had come all the way from Mexico and still cost less than a dollar a bottle.

Our second round was Tiger beer, which I'd seen in the States, and our third was Bintang, which I hadn't. We were doing quite well in the male-bonding department, Ku Min and I, and hadn't found it necessary to say anything further about the government, and consequently had had no need to spit on the floor.

"This woman," I said. I leaned forward, lowered my voice. "Aung San Suu Kyi. We hear much about her in America."

"Ah," he said.

"You think she is good?"

He took his time answering. "For Burmese she is good," he said at length.

"And for Shan?"

"Shan supposed to have independent state. Supposed to have own government."

"The deal they signed with the British in 1947," I said. "The Panglong Agreement."

"You know about Panglong?"

I knew that the Shan leaders had signed away their hereditary rights and never felt they got the autonomy they bargained for. They'd been in a state of intermittent rebellion ever since. These days SLORC had the lid back on the kettle, but that didn't mean they'd stopped simmering.

Aung San Suu Kyi was all right, Ku Min allowed. She was a good person, and if she ran things the Shan would probably have more autonomy, if not the outright independence they'd bargained for.

But what difference did it make? "She got no power," he said. "Gov'ment say stay in house, she stay in house. Gov'ment say nobody go see, nobody go see. She good, she bad, what difference?"

And what if something happened to her?

He rolled his eyes at the very thought. "Be very bad," he said. "Not good to be in Rangoon when that happens. People be very set-up."

"Upset."

"Good, yes. People be upset. Go peanuts. Is right? Go peanuts?"

"Go nuts," I said. "Or go bananas."

"Go bananas," he said, enjoying the phrase. "Something happen to Suu Kyi, Burmese people go bananas."

So the Chief was right, I thought. All I had to do was kill her.

Chapter Nine

No, of course I wasn't going to kill her. In the first place, it's not the sort of thing I do. I'm a long ways from nonviolent, although I like the idea of nonviolence. But I'm certainly not an assassin.

Assassination, according to Bobby Kennedy, never solves anything. Well, I'm not too sure about that. You could argue rather forcefully that assassination had solved Bobby Kennedy. And, just as I've wondered how history might have been different if the Kennedys had not been gunned down, so I've wondered what difference a well-placed bullet or bomb might have made with Hitler or Stalin as the target. It was a little late in the game by the time Von Stauffenberg and his pals tried to take out the Führer, but suppose someone had nailed the son of a bitch in, say, 1930, or '35 or '40. Would we have been spared Auschwitz? Might we have avoided the Second World War altogether?

Recently, in the course of catching up with current events, I'd read about the Gulf War and wondered why nobody had thought to knock off Saddam Hussein. Surely it had to be more cost-effective than sending a whole army halfway around the world, and more humane than bombing hospitals in Baghdad, or burying enemy infantry battalions in the sand. And, if it was simply too difficult to pull off in the beginning, why not do it at the end, when the Iraqi army was reeling? Just drop in an airborne unit with instructions to find him and string him up. Down the line you could always attribute the action to dissident Iraqis. There had to be a few of those around, and if you just kept quiet about the whole thing, some of them would very likely jump up and claim the credit anyway.

I wouldn't call myself a big proponent of assassination. I think it's tactically unsound most of the time, and I didn't need the bald-headed guys in the red robes to tell me it was bad karma. But it still has the same thing going for it as capital punishment—i.e., it's a good bet that particular son of a bitch won't give you any more trouble. Right or wrong, humane or barbaric, it's unquestionably final.

That didn't mean I favored knocking off some of the good guys as a way to achieve their goals. That might make sense if the end justified the means, but it doesn't. And even if you thought it did, what kind of ninny would want to assassinate Aung San Suu Kyi, who, according to everybody in the world but the SLORC generals, was a sort of cross between Mother Courage and Mother Theresa?

No, I don't think so.

—〰—

So what was I doing in Burma? Why, feeling that way, had I caught the noon balloon to Rangoon?

I could say I'd always loved to travel, and I'd had a yen to see Burma since I read the Kipling poem. (As a boy, I was especially fond of that couplet that goes "On the road to Mandalay / Where the flying fishes play." For some reason I always pictured them playing gin rummy.) I could say, too, that I'd been spending too much time around the house lately and I was long overdue for a change of scene.

All true, and all beside the point. I'd accepted the assignment because, the way I looked at it, I didn't have any choice.

If I didn't go, they'd send someone else.

I never knew how many men worked for the Chief when he was working for the government, and I couldn't guess how many had followed him into private service, or whom he might have recruited recently. But I damn well knew I wasn't the only arrow in his quiver. After all, he'd managed without me for twenty-five years, and if I didn't want to go to Burma, someone else would.

And my replacement would very likely get

the job done.

Because it didn't strike me as all that hard to do. SLORC's flunkeys were keeping people away from Suu Kyi, and they said it was for her own protection, but I don't think they really expected anyone to believe it. They wanted to keep her away from her supporters, and from the journalists and TV cameras. While they were busy trying to attract tourists, they didn't need clips of her on the evening news, holding court on her front porch and telling the world not to visit lovely Myanmar after all. Now that they were opening up to foreign trade and investment, the last thing they wanted was Suu Kyi, Nobel laureate and darling of the media, calling for economic sanctions against her homeland. If they couldn't muzzle her, they just might have to kill her themselves.

Isolating the woman, albeit in the guise of protecting her, was a far cry from providing her with any real protection. They might block off her street, but I couldn't believe it would be all that hard to slip around the barriers, or to get access by going over rooftops or through backyards. SLORC might not want her dead—if they really wanted her dead, she'd already *be* dead—but neither did they think there was any real threat. Since they were her only enemy, where was the danger?

My assignment was to kill her. And my own personal mission was to accept my assignment and fail to carry it out. That was child's play—any fool could spend a couple of weeks visiting pagodas and releasing birds and slurping noodle soup—but if I did it right I could make it clear to the Chief and his mysterious billionaire that I had given it my best shot, that it was a practical impossibility, and that perhaps there might be a better way to achieve one's ends in Burma. Because otherwise I'd just be postponing the inevitable, and they'd send someone else later on to do what I'd been unable to do.

The only problem was that I didn't know how I was going to pull this off. Especially in light of the warning on the bottom of the bird cage.

Leave Burma or die.

Terrific.

It was dark by the time we left the noodle shop. I hadn't seen any other Westerners in the place, but neither had any of the other patrons registered much surprise at seeing me there. The Burmese, I could see, were an unfailingly polite lot. An-ah-deh was consistent with the whole feel of the country. They didn't want to make anyone uncomfortable.

I paid the check, as I'd taken it for granted I would do, and I was surprised to discover that Ku Min had assumed we would split it. With all the beer we'd had, it still came to less than ten dollars for the two of us, so you couldn't call it a grand gesture on my part. But it reinforced a decision Ku Min had already made: I was a genuine good fellow, and the closest thing to a brother Shan.

"You must come to my country," he said, as we stood outside the little restaurant. "You know what I mean when I say my country?"

"The Shan state," I said.

"The *independent* Shan state," he said.

"Of course."

He swayed, and grabbed a lamp post to steady himself. We had swallowed beer from all over the world, and it was not without effect, on his body as well as his spirit. "You are my friend, Evan. You are my brother."

"The Shan must be free," I said.

"Yes!"

"Free of SLORC," I said, and I spat, and he cried out with delight and spat himself.

Maybe he wasn't the only one feeling the beer.

He had invited me earlier to accompany him to a boxing match—he hadn't known the word for it, nor had I understood when he said it in Burmese, so he'd mimed it, throwing punches at the air. I'd turned him down then, and I did so now when he repeated the offer. I could imagine what boxing was like in this gentle Buddhist land. No doubt some physical equivalent of an-ah-deh applied, and you took pains to avoid striking a blow that would cause your opponent to lose face. The end result was probably more like ballet than boxing, with the winner the one who had not actually struck his opponent, but whose blows had missed their mark in the more artful manner.

"Evan," he said, his eyes moist in the light of the street lamp. "Evan, my Shan brother, how I find you again?"

"Our paths will cross," I said. And we embraced, and he went one way and I went the other.

GET OUT OF BURMA OR YOU DIE

I stood beneath another street lamp on another street and read the note again, not that there was much chance I'd forget what it said. But maybe there was a clue for me in the words themselves or the way they were written.

Printed, that is. In block capital letters that looked clumsy to me, or awkward. As if the author of the note were unaccustomed to the Latin alphabet? Or as if he had deliberately used his left hand (or his right hand, if he chanced to be left-handed) to disguise his handwriting. People did that in ransom notes, I seemed to recall, and in the messages they shoved across the counter at bank tellers, PUT ALL THE MONEY IN THE SACK, that sort of thing. I couldn't see how any of that fit the present circumstances, and decided not to try reading too much into the seven words in front of me. The message itself was plain enough. I didn't have to go rooting around looking for subtext.

But had the note been meant for me? Young Master Shit, the bird salesman, had been recruited for the occasion, and who was to say that all Westerners didn't look alike to him? Maybe he'd given the bird to the wrong person.

No, I decided, that wouldn't stand up at all. The envelope, which was just too bird-limed to hang onto, had had my name on it, in the same spidery letters as the note it contained. I had been instructed to be in a certain place at a certain time, and a few minutes after the appointed hour a kid gave me an envelope with my name on it. No matter how much beer I'd had since and irrespective of its country of origin, I couldn't sell myself on a case of mistaken identity. TANNER EVAN was what it said on the envelope, and, last I looked, that was me.

No comma between TANNER and EVAN. That suggested an Asian hand had printed those letters. An American would have written EVAN TANNER. A European might have put the last name first—a Viennese, I thought, would have made it HERR DOKTOR EVAN TANNER—but there would have been a comma if the Tanner had preceded the Evan.

But how did I know that there wasn't? I'd have had to scrape away a lot of birdshit to find out. It hadn't seemed worth it at the time, and it didn't seem worth it now, not that I still had the option.

My friends in Burma, the contacts of my contacts in Thailand and Singapore, were the source of the rendezvous at four-thirty in Shwe Dagon Pagoda. There was no getting around it. The people I was looking to for assistance had responded with threats. Nothing veiled about it, either. No an-ah-deh type niceties. Get out or get killed—just that and nothing more.

Unless....

Wait a minute. Was it a threat or a warning? It made just as much sense either way. Suppose my friends had learned that the other side was on to me, and that I was likely to be killed if I hung around. They'd want to warn me, but they might be afraid to make direct contact with me, for fear that SLORC had me under observation. That would explain the whole business with the boy and the bird cage.

Sure, that made sense. If they wanted to intimidate me, why send a boy and a bird to do a man's job? It wouldn't even take a note. Just a couple of dangerous-looking men (assuming a man in a skirt could look dangerous) telling me to get out of town if I knew what was good for me.

So it was a warning, not a threat. Unless, of course, the Burmese preferred gentle threats, with no loss of face on either side....

It was hard to say for sure, hard to tell a threat from a warning. And it was even harder to figure out what to do next.

For starters, I kept moving.

I walked a lot, for the exercise and to walk off the beer, and to transform an acquaintance with maps and guidebooks into a real feel for the city. I didn't want to stray too far from central Rangoon, but I could stay within the immediate area and still wear out a lot of shoe leather.

And I paused from time to time—to buy a few kyats' worth of tamarind candies from a vendor, to snack on fried vegetable rolls at a hole-in-the-wall around the corner from the National Museum, to duck into a teahouse and sip a pot of tea while two men at the next table puffed on cheroots and played a passionate game of dominoes, slapping the tiles down with a vengeance.

In the swank bar of the Traders Hotel I had a whisky and soda and spoke French with a wine salesman from Nice. He had been all over Southeast Asia and disliked it all, but he especially disliked Burma. "If you think that this city is disgusting," he said, "and believe me, I do—well, Mandalay is far worse. The sanitation is primitive, the cuisine is lamentable, and the women are neither skilled nor attractive. Have you noticed the pale circles on their cheeks? They paint them on to make themselves beautiful. They look like clowns in the circus."

He was glad of my company because I spoke French, and he was starved for conversation in his own language. He got plenty of it in Laos and Vietnam, but lately he'd been in Singapore and Bangkok and Jakarta, where he'd had to speak English. "Everywhere English," he lamented. "What a stupidity. If there must be a single language spoken throughout the world, certainly it ought to be French."

"The language of Voltaire," I said. "Of Racine, of Corneille, of Moliere. The tongue of Victor Hugo, of De Maupassant, of Proust and Sartre and Camus."

"Ah, my friend," he said. "You are an American. And yet you understand."

"Mais certainement," I said.

When I left the Traders Hotel, I got disoriented for a moment. (Or disasiaed, I suppose, to be politically correct.) I turned left when I meant to turn right, and walked half a block before I realized it. Whereupon I turned around and headed back where I'd come from.

And realized I was being followed.

I don't know why it took me so long. I haven't had a great deal of experience at following or being followed, and it's not something I have on my mind much. But I should have this time around, especially after the threat or warning, whichever it was, that I'd received that afternoon at Shwe Dagon. There were people who knew I was in Rangoon, and some if not all of them were not happy about it, so it was a good time for me to grow eyes in the back of my head.

The only eyes I had faced forward, and I hadn't done a great job of using them. I'd probably been followed all day, and the first inti-

142

mation I had of it was when I spun around abruptly on Sule Pagoda Road and, half a block away, somebody darted into the shadows of a doorway.

You'll go to ground, the Chief had said, and it seemed to me I should have done that right off. Even if I wouldn't be sleeping in it, I needed a place to hole up, a room where I could shuck off my backpack and unsnap my Kangaroo and kick off my shoes and relax. But first I had to make sure no one knew where my refuge was, and that meant giving the slip to the man in the doorway and any little helpers he might have brought along.

It would be easier, I thought, to dispose of a tail in a city I knew. It's a cinch in New York, with so many public buildings with multiple exits. And there's the subway—you can hop on and off, and if you time it right your shadow has to ride forlornly on to the next stop. Ditch him on the train at Columbus Circle, say, and he's stuck until the train gets to 125th Street, just over three miles away.

In the present instance, however, I didn't know the city at all, and the man or men on my tail presumably did. So I would have to be clever, and for starters I couldn't let my pursuer know that I knew I was being pursued. I had to lose him without looking like I was trying.

That meant walking on at a leisurely pace and not looking back to catch a quick glimpse of him. It's not as easy as it sounds, though, especially when you don't know who the bastard is or what he's got in mind. It's one thing if he's just a snoop, trailing relentlessly after you, content to keep his distance. It's something else if he's stalking you, waiting for the opportune moment to close the distance between you and slip a knife between your ribs.

And the latter was a real prospect, if not an appealing one. I had been threatened or warned that I would be killed if I didn't leave Burma. And I hadn't left Burma. And here I was, walking down a darkened street in an unfamiliar city, with someone tagging along in my wake.

I pressed on for a block or two, turned left, walked another block, turned right. I was on a main street now, with empty taxis trolling for fares. I hailed one, jumped into the front seat beside the driver, who looked quite startled.

"Take me somewhere east of Suez," I said, "where the best is like the worst."

He looked straight ahead, avoiding my eyes entirely. I wasn't looking at him much, either, after a quick glance. I was too busy looking out the back window.

"Just drive around," I said, and handed him a two-hundred-kyat note. "I want to see Rangoon."

I had to spell it out, but he got the idea, and by the time he pulled away from the curb, my shadow was in a cab of his own and ready to resume pursuit. That was good. I wanted to lose him, but I didn't want it to look as though that was what I was doing.

And I wanted to get a look at him.

The poor cab driver thought I wanted a sightseeing tour, and pointed out this pagoda and that public building, all in an accent that would have been hard to make out if I cared to try. I didn't have the heart to tell him to shut up.

Then he said, "That guy following us."

How had he noticed? The son of a bitch had been tracking me for hours before I got a clue.

"Like in the movies," he said with satisfaction. His English was much better now that he had Hollywood films on his mind. "Cocksucker. You want, I lose him."

First, I explained, I needed to know who he was. He thought that one over and hatched a plan. I rolled my window all the way down, held my backpack on my lap. He picked out the place where we would make our move, a narrow and poorly lit alley off a street that wasn't much to begin with. We were a hundred yards or so into the alley when another car turned in after us and immediately cut its headlights.

"Stupid," he said. "He think we not see him. But now he don't see us." He hit the brake. "Now!" he said. "Go!"

And I went, tossing my backpack out the window, thrusting myself feet first after it. The car was moving again before I hit the ground, and from a hundred yards back it must have looked as though he'd feathered the brake pedal to avoid running over a cat, or to dodge a pothole. My door never opened and the

145

dome light never went on, and he'd picked a nice dark place to do it. I had a reasonably soft landing on a patch of bare earth, and I stayed down and rolled deeper into the shadows.

I wasn't sure where my backpack had wound up, but I could wait to find out. Right now I wanted to make the most of my chance to spot my shadow. He'd be in the back seat, and he'd probably be leaning forward, his attention concentrated on the car in front of him. It would be a great opportunity for me to get a look at him, except for the very factor that had made it easy for me to give him the slip.

Namely the lack of light. A dark alley was the perfect setting for Act One of our little melodrama, but Act Two ought to be taking place on a main thoroughfare, with dozens of bright lights blazing.

Well, that wasn't going to happen. In the dark I wouldn't get much of a look at him. The best I could hope to do was tell if he was a local or a Westerner, and I wasn't by any means sure I could do that. That was one flaw in the plan. Another was that sooner or later he'd catch up with my cab and see that I wasn't in it, and he'd know I found some cute way to get away from him, and I'd hoped to keep him from realizing I was on to him.

And the third flaw was that I'd landed on my right shoulder, and I could tell it was going to hurt worse than root canal in a couple of hours.

All this takes longer to tell than it took to happen. Because I crouched there in the dark, waiting, and the pursuit vehicle made its deliberate way through the alley. It seemed to stop for an instant when it was right in front of me, but I think that was just my perception of the moment, as if it were a stopframe, frozen in time.

The guy in the backseat was facing forward, one hand on the back of the seat in front of him. His face was in profile, but the cab's interior was too dark for me to make out facial features, and far too dark to provide a hint of his skin color. All I saw, really, was a dark face and an even darker head of hair.

And a blaze of white at the temple.

Chapter Ten

I had a mini-flashlight in the Kangaroo strapped around my waist, keeping my Swiss Army knife company. It would have been handy for getting out of the alley, and I opened the zipper of the Kangaroo, groped around until I found the light, and then, reassured by its presence, decided to leave it there. Spurgeon's cab might well circle the block and make another pass at the alley before I cleared it, and I wanted to be able to disappear into the shadows if I had to.

Meanwhile, I did what I could to avoid falling on my face. The alley was evidently where the citizens of that part of Rangoon stored their spare stumbling blocks, and it's hard to keep from getting tripped up by objects in your path when you don't know they're there. I stubbed my toe a couple of times, and almost fell more than once, but I stayed on my feet. It struck me as a good thing I wasn't traversing holy ground. The trek would have been murder without shoes.

At the mouth of the alley I looked both ways without knowing exactly what I was looking for. I saw cars passing in both directions, and any of them could have been Harry Spurgeon's cab. If it had had any distinguishing marks or characteristics, I hadn't noticed them.

Unlike the man himself, who sported a distinguishing mark on either side of his head. That patch of white hair was as vivid and unmistakable a field mark as the white feathers on a magpie's wing or the eponymous scarlet of the red-winged blackbird. I hadn't really given Harry a thought since we'd shared that cab from the airport. Now, suddenly, I could think of nothing else.

And now, of course, it all seemed obvious. The way he'd so neatly picked me up when I cleared Customs, the way he'd suggested our sharing a cab. He was a type, the old Burma hand, knocking around Asia at his employer's behest, grumbling a little about each country's less palatable idiosyncrasies, and making the best of it all the while. Bluff, open, friendly, especially to another English speaker—

And determined to dog my footsteps all around Rangoon.

But who the hell was he? A player on the other side, I had to assume, but what other side? What *were* the sides in this particular game without rules? And how many sides were there?

I had a million questions and I couldn't come up with answers to any of them. When I tried, all I got were more questions.

All I knew was that I didn't see Harry anywhere right now, and I wasn't inclined to wait for him to show up. Before I'd spotted him, and long before I knew who he was, I'd been planning to go to ground.

It seemed like a better plan than ever now.

The Char Win Guest House was a four-story frame building on Mahabandoola Street. I liked the name of the street—it had such a nice musical cadence to it I was surprised SLORC hadn't changed it. And, sipping a beer in the café across the road, I decided I liked the looks of the Char Win as well. What I especially liked was that, while I drank my bottle of Mandalay (and it was watery and tasteless, as Ku Min had said it would be) I saw four couples make their way up the half flight of wooden steps and into the guest house. In two instances the couples were mixed, with the woman Asian and the man a Westerner. All four couples were traveling light, unencumbered by luggage.

My kind of place.

I climbed the stairs myself. The lobby held

149

two wicker chairs and a sad little palm tree. The fellow behind the counter looked as though he'd spent all his life staying away from sunlight and fresh air. He had sunken cheeks and a very tentative mustache, which he worried with a forefinger as he studied me.

"I want room," I said in what I hoped was basic Burmese.

It was hard to tell if he understood me or not. He peered at me, picked up a cigarette from a glass ashtray, drew deeply on it. In English he said, "You bring girl?"

I shook my head.

"You got girl coming?"

"No."

"You want girl?"

"I want a room," I said. "To sleep."

He nodded, looking neither pleased nor disappointed. He consulted what I suppose was the register, then reached to take a key from a hook. "Twenny dollar," he said.

"Ten," I suggested.

"Twenny."

"Fifteen?"

He shook his head sadly. I found a twenty-dollar bill and gave it to him, and he looked it over carefully. He said, "Passport?"

I just looked at him. He held my glance for a long moment, then shrugged elaborately. The bill went into the breast pocket of his pale green shirt. He handed over the key, pointed at the stairs. "Room Six," he said. "First floor."

First floor meant one flight up, as it does just

about everywhere but the United States. I climbed the stairs and found my room. The key was an old-fashioned skeleton type, with a brass oval attached to it, stamped with what was either a 6 or a 9, depending on which way you held it. I had trouble fitting the key in the lock, and had just about convinced myself he'd given me the wrong key when it slipped in the final quarter-inch. I turned it and opened the door.

I wasn't expecting much, and that was exactly what I got. The room was very small, just a cubicle, really. There was a single bed, an old iron bedstead, the paint flaking from the metal panels of the headboard. There was a small mahogany table and a desk chair with a cane back and seat. The seat needed some repair, but probably wasn't worth fixing. The floor was uncarpeted wood, ill used by time.

There was a window that looked out onto the litter-strewn backyard. I'd have closed the curtains if there had been any. I switched off the light instead, set my backpack on the rickety little chair, and sat down on the bed. The mattress was thin and the springs groaned. I stretched out on the bed—I kept my shoes on, what the hell, I wasn't in a pagoda—and wished I had something to read. Except there wasn't enough light to read by. Not now, with the light off, of course, but not with the light on, either. There was no lamp, just the one-bulb ceiling fixture, and the bulb couldn't have been more than twenty-five watts. And it was a long ways off, too; the one nice thing about the room was its twelve-foot ceiling.

We'll, I'd gone to ground. Now what was I supposed to do?

I settled my head on the pillow and tried not to think about lice. The room wasn't exactly filthy, although it would have been going some to call it clean. But over the years I'd found myself in a lot worse places.

Maybe I should have asked him to get me a girl. This was no room to take a decent woman to, or even an indecent one, but maybe you got a more spacious room if you were going to be sharing it.

I closed my eyes and thought about Harry Spurgeon. But I didn't want to think about him, not now. I tried instead to slip into the state of relaxation and meditation that I use as an alternative to sleep. By tensing and relaxing different muscle groups in turn, I get into a state that helps knit up the raveled sleeve of care. It's not quite the restorative that eight hours of unconsciousness provides, but it's an acceptable substitute when you haven't got a working sleep center in your brain.

I started to ease into it, then lost it when tensing the muscles in my shoulder sent a stab of pain through me. The shoulder I'd landed on was going to hurt, all right. I rubbed it a little, to no apparent purpose, then started over from the beginning. Feet, ankles, calves, thighs, fingers, hands, arms—

There was a knock on the door.

I stayed where I was, breathing slowly and deeply, trying to concentrate on the light tin-

152

gling sensation in my hands and feet.

Another knock.

Go away, I thought. And then I heard the knob turn and realized the lock was the sort that you had to lock with the key, and I hadn't.

The door opened. In an instant the woman who'd opened it slipped inside and pushed it shut, pressing her back against it. I couldn't see much in the dim light, only her silhouette against the door. She was about five-six and slender, and her hair was long. That was all I could tell.

"Please," she said.

I didn't say anything. I didn't move, either, just lay there on my back.

"You are European?"

"American," I said.

"That is even better."

I guess the U.S. Information Agency would have been glad to hear that. It's always nice to know our image in the Third World is improving. Still, I had the feeling I ought to nip this conversation in the bud.

"The clerk has made a mistake," I told her.

"He has made many mistakes," she agreed. "He would not be here otherwise."

I couldn't argue with that. I said, "I told him I didn't want a girl tonight."

"Oh," she said. There was a silence, which I thought I probably ought to fill with an apology. But I didn't, and at length she said, "But I am not a girl, not in the sense you mean. Of course you would think that. What else would you think when a woman comes to your door?"

If the clerk had sent her, I thought, she wouldn't have entered so furtively.

"I am not a prostitute," she said. "Perhaps I would be better off if I were, but I am not. If you want me to go, tell me."

"First tell me what you want."

"May I turn the light on?" She worked the wall switch without waiting for permission, and now I got a good look at her. She turned out to be Eurasian, and I wasn't greatly surprised. Her English was fluent, even educated, but it was strongly accented and I couldn't place the accent.

Whatever it was, it seemed a match for her appearance. She had straight blond hair that hung to her shoulders and a heart-shaped face with a broad, high forehead and cheekbones that were almost severe in their prominence. A lot of Slavic blood showed in her face, but the Asian was evident around the eyes and mouth, and in her complexion. I was so busy cataloging the various elements that it took me a minute to notice that, when all was said and done, she was not merely exotic. She was beautiful.

Her looks were the sort that made you sit up and take notice. I'd already taken notice, and now I sat up. I must have winced, because she asked me what was the matter.

"My shoulder," I said. "I hurt it in a fall."

"A long time ago?"

"About an hour."

She came closer, set my backpack on the

floor, and sat on the cane chair. She said, "Do you have anything to drink?"

"No."

"It would probably do you good."

"It generally does," I said.

She took a breath. "That is one reason I came here," she said. "I was at my window when you came into the hotel. I thought you might have some whiskey."

"I wish I did."

"Yes, I wish it, too."

"I might have bought a bottle," I said, "but I didn't see it for sale anywhere."

"Buddhists," she said.

"They don't prohibit alcohol, do they?"

"They discourage drunkenness," she said. "The Fifth Precept is opposed to intoxication."

"Well, so am I," I said, "but that doesn't mean I don't like a drink now and then."

"They sell whiskey in the big hotels," she said. "But not in a place like this. And it is very expensive."

"I see."

"What is your name?"

"Evan."

"Evan. It's American?"

"Well, the name is Welsh originally, the Welsh equivalent of John. Like Ian in Scottish, or Ivan in Russian."

"Evan. My name is Katya."

"Russian?"

"The name is Russian. I am—I don't know what I am. So many different things. Katya is a diminutive."

"For Katerina."

"Yes. In English it would be Katherine. What would you say for short, Kathy?"

"Or Kitty," I said. "Or Kate."

"Kate," she said, trying it out. "That is so quick, is it not? So sudden, like fingers snapping. Kate. It is almost harsh."

"Katya is a pretty name."

"Maybe you'll call me Kate. Maybe I like it. I don't know." Her forehead darkened. "Or maybe you will not call me anything at all because you want me to go."

"No," I said. "I don't want you to go."

"If we had some whiskey," she said, "we could go to my room and drink it. My room is larger than yours."

"Almost anything would be."

"And not so barren. There are some pictures on the walls, a bit of rug on the floor."

"It sounds cheerful."

"No," she said, "it is not cheerful. It is sad, like everything in this place. But it is a little better than this. Evan, could you give me some money? I will go buy whiskey."

"Where will you go?"

"There is a night market a few hundred meters from here. They sell whiskey at one of the stalls, but you have to know to ask for it. It is not very good whiskey. It is made in Burma, so how good could it be? But it is whiskey."

"How much is it?"

"Six hundred kyat. Five dollars if you pay in hard currency. I am not trying to cheat you, Evan."

"I didn't think—"

"Of course you did. A woman comes into your room and asks you for money, what else are you to think? But I am not after your money. You are welcome to come with me to the market. But I do not think you wish to leave the hotel. I saw your face when you crossed the street, and I sensed that tonight you do not care to be where people can see you."

"Well," I said, "you're right about that."

"Come to my room, Evan. I will look at your shoulder. And you can rest while I go for the whiskey. You will be more comfortable there than here."

I sat on her bed and looked out the window, and I watched as she left the hotel and walked purposefully down the street. She turned at the corner and disappeared from view.

Her room was nicer than mine, just as she'd said. It was larger, and the bed was wider and the mattress thicker. She'd taped some pictures cut from magazines on the green-gray walls, and there was indeed a scrap of worn carpet on the floor. There were two chairs instead of one, and a small chest of drawers that held her neatly folded blouses and longyis. There was no closet, but a row of pegs on the far wall held other garments, and several pairs of shoes and sandals were lined up beneath them.

I was turning the pages of a year-old copy

of *Paris Match* when the door opened and she burst in, carrying a bottle wrapped in a sheet of newsprint. She unwrapped it, a flattened one-liter bottle, and filled the two glasses from on top of the dresser.

"Ayet piu," she said, handing me one. I thought that was the local equivalent of *Cheers!* or *Prosit!* or *Here's mud in your eye!*, but it turned out to be the name of what we were drinking. The name meant white liquor, and when I'd had much the same thing ages ago at a Macedonian get-together in Tennessee, they'd called it White Mule. In the west of Ireland it's poteen, and other cultures call it other things, but whatever you call it, it tastes like fusel oil and kicks like, well, like a white mule.

"Ayet piu," I said, even if it wasn't a toast, and we both drank. "Piu," I said, and shuddered. I wasn't repeating the last name of the stuff, either. I was giving my considered opinion of its bouquet and flavor.

"It is terrible," she agreed. "But it performs the task."

"Performs the...oh, right. It gets the job done."

And I have to say it did. As warm as it was in Rangoon—and it hadn't cooled off much in the evening, either—I'd been starting to feel the chill that never entirely left my bones. But the ayet piu got right in there and fought the good fight. It smelled foul and tasted worse, but it got the job done.

I was working on my second glass of the stuff

158

when Katya sat next to me and told me to take my shirt off. She clucked with concern when she saw my shoulder, and I could see why. It was already turning an interesting color. Her fingers probed the sore spots, and she didn't have to press hard to make me cry out.

"How did you do this, Evan?"

"I was getting out of a car."

"You said you fell."

"It was more of a dive," I said. "I went through the window."

"Were you cut? Was it a bad accident?"

"It was the side window," I said, "and it was open." And I added a few words of explanation, without getting around to the question of why I'd thought it a good thing to leave a car in such an unorthodox fashion.

"But it's just a bruise," I said. "It'll look bad tomorrow and worse the next day, but then it'll start getting better."

"I envy you," she said.

"Why?"

"Because in two days you will start getting better. Days and weeks and months pass, and it never gets better for me."

"What's the matter, Katya?"

"What is the matter? I am in Rangoon."

"I guess you're not thrilled to be here."

"I hate it," she said.

"Why do you stay?"

"I stay because I can't leave. To leave one needs papers. A passport, a visa to enter another country. One needs money for a ticket. I have none of these things. Christ, I had to beg you

159

for five dollars for a bottle of bad whiskey."

"It's not that bad," I said. "I'm starting to like it."

"Well, I am not starting to like Rangoon. Or this—this castle I live in." She extended a hand. "Look at it. I brought you upstairs because it is nicer than your room. But your room was just to sleep in. I *live* here, day after day after day. Look!"

"How long have you been here, Katya?"

"Forever."

"That long," I said.

"I do not even know how long," she said. "I would have to count the months. What does it matter, Evan? You don't want to hear my story, do you?"

"Why not?"

"It is not so interesting," she said. "And my English is not so good, I am thinking."

"Your English is just fine," I said. "But what's the easiest language for you to tell it in?"

"I suppose Russian. But it is not so good Russian, I am thinking. I have never been to Russia, so how do I know if it is good?"

In Russian I said, "Why don't you tell me your story, Katya?"

Her eyes widened. "You speak Russian?"

"A little bit."

"It would be good to talk a little in Russian," she said. I suppose her Russian was accented, but I could follow her well enough. "If you are bored," she said, "just close your eyes and go to sleep. I will tell myself you are deeply con-

160

centrating."

"I won't be bored," I said. "And I won't drift off. I won't even close my eyes."

She could have been reading the Rangoon phone book, if they had one, and it wouldn't have put me to sleep. Because nothing does. But I can't imagine how anyone could have dozed off listening to her story.

Her paternal grandfather was a Russian nobleman who led a brigade of Cossacks against the Bolsheviks in the fighting that followed the 1917 revolution. When the Red victory was inevitable, he escaped through Siberia into China, eventually reaching Nanking, where he met and married a Chinese girl, the daughter of a minor war lord.

A son born of that marriage fought with Chiang Kai-shek, first against the Japanese, then less successfully against Mao's forces. When the Nationalist army withdrew to Taiwan, he went in the other direction and wound up in French Indochina. He joined up with the French, and he was with them when Ho Chi Minh's men defeated them at Dien Bien Phu.

"My family," she said, "is never on the winning side. It is a great failing of ours."

When the French surrendered, her Russian-Chinese father slipped out of the country in the company of a much younger woman, herself the illegitimate offspring of a liaison between a French merchant and a Vietnamese actress. The two wound up in Vientiane, in Laos, where they opened a restaurant and nightclub. It flourished, but then the political climate changed and they had to leave the country. They were in Thailand, among other places, and had wound up in Sri Lanka sometime in the early 1960s. They were there in 1964, when Katya was born.

"So now you know how old I am," she said.

Katya's childhood in Sri Lanka was a pleasant one. They lived in a large house in the hills overlooking Columbo, with a whole retinue of Tamil servants. Katya had a Russian nanny, herself the granddaughter of an exiled countess, and grew up speaking the language. She went to a school run by French-speaking nuns, and was fluent in that language as well, along with Sinhalese.

Then there was a change of political fortune. Her father, who had thus far led a charmed if ill-starred life, had run out of luck. He was imprisoned on trumped-up charges, tried, convicted, and executed. All of the family holdings were confiscated, and Katya and her mother, accompanied by the servants, fled to the Indian mainland. There her mother formed an alliance with a Portuguese expatriate who had been the deputy governor-general of Goa until India took over the Portuguese colony.

The story got hazy at that point—or I did, or Katya did. The ayet piu may have had something to do with the haze. I was beginning to like it, but she had a true thirst for the stuff, and was doing a good job of killing the bottle.

"Evan," she said. "In Russian that is Ivan. I could call you Vanya."

"You could," I agreed.

"Kiss me, Vanya."

I suppose she must have tasted of ayet piu, which is a hell of a thing to say about a person. But you couldn't prove it by me. I had enough of the stuff on my own breath to keep me from detecting it on hers. I took her in my arms and kissed her, and felt the soft womanly warmth of her against me. I felt a stirring, and wondered if it might not be a good time to end the Noble Experiment of celibacy. She was drunk, and to have it off with a woman in such a condition was ethically questionable. In Victorian times they called it gallantry, in my own youth it was considered caddish if expedient, and nowadays a lot of people labeled it rape. I didn't think Katya would call it that, I think it was what she had in mind when she brought me to her room, but I still wasn't sure what I wanted to do.

"My little Vanya," she said, and smiled lazily. And then she solved my ethical dilemma by passing out.

That did make it easier. I might have been able to rationalize the seduction of a drunken Katya, but an unconscious Katya was something else entirely.

There was a little of the clear liquid left in the bottle, and I left it in case she needed it

163

first thing in the morning. I unbuttoned her blouse and took it off, untied her longyi and eased it down over her hips. I'd read somewhere that men were as naked under their longyis as Scotsmen are under their kilts, but that source had had nothing to say about female under-garments or the absence thereof. I could now state authoritatively that Russian-Chinese-French-Vietnamese women residing in Rangoon didn't let anything come between them and their long skirts.

She lay on her back, her blonde hair spread on the pillow, and I drank in the sight of her. I kissed her gently on the mouth, and what worked with Sleeping Beauty had no dis-cernible effect upon Katya. She didn't move a muscle.

I drew the sheet over her and covered her to the throat. I switched off the little lamp—the overhead light was already off—and, not without reluctance, let myself out of her room.

~

I left her door unlocked. Halfway down the stairs it occurred to me that I could have tried locking it with my key. There was a good chance that most of the keys at the Char Win fit most of the locks. But if that was so, why bother locking the door in the first place?

I'd left my own door unlocked again, I saw, although I could have sworn I'd taken a moment to lock up before I went up to Katya's

164

room. But when I gave the knob a turn and the door a push it opened inward. Maybe the key had turned without engaging the tumbler. Something wasn't working right, either the lock or my memory, but I couldn't see that it mattered.

I slipped inside and reached for the light switch. And stopped when I saw that there was somebody sleeping in my bed.

Classy hotel, I thought. It was a variation on an old Henny Youngman joke—you get up in the middle of the night to go to the bathroom, and when you get back there's another guest in your room.

How had it happened? Well, maybe they put him in Room 9 and he held the key upside down. Maybe the clerk, on his rounds, checked my room and found it empty and thought he could fit in an extra off-the-books rental. Maybe Katya, with a nod and a wink, had told him during her ayet piu run that I'd be upstairs in her room.

Didn't matter. He was there, and the bed was far too narrow for two people, even if they loved each other. The night was almost over—there had been a lot of rich detail in Katya's story, and the hours had flown during the telling of it. It was almost dawn, and time for me to get busy doing...well, whatever I was going to be doing. I could leave now, or, if I wanted to wait another hour or two, I could go back upstairs and perch on a chair in Katya's room.

I opened the door to let myself out. Then

I remembered the backpack. I'd put it on the chair, but Katya had moved it so that she could sit down. And there it was, on the floor where she'd placed it.

So I slipped inside again and went over to get the pack. And that brought me close enough to the bed so that, with only what little light filtered in through the window, I could have a look at the someone who'd been sleeping in my bed.

It wasn't Goldilocks. This sleeper's hair was dark. All except the patch of white at the temple.

Spurgeon! Harry Spurgeon, asleep in my bed!

Well, not exactly. Staring hard at him, I realized he didn't seem to be breathing. I leaned in, listening, and still couldn't hear anything. I reached out a hand and touched him. His forehead was still warm—it takes a while for a body to lose heat, especially in the tropics—but I could tell I was touching a dead man.

He was lying on his stomach, the side of his face pressed to the pillow. I rolled him over to get a look at his face and found I was wrong on a second count as well. Not only wasn't he sleeping, but he also wasn't Harry Spurgeon.

I got my little flashlight from my Kangaroo and made sure. He wasn't Spurgeon, and he didn't even come close. This man was Asian, for openers, and he was shorter and slimmer and darker than the hearty fellow who'd picked

166

me up at the airport. In fact, the only similarity between the two men was the white hair at the temple.

And that was a fake. A close look with the help of the flashlight showed the hair had been bleached, with the effect heightened by the application of what looked like white shoe polish.

Who was this faux Spurgeon? And what was he doing here? And how had he died?

The last question was the easiest to answer. Whoever had stuck the knife in him had left it there, wedged between his ribs. The wound must have been instantly fatal, as there was hardly any blood.

I patted him down, looking for ID. His pockets were empty except for a single well-worn forty-five-kyat note. Something made me roll him over again, onto his face, and when I ran my hands over him I felt a bulge in the small of his back. I tugged his shirt free from his pants—he was wearing dark Western trousers, this Spurgeon imitator—and found an oilskin packet fastened to his skin with plastic-coated tape.

I ripped it free, stuffed it into my own pocket. And heard a car draw up somewhere outside, brakes squealing. And more noise in the pre-dawn stillness—men shouting, their boots slapping on wooden stairs, their voices loud and angry in the lobby.

Time to get the hell out.

I heard them on the stairs and beat them to the door, turning the key and sliding the brass bolt across as well. While they hammered at the door I rushed to the window, flung it all the way open, and tossed my backpack out. More hammering at the door, and they were fiddling with the lock, trying to get a key in while the key I'd left there blocked the way. In a minute or two they'd lose patience, I knew, and they'd kick the door in, and that would be about as difficult as shoving in the side of a cardboard box.

I sat on the windowsill, my legs outside. I got turned around so that I could get a grip on the sill and lower myself partway before letting go. My shoulder ached, and when my hands were supporting my body weight, the ache in my shoulder became something more than an ache. It felt as though my arm was being yanked out of its socket.

Could I just stay there? Maybe they'd confine their search to the room, maybe it wouldn't occur to them to look out the window—

Yeah, right. I heard them hammering at the door—more forcefully, it seemed to me—and I took a deep breath and let go.

Chapter Eleven

One of the things that had struck me during my months of catching up with the news of the world was an experiment the city of Chicago had tried a few years ago. Someone had determined that street-level drug dealers made a lot of their arrangements via public telephones. So the city ordered the removal of all pay phones in drug-infested areas.

That struck me as something like draining Lake Michigan because mosquitoes breed in it. And of course it didn't inconvenience the dealers for longer than it took them to run out and get cellular phones. But it certainly made it a lot more difficult for the rest of the public to place a call.

I wondered if the same keen civic intelligence was at work in Rangoon. If there was a phone booth anywhere in town, I couldn't find it. New York has pay phones at almost every corner. Three-quarters of them don't work and the rest have people lined up waiting to use them, but at least they're there.

And I wanted to make a phone call. I knew one man in Rangoon, and I even knew where he was staying. He was all mixed up in whatever it was that I was mixed up in, and I'd been followed earlier by someone who was either him or his double, and I knew he had a double because that's who I'd just found in my bed, deader than your average New York pay phone. I wasn't sure what I was going to say to Harry Spurgeon, but I couldn't think of a better place to start.

⟋⟍

The one-story drop hadn't done any further damage to my shoulder, though it certainly didn't do my ankle any good. I landed on both feet and managed to stay upright, and I grabbed my backpack and got my arms through the straps. The pack felt a little heavier than I remembered it, but I figured that was me. I was probably a little weaker than I'd been at the beginning of the evening.

I limped a little leaving the alley behind the guest house. I figured there might be some cops out front—I could only assume those were cops hammering on my door, and didn't want to hang around to test the hypothesis. Nor did I want to meet any of their fellows, so I worked my way through backyards instead and wound up on a different street. And decided I ought to call Spurgeon, and went looking for a phone.

I don't know what I could have done if I'd found one. The small change in Burma, all the way down to a single kyat, was in the form of paper money, and you couldn't stuff it in a telephone. Maybe they had tokens, or plastic phone cards. Then again, what did they need them for if they didn't have phones?

Of course I could just turn up at the Strand and ask for him at the desk. But the more I thought about it, the less I liked the idea. I didn't know what his agenda was or how I fit into it, but he damn well had one. I wanted to talk to him, but from a distance.

I bought some sticky rice and a couple of steamed buns from a vendor. He didn't have any English and my Burmese didn't include the word for telephone, so I asked my question by pantomime, holding an invisible receiver to my ear and making dialing motions.

"Hotay," he said.

That meant hotel, and I tried the first one I came to. The clerk was Chinese—from Singapore, I guessed—and his English was fine. Yes, he said, they had a telephone available to the public. There was only one problem. It wasn't working.

"Phone system very bad in Myanmar," he explained. "Almost never possible to call through to Mandalay. Other towns, forget it."

"I wanted to call someone in Rangoon."

He picked up the phone behind the desk, checked it a couple of times, shook his head. "Not possible now," he said. "Maybe they fix it in an hour, maybe a few days."

"If I tried another hotel—"

"Be same story. Is the whole system, not just hotel." Whereupon the phone rang, and he picked it up, rattled off a conversation in Chinese too rapidly for me to follow, and hung up. "A guest," he said. "Hotel system works fine. You want to talk to someone staying here, no problem. Anybody else, forget it."

"I tried to call," I told the young woman at the Strand's registration desk. "From Delhi yesterday, and then from the airport just now. But I couldn't get through."

171

"It is a problem," she said.

"So I don't have a reservation. I hope you have a room for me. I'll be staying three nights, possibly longer."

She had a nice room on the fifth floor, she told me, and she gave me a card to fill out. I signed in as Gordon Edmonds and made up a street address in Toronto and a Canadian passport number. My luggage would be along later, I explained. It had missed one of the connecting flights, but I'd been assured the bags would catch up with me here in Yangon, and that the airlines would deliver it to the hotel.

She asked to see my passport, and a credit card. I patted the money belt beneath my clothes and explained I couldn't get at either very easily but that I'd bring them to the desk as soon as I'd had a chance to wash up. She decided that would be fine.

I rode up alone in the elevator. It was a beautiful hotel, and I could see why Spurgeon was partial to it. I'd have been happy to stay there myself, but for the fact that a hotel room is largely wasted on a man who doesn't sleep.

I'd only come here now because I wanted to use the phone.

～

And that was the first thing I did.

"Mr. Spurgeon," I said, and spelled the name. After a long moment the phone rang, and after two and a half rings he picked it up.

172

"Mr. Spurgeon," I said again.

"This is Harry Spurgeon."

"And this is Evan Tanner," I said. "I don't know if you remember me, but we shared a taxi from the airport."

"Of course I remember you, Tanner. I hope you're enjoying Rangoon."

"As much as possible," I said.

"And you got to Shwe Dagon Pagoda all right?"

"I did."

"And took your shoes off, I trust."

"Yes, and put them back on again once I got out of there."

"Wound up with the same ones you started with, did you?"

"I think so, yes."

"That's good," he said. "One wouldn't care to be walking around in another man's shoes."

"One wouldn't," I agreed.

"And you found a place to stay? Something modest but not too modest, I hope."

"The first place I tried was a little too bare-bones for me," I said. "It turned out to be less private than I would have liked."

"I daresay that was unpleasant."

"It was," I said, "so I moved to someplace a little more upscale."

"A good idea, I'd say. What's the name of it? I always want hotels to recommend to associates."

"I'm in it right now," I said, "and I'm damned if I can remember the name of it. It's three or four one-syllable words strung together, and it sounds like a dish you'd order in a Chinese restaurant. Wan hung lo? Hu flung dung? I don't know, something like that."

He chuckled. "But you're comfortable there," he said. "That's the main thing, isn't it?"

"It is," I agreed.

"And I'm glad you thought to call me."

"I've been trying for hours," I said. "I gather there's been a problem with the phones."

"Ah, well," he said. "Burma, you know."

"I thought perhaps we could meet."

"Talk things over."

"Yes."

"See where we stand."

"Exactly."

"Good idea," he said. "Should we meet at your hotel, do you think?"

"I don't even know the name of it."

"I suppose you could always find out and ring back."

"Of course I might not get through if I ring back," I said. "Burma, you know."

"Quite. Would you want to come here?"

"The Strand, do you mean?"

"It's better than trying to meet at a pagoda," he said.

"At least we can wear shoes."

"We can. I'd tell you to pop by right away, but I'm afraid I have an appointment. Do you want to come for lunch?"

"That would be fine."

"Hang on," he said. "I've a better idea.

They do an English tea here better than you could get at home. Better than *I* could get at home, I should say. I've no idea what you could get at home."

"Any number of things," I said, "but not much in the way of a proper English tea."

"Four o'clock, then," he said. "Just say you've come for tea. They'll show you where to go. Until then, Tanner."

I can't say my mouth started watering at the thought of a proper English tea, with watercress sandwiches with the crusts cut off and similar dubious delicacies. But the Strand also boasted a proper American bathroom, and as soon as I got off the phone with Spurgeon I went and drew myself a proper American bath.

I wasn't sure whether I was going to stay put until tea time. That was the safest and simplest way. I could hang out in air-conditioned comfort, letting room service keep hunger at bay, and slipping downstairs when four o'clock rolled around.

But would the sweet young thing at the desk let me stay that long without showing her a passport and a credit card? I had both, but they were in my name, and not the one I'd signed at registration. I could come up with cash in lieu of a credit card, but how could I get around showing her Gordon Edmonds's Canadian passport?

I lowered myself into the deep claw-footed

175

tub and decided I could jump off that bridge when I came to it. The hot water was just what my shoulder needed, and wouldn't do my sore ankle any harm, either. And, in combination with soap, it was just the ticket for the rest of me, or at least for the outside surface thereof.

I'd have gladly stayed in that tub until it was time to dry off and meet Spurgeon for tea, but I knew I couldn't do that. I soaked for as long as I dared, hopped out, toweled dry, and had a quick shave. I looked a lot less grubby, and God knows I felt a lot less grubby. Insomnia, all things considered, doesn't save the traveler as much money as it might. Even though you don't need a bed to sleep in, you still have to have a place to wash up.

I got my backpack from the chair where I'd left it and dumped it out on the bed, picking out clean clothes to wear. Clean undershorts, clean socks, a clean shirt, clean khakis—I was going to be clean from head to toe, and God knew when I'd be able to make that claim again, since the chance I'd be able to wash anything out between now and my return home struck me as remote.

Well, what better venue for cleanliness than tea at the Strand?

I laid out what I was going to wear and put everything else back in my pack. Then I'd get dressed, and then—

Hello!

What had we here? It was a parcel about the size and shape of a brick, although it didn't seem as heavy as a brick. It weighed, at a guess, a pound or two. I hefted it in my hand and decided it was closer to two pounds than one.

Maybe just a little more than that, I decided.

Maybe 2.2 pounds, say. One kilogram, if you're feeling metric.

All wrapped in foil and neatly sealed with tape.

Now where had this come from? I certainly hadn't brought it with me from New York. It was the sort of thing I'd remember packing.

And it certainly hadn't been in my pack when I cleared Customs the previous morning at Yangon Airport. It was the sort of thing the inspector would have noticed, and I had a feeling he'd have made a fuss about it.

From then on the pack had stayed on my back, the zipper zipped shut. Until I set it down on a chair at the Char Win, where it stayed until Katya shifted it to the floor. And that's where I found it when I returned to my room. It had company—the dead man with the Spurgeonesque whitened temples—but it appeared undisturbed.

Yet, when I picked it up, it had seemed heavier. And well it might, I thought, having grown in weight to the tune of a kilo.

A kilo of what? Well, I didn't know. But I could all too easily guess.

I stood there, stark naked, and decided I would have to do something about the foil-wrapped brick-shaped kilo of something or other. But I wasn't sure what to do, and whatever it was could probably wait until I had clothes on.

I put down the package and picked up a pair of undershorts. And someone picked that moment to commence shouting my name and pounding on the door.

Not my name, actually.

Gordon Edmonds's name.

Well, that was something.

"Just a minute!" I shouted, and ran to the door and made sure the chain bolt was on. "Give me a second! Be right with you!"

"Mr. Edmonds, open the door!"

"Right-o," I cried, wondering if that was something Canadians said, wondering why I thought it mattered. "Just out of the tub!" I added. "Be with you in a jiffy!"

I'd dived out a car window and dropped from a first-floor guest-house window, but this time, damn it to hell, I'd taken a room on the fifth floor. Was there, by some lucky fluke, a fire escape? Or a ledge wide enough to cling to?

No and no.

"Please open door right now!"

"Yes!" I sang out. "Right now! Wish you'd let me get decent, but I daresay you're in a bit of a rush, and I wouldn't want to throw your timetable out of kilter. Know how annoying that sort of thing can be."

They had the door unlocked and were just about to hit it hard enough to smash the chain bolt when I reached it, unhooked the chain, and drew the door open. I had my clean khakis on, although I hadn't managed to run the belt through the belt loops. Nor had I put a shirt on.

And I was barefoot. If we were going to visit a pagoda, I was dressed for it.

"Come in," I said. "Come right in, make yourself comfortable. Sorry I'm not properly dressed, but I sensed that you were in a bit of a hurry. Now then, what seems to be the trouble?"

Chapter Twelve

There were four of them, all men, all dressed in smart khaki uniforms, the trousers sharply creased, the shoes polished. Two held automatic weapons and looked as though it was all they could do to keep from pointing them at me and letting off a burst. The other two were officers, with no weapons in their hands but holstered pistols on their hips. One was the little master of an-ah-deh who'd steered me away from Aung San Suu Kyi's house. The other, with an extra chevron on his sleeve, looked to be in command.

"Your papers," he said.

"My papers."

"Your passport."

"Oh, right," I said. "Didn't I leave it with

179

the girl at the desk downstairs?"

"She say not."

"Well, I suppose she's always been truthful in the past. Oh, right," I said, digging it out of my Kangaroo. "Here we are."

The man in charge let his segundo take the passport from me and inspect it before passing it on. Then he had a look at it himself, and then he had a look at me.

"Evan Tanner," he said.

"Yes."

"You gave other name downstairs."

"Well, yes," I admitted.

"Edmonds."

"Yes, Gordon Edmonds."

"Canadian."

"Yes, that's what I wrote."

"Put passport number. Different number from this."

"Yes," I said. "I can explain."

They looked at me.

"You see," I said, "I didn't want my competitor to know what I was up to. I'm a businessman, and one of my rivals has a representative in Rangoon, and I didn't want him to know where I was staying."

"So you use false name."

"That's right."

"Who is Edmonds?"

"No one, really."

"You just make him up."

"Yes. Silly of me, I suppose. I thought I'd be a Canadian, you see, and I tried to think of a Canadian name, and all I could think of was Gordon Lightfoot. The singer?"

They didn't seem to have heard of him.

"Well, he had a big hit with a song called 'The Wreck of the Edmund Fitzgerald.' About a ship that sank in Lake Superior some years ago. Gordon and Edmund, you see. Gordon Edmonds. I don't suppose it sounds particularly Canadian, but—"

"You are here on business."

"Yes."

"It says tourism on your visa."

"Yes, well—"

"What business you in?"

"I'm an importer."

"What you import?"

"Coffee, mostly. You see—"

"No coffee in Myanmar."

"But that's just it," I said. "You don't grow any coffee here, and I'm sure there are hillsides in this country that would be perfect for coffee plantations."

I nattered on in this vein, making it up as I went along, and it began to sound pretty good to me. Why not grow coffee in the mountainous regions? There were areas of the Shan state, for example, that ought to provide an ideal climate for its cultivation. It might not have the dollar-per-acre return of opium, but it could still prove profitable, and caffeine was a more socially acceptable drug than heroin, and—

"I think you have something beside coffee," said the man in charge. He pointed at my backpack, still reposing on the bed, and let off

181

a burst of Burmese too rapid for me to make out. One of the men opened my pack, and the Number Two officer began to go through my things.

"You are drug trafficker," said my interrogator. "Yes?"

"No."

"You come to Myanmar, buy drugs, sell drugs. Destroy moral fiber."

"Never," I said. "I'm all for fiber. I know how important it is."

"You got drugs in pack."

"They searched my belongings at the airport when I got here," I said. "They didn't find anything."

"This time," he said confidently. "This time we find."

But they didn't, and it didn't make him happy. There were some more rapid-fire exchanges with his subordinates, and you didn't need to know the language to realize he was pissed off—at them, at me, and at the stars in their courses.

He barked a command, and they pulled drawers out of dressers, ran their hands over the bare closet shelves, crawled around looking under the furniture. And they came up empty.

Well, Burma, I thought. What could you expect from the Third World? His American counterpart would have come well prepared, with some contraband of his own to discover if he couldn't find any of mine. But this crew was so sure they'd find that foil-wrapped brick in my knapsack that they didn't have a Plan B.

"I don't know what you're looking for," I said reasonably, "but it doesn't look as though you're going to find it. Why don't you tell me what it is and perhaps we can look for it together?"

"Shut up," he said.

I opened my mouth, considered, and closed it.

"That. What is that?"

He was pointing at my waist. "It's a Kangaroo," I said. "A fanny pack, they call it, because if you turn it around"— I demonstrated—"it rides on your fanny. Of course, they don't call it that in England because a fanny is something different over there. I don't know what they call it in Canada."

He held out a hand. Obediently I unclasped the Kangaroo and gave it to him. He opened it and shook out its contents onto the bed. No foil-wrapped brick, but how could there be? The brick was substantially larger than the exterior dimensions of the Kangaroo pouch.

"Now take off clothes."

"Couldn't you just pat me down?" I patted myself down to give him the idea. "Nothing here," I said. "Nothing at all."

"Take off clothes," he said again, and one of his men aimed a gun at me.

I took off my clothes. My pants, really, because that was all I was wearing. And my undershorts.

183

And, at his insistence, my money belt.

"American currency," he noted.

"Well, yes. I suppose I'll be sorry I didn't take traveler's checks, but—"

"Now you bend over."

I braced myself, as one does for a routine prostate examination, and I wrestled with every man's two great fears at such a time—that it will hurt, or, worse, that it will feel good. Neither came to pass. The procedure, let us say, was not overly invasive.

"Put on clothes."

"With pleasure," I said. I got into my shorts, then reached out a hand for my money belt. He just looked at me. "I guess that's a no," I said, and put on a shirt and trousers. I picked up my belt, and he took it away from me.

"It's just a belt," I said. "To keep my pants up."

He put the end through the buckle, draped the noose he'd thus formed around his neck, and mimed hanging himself. "Not safe," he said.

"But that's ridiculous," I said. "You can't expect me to walk around without a belt."

He looked at me.

"Oh," I said.

He bent over the bed, sifted through the articles he'd shaken out of my Kangaroo. He opened the little flashlight, examined the batteries. He checked out my Swiss Army knife, as if contemplating a concealed-weapons charge. Then he picked up a foil-wrapped condom and thrust it at me.

"You are on sex tour," he said. "Come to

184

corrupt women of Myanmar."

I didn't even try to answer that one, and he threw the offending article back on the bed.

"You drug trafficker," he said. "Yes?"

"No."

"I think yes."

An-ah-deh seemed to have gone by the boards, so I figured to hell with it. "I think you're full of crap," I said. "I don't approve of drugs, let alone traffic in them. I hardly ever take aspirin for a headache, and I certainly don't—"

"What's this?"

"Lariam," I said.

"Say again?"

"Lariam, just like it says on the wrapper. They're malaria pills."

"Malaria pills?"

"Well, anti-malaria pills, actually. You don't get malaria from a pill. You get it from a mosquito."

The Lariam tablets, like the condoms, were individually wrapped in foil packets. There were more of the Lariam, though. I had to take one a week while I was in Burma, and was to continue the regimen for four weeks after I got back home. They contained mefloquine, the prophylaxis of choice now that most strains of the disease were resistant to chloroquine. (If you build a better mousetrap, someone once told me, God will build a better mouse.) Lariam wouldn't prevent infection, but it would kill the parasites once they got in your bloodstream, before they could be fruitful and mul-

185

tiply. And it would remain effective, I suppose, until evolution unfailingly produced a new strain of Lariam-resistant little buggers.

The man in charge tore open a packet, took out the pill it had contained. He touched the tip of his tongue to it.

"Bitter," he announced.

"Well, of course it's bitter," I said. "They're not after-dinner mints."

"Very bitter," he said accusingly.

"Very bitter indeed," I agreed. "After all, they're quinine."

"Quinine?"

"A form of it."

"I think heroin," he said.

"Oh, right," I said. "That's very amusing. Heroin for malaria protection."

"No need for quinine," he said. "There is no malaria in Myanmar."

"I know," I said, "and it don't rain in Indianapolis in the summertime." He stared at me. "It's a song," I explained. "Little green apples? Roger Miller? Never mind."

"Heroin," he said authoritatively. "But we see. Send pills to laboratory, test them. See if they quinine or heroin."

"Fine," I said. "You take them, and let me know what you find. Meanwhile I'll just continue to enjoy your beautiful city and—"

"You come," he said. "You go to jail now."

"Jail?"

"For little while," he said, "until we get report from laboratory. If pills are what you say, then you will be deported from Myanmar

186

and returned to your own country."

"But why? For telling the truth?"

"For giving false information when registering at hotel. For claiming to be tourist on
visa application and pursuing commercial
interests."

"Oh," I said.

I waited until we were crossing the lobby to
ask what would happen if the pills were heroin.

"Then you a drug trafficker," he said. "And
we hang you. Not with belt, though. We use
rope." And he said something in Burmese—
a translation, I suppose. And everybody had
a good laugh.

Chapter Thirteen

The cell was a cage built into a corner of
the room. It was a perfect ten-foot
cube, with the floor and ceiling and
two walls making up four of its six sides.
Steel bars formed the other two sides, with a
door fashioned in one. It had swung open to
admit me, and had swung shut with me safely
inside. A padlock the size of a man's hand
assured it would not swing open again.

There was a mattress in one corner of the
cell and a chamber pot in the other. That
would have been fine for one person, but
there were two of us. My companion was sitting cross-legged on the mattress when they
shoved me into the cell, and he didn't change

position or utter a word until they left. Even then he remained silent until I looked up at a sound of rhythmic thumping overhead.

"He's dribbling," he said. "The guard. Dribbling a basketball. Didn't you see what they had on the ground floor? There's a basketball backboard and a few other odds and ends of athletic equipment. When he can't stand sitting at the desk and staring at me, and when he doesn't feel like stretching out on the couch and ignoring me, he'll go upstairs and shoot baskets. I don't know if the ball ever goes through the hoop. There's no clue from the sound if he's missing or making his shots."

"You're Australian?"

He grinned. "The accent, right? Yeah, I'm from Melbourne. And you're a Yank."

"From New York."

"Never been there. Always wanted to go. What did they get you for, mate?"

"Lariam," I said.

"Lariam," he said. "What the fuck's Lariam?" His eyes widened. "You mean for malaria?"

"Against it, actually."

"Stone the crows," he said. "You can get high on Lariam?"

"I don't think so."

"Then what do the sodcutters care if you take it?"

"They're going to analyze it," I said, "and see if it's heroin."

"Is it?"

"No, of course not. But I'd guess the lab report will say whatever they want it to say.

If they just want to deport me, they'll say it's Lariam. If they want to kill me, they'll call it heroin."

"Kill you," he said. "Would they do that?"

"I hope not."

"Stone the crows." He got to his feet, a very tall and slender young man with shaggy hair and a full beard, all of a reddish blond. "What we'll do," he said, "is we'll sleep in shifts."

"I won't be able to sleep."

"You think so now," he said, "but wait until you've been here a couple of hours. If the heat doesn't put you to sleep, the boredom will. Don't suppose you've got a cigarette, do you?"

"I don't smoke."

"Very wise. Fucking things'll kill you. Wouldn't help if you did, because the sodcutters'd confiscate 'em, same as they did mine. Took me belt and shoes, too. Yours as well."

"Yes."

"So we won't hang ourselves, though how could you? Nothing to hang from. And the shoes are a right puzzler. Mine didn't even have laces, they were slip-ons, and they took 'em anyway."

"I think they've got something against shoes," I said. "Not just in monasteries and pagodas. I think they disapprove of them altogether."

"You ask me," he said, "they hate the whole idea of feet. Fucking sodcutters would be hap-

189

pier if everybody was cut off at the knees. We'd all be scooting around on little wheeled platforms, eating rice and kissing Buddha's arse."

"There's a picture," I said.

"It is, isn't it? Name's Stuart, mate."

"I'm Evan."

"And you're a Yank and I'm an Ozzie, and here we are in a fucking jail. Not even a proper jail, either. A concrete block shithouse of a building with a sodcutter playing basketball on top of our heads."

"I wish he'd stop."

"Oh, he will. Then he'll come downstairs and sit over there and stare at us, and you'll wish he'd go upstairs and dribble some more."

"How long have you been here, Stuart?"

"I dunno. I can't say what day it is, and don't tell me because I don't know what day it was when I came here. I don't think it's two weeks yet, but I can't be sure. See, day and night's all one here, 'cause there's no window to let the sun in and no clock on the wall. And they have the light on all the time."

"They must have more than one guard."

"There's another chap, or maybe two of them. It's hard to tell 'em apart. They all do the same. Bring a tray of food now and then. Empty the slop jar now and then. And go upstairs now and then and play fucking basketball until you want to scream."

"What are you in for, Stuart?"

"I'm ashamed to tell you."

"Keep it to yourself if you'd rather," I said. "But I've been around some. I don't shock

190

easily."

"Oh, this won't shock you, Evan. And I don't mind saying. It's durian."

"Durian?"

"Durian."

"Is it an Australian word? Because it's a crime I've never heard of."

"I was eating durian," he said.

"Eating it."

"Yes."

"Is it some kind of drug?"

"No."

"Or an endangered animal species? Is it like eating whooping cranes?"

"Jesus, no. It's a fruit."

"Oh, right," I said. "I thought it sounded familiar. What's wrong with eating it? Does it get you high?"

"Not like drinking pints does." He sighed. "I say, mate, you wouldn't have a pint in your back pocket, would you? Nice frosty pint of Foster's?"

"I'm afraid not."

"Like I thought. Can't even get Foster's in this sodcutting country. Just the local brew. Mandalay. Tried it yet?"

"Yes."

"Tastes like piss, don't it?"

"I don't know."

He frowned. "Thought you said you tried it."

"I did," I said. "But I never tried the other."

"The other." He thought about it, then let out a whoop. "Stone the crows! You never tried piss. Jesus, I never tried it meself. Never hope to try it. Mandalay beer's as close as I ever hope to get."

"Same here," I said.

"S'funny how people will say that. 'Tastes like piss.' But how would they know?" He shook his head in wonder, then lapsed into thoughtful silence. I had to ask him why he'd been arrested, then, for eating fruit. Was it stolen?

"Nope. Bought and paid for."

"Legal for them to sell it to you?"

A nod. "And legal for me to buy it. Oh, I don't mean to make you drag it out of me. I was eating it in my hotel room, and you can't do that."

Now I remembered what it was about durian. "The smell," I said. "It smells, doesn't it?"

"It does," he said. "Has the most almighty pong you ever smelled in your life. You get a whiff of it and you think a man'd have to be stark mad to put it in his mouth. Then you get a taste of it and it's so good you don't care a fuck what it smells like."

"What *does* it smell like?"

"Like sex," he said.

"Like sex?"

"Like sex, but that's just part of it. Imagine if you and a really trashy Sheila was to smear yourselves head to toe with limburger cheese and then have sex on top of a heap of rotting fish."

"Oh," I said.

"That's a fair description of the smell. The taste is something different."

"It would have to be," I said, "or no one

192

would ever have a second bite of it."

"I can't describe it," he said, "but once you taste it, all you want to do is have more of it. I bought a single durian—it's a sort of a melon, like—and I took it to my room and ate the whole thing. And then I went out and bought two more."

"But it doesn't get you high?"

"Not like a drug will, or a couple of pints. It's just good, is all, and you're so glad to be eating it you've got room in your mind for little else. And in no time at all you don't mind the smell, and the time comes when you begin to like it."

"It must taste wonderful," I said.

"It does."

"And it must smell terrible."

"It does that as well, and it's a smell that lingers. The hotels have rules against bringing durian into your room, because once you do it's ages before they can rent the room again, because it pongs so bad."

"But you didn't know about the rule?"

"I knew," he said. "But I thought, what harm? So I'll open a window after, air the place out. I was three days and three nights eating durian in that room. They'll be three months fumigating it and airing it out."

"Oh," I said. "Still, to jail you over it—"

"They want damages," he said. "For all the nights they can't rent the room, plus the cost of clearing the smell out of it." He cupped his beard in his hand, sniffed deeply. "There's still a whiff of it in me whiskers," he said, "if you want to get the sense of it."

"That's all right," I said. "How much do they want from you?"

"Five thousand U.S.," he said, "which is absurd, but I'd say they'd take less. But all I've got is a couple hundred and me ticket home, and they've taken that away from me along with me shoes and me belt. And who's going to send me that kind of money?"

They'd let him try to call home, on a rare day when the phones worked, but getting through to Australia had proved to be impossible. He'd written letters to everyone he knew back home, and they'd taken the letters, and he could only suppose they'd mailed them, but God knew when they'd get there.

"And what are me mates going to think? 'Oh, that Stuart, he spent all his cash on drink and whores, and now he wants to cadge the price of the next girl and the next few pints.' Catch them falling for that line, eh?"

"The Australian consulate," I suggested.

"Oh, right. Would the U.S. consulate lend you a few thousand to pay for stinking out a hotel room? Well, neither would ours."

Somewhere in the course of his recitation the basketball stopped bouncing, and a few minutes after that our guard made his appearance. He was short for a Burmese and even shorter for a basketball player, and I didn't suppose he got too many chances to dunk the ball.

He sat at the desk and watched us for a while, then picked up a magazine and turned its pages. He'd evidently lost interest in us, and it didn't take me long to lose interest in him.

It was getting on for tea time, I thought. That reminded me how long it had been since my breakfast of steamed buns and sticky rice. I kept hunger at bay by thinking about Harry Spurgeon. Was he at a table in the Strand's lounge, having his tea? He might well be, I decided, but I rather doubted he was glancing at his watch, wondering what on earth was keeping me.

Had he sent the cops a-knocking on my door? That made the most sense. If he knew the phones were out all over town, he could have figured that my call would have had to have come from within the hotel. Once he knew that, it was a fairly simple matter to check with the desk and fill in the rest of the puzzle. Yes, Mr. Spurgeon, we did have a recent check-in fitting that description. A Mr. Edmonds, a Canadian gentleman, and he'll be coming down soon to show us his passport and a credit card, neither of which was close to hand when he checked in.

Maybe calling him from the Strand wasn't the best idea I ever had.

But what else could I have done? Lurked across the street from the Strand, hoping he'd show up? And what if he did? Then what?

I still didn't know where he fit in, or even

195

where *I* fit in. What exactly had happened last night? Someone had been shadowing me, someone I'd presumed to be Harry Spurgeon because of his whitened temples (which I was beginning to think of as whitened sepulchres, but that was wrong). But my tail could as easily have been the Spurgeon manqué, the Burmese fellow who turned up dead in my bed at the Char Win Guest House.

Scenario: X, a Burmese man who is attempting for reasons of his own to look like Harry Spurgeon, has the job of shadowing me. I give him the slip, but he circles the block and picks me up again without my spotting him. For camouflage, he picks up a prostitute and checks into the Char Win, where he goes to my room and plants a foil-wrapped brick-shaped package in my backpack.

Then the prostitute, revealing a heart of something other than gold, stabs him to death, goes through his pockets, takes his money, and leaves him there.

Or try this: Spurgeon is on my tail, and I ditch him successfully when I dive out of the taxi. But his backup man, X, stays with me. They hook up together, slip into the hotel together, and enter my room, where Spurgeon murders his partner, whitens his temples, tucks him into bed, stuffs the brick into my backpack, and takes off.

Or, as an alternative—

Never mind. You get the idea. I had too little in the way of data and too resourceful an imagination, and I could thus concoct no end of scenarios, one as plausible as the next. None of them made much sense, and all of them raised more questions than they answered.

———~———

"Feeding time," Stuart said. "Here comes the bloke with the key, and there's Gran with the tray."

"You don't sound enthusiastic."

"See how enthusiastic you are, mate, when you see what's on the tray."

Our guard unlocked the massive padlock, then unholstered his gun and pointed it in our general direction while he swung the door open. Then a little old Burmese lady, shrunken and wizened, brought two trays of food, one at a time, and set each in turn on the floor of our cell. Then she turned without a word and left the room, and the guard swung the barred steel door shut and went back to his desk and his magazine.

Stuart took a tray and sat on the edge of his mattress. "What have we here?" he said. "Why, I do believe it's chopped muck with rice. How unusual."

"It doesn't smell very nice," I said.

"Nasty pong, eh? Doesn't smell as bad as durian, but it doesn't taste as good as durian. Tastes like old lawn clippings."

"And smells," I said, "like a goldfish bowl."

"With the fish floating belly up," he said. "That's the fish sauce. They put it on everything."

"It's the same in Vietnam," I said. I dug in.

197

"But it tastes better in Vietnam."

"It tastes better in Burma," he said, "in a proper restaurant. I don't suppose jailhouse food ever gets a star in Michelin. Poor old thing that brought it, I wonder if she cooks this muck herself."

"It's amazing enough that she brings it. She looks about a hundred years old."

"She's actually twenty-one," he said. "It's the diet that does it."

I put my fork down. "I don't know if you noticed," I said quietly, "but our friend over there didn't fasten the padlock."

"I didn't notice. Are you sure?"

"See for yourself. But don't let him see what you're doing."

"I can see it from here. You're right, mate. He forgot to lock up."

"Has he done this before?"

"Not since I've been here."

"We could walk right out," I said.

"On our tippy toes," he said. "He's between us and the door, and he's got a gun."

"I know."

"In fifteen minutes or so he'll collect the trays," he said, "and he'll see the door's unlocked, and he'll lock it."

"I suppose so," I said.

"You've not finished your food, Evan."

"No."

"If you're done with it, shove it over."

"I didn't think you liked it."

"I fucking hate it. But wait till you've been here a few days. You'll be cleaning your plate and wishing for more."

"I was in a Turkish jail once," I remembered.

"Stone the crows. Like *Midnight Express*?"

"Before *Midnight Express*."

"Couldn't be. Years ago, that was. You'd have been a babe in arms."

There might be a time when I'd want to tell him about my sojourn in Union City, but not this early in our relationship. "Before I knew about *Midnight Express*," I said. "They fed me the same meal every day. Pilaf, pilaf, and pilaf."

"Sounds like a Russian law firm."

"I suppose it does," I said. "But the thing was, it was great pilaf. Really tasty. It was still jail, and it was no picnic, but I got so I looked forward to mealtime."

"If they gave you durian three times a day," he said, "I could stand this place." He thought about it. "No," he said, "I take it back. I still couldn't bear it."

I held a finger to my lips, then pointed at our guard. He had emerged from behind the desk, but he wasn't shuffling over to collect the trays. Instead he turned and headed for the stairs.

"He's left it unlocked," I said.

"So? Any second now you'll hear that sod-cutting basketball. Thump thump thump as he dribbles. Clink as it hits the backboard, thump as it hits the floor. Then another round of thump thump thump."

I waited. "I don't hear it," I said.

"Maybe he's using the toilet."

"And maybe he went out for a beer," I said, "or to check what's playing at Loew's Maha Bandoola."

"What are you doing?"

"Getting the hell out of here," I said.

"He'll spot you."

"I don't think he's there."

"But—"

"And what if he is? All he can do is bring us back and lock us up. But I think he left the door unlocked on purpose. I think he's supposed to let us out."

"So we can be shot trying to escape?"

"If they wanted to shoot me," I said, "they'd have done it already. I'm going, Stuart."

"You've got no shoes," he said.

"So?"

"And no belt. We're both of us barefoot and beltless. What are you going to do, race around on tiptoes with one hand holding your pants up?"

"If I have to."

"Even if you get away," he said, "then what will you do? You've got no money and no passport. No ticket home, no credit card, no place to stay."

"No Lariam tablets," I added. "No clean underwear. No Swiss Army knife. I don't give a damn. I'm out of here."

"But where will you go, mate? What will you do?"

"I'll—"

"Yes?"

"I'll think of something," I said.

Chapter Fourteen

There was a different clerk behind the desk of the Char Win. The fellow last night had had a mustache, albeit an unimpressive one. This one was clean-shaven, and better fed.

That improved the odds. I'd been trying to think of a way to get past him, but all the likely strategies—taking a room, hiring a girl as camouflage—would cost money. And I didn't have a single kyat between me and starvation.

A handful of gravel against Katya's window might have worked, but her window was two flights above ground level, and there wasn't a whole lot of gravel around, anyway. Besides, she had a front room, and I figured I'd attract more attention standing on the pavement chucking stones at a window than I would just walking right past the clerk as if I owned the place.

Which is what I did.

It worked, too. It would have been trickier if the clerk had seen me before. And it would have been dicier still if I hadn't had shoes.

～

"Evan!" She flung the door open. "Come in. I didn't know if I would ever see you again."

For my part, I hadn't known if she would remember my name. What a nice surprise for both of us.

"I woke up," she said, "and you were gone. I do not even remember when you left."

"You were sleeping."

"This is embarrassing, but I must ask you. Did we—?"

"We didn't."

"I don't know if I am glad or sorry. I wanted it to happen, but if I do not remember it, then perhaps it is better that it did not happen. It is a puzzle."

"Like the tree," I said.

"What tree?"

"Berkeley's tree," I said. "The one that didn't fall in the forest. Don't worry if that doesn't make sense. I just got out of jail and I'm a little confused."

"Jail! What happened?"

"That's not going to make much sense, either," I said. "But I'll tell you."

"I didn't really think they were going to hang me," I said. "If they wanted me dead, all they had to do was put a bullet in the back of my head and toss me into an unmarked grave. I figured they were going to deport me and just wanted to wait until they decided what kind of spin to put on it."

"But they let you escape."

"Well, someone did," I said. "Either the

guard was acting on instructions or somebody bribed him to leave the door unlocked
and desert his post. Or there's a slim chance
he actually forgot, and he was around the
corner squatting over a hole in the floor while
I made my getaway. To tell you the truth, I
don't much care which it was. I was in jail and
now I'm out, and out is better."

"Where did you get the shoes?"

I looked at my feet, newly shod in a pair of
stout brown wingtips. "I got them at a pagoda,"
I told her, "but don't ask me which one. At
the entrance there was a whole row of them,
and people taking shoes off and putting shoes
on, and I picked out a likely pair and walked
off with them. Walked off *in* them, I should
say."

"Do they fit?"

"Not terribly well. Even with the socks that
came with them, they're going to raise blis-
ters before long. But I didn't have money to
buy shoes, and I couldn't walk around barefoot."

"So you stole some tourist's shoes," she said,
and giggled. "Imagine the look on his face!"

"It'll cost him the price of a pair of shoes,"
I said, "and he'll dine out on the story. These
were ready for new heels, anyway."

"Oh, I am not worried about the man,"
she said. "But I am worried about you, Evan.
What are you going to do now?"

"I'm going to get out of Burma."

"And you came here." Her eyes lit up.
"You are going to take me with you!"

"Uh," I said.

"Say yes, Evan! Please?"

"I don't even know how I'm going to get out," I said. "I don't have any papers and they'll be looking for me at the airport. I'll have to go across the border into Thailand or Laos. It'll be dangerous, and it won't be comfortable."

"I don't care about danger. And I am already uncomfortable. Evan, take me with you."

I'd expected the request. Truth to tell, I had been counting on it.

"Well, all right," I said. "I'll give it a try. If you can accept the dangers and the hardships—"

"I welcome them!"

"And if you can do something for me first."

The sun was setting by the time she got back. The door burst open and she came in, her face flushed. "That was exciting," she said. "Vanya, I have not had such excitement in ages!"

"Did you have good luck?"

She opened her handbag, drew out first the foil-wrapped brick, then the oilskin packet I'd removed from the man I'd found in my bed.

"I was very good," she said, pleased with herself. "I thought my clothes might be too shabby, but the dress was Western, and that helped. And my grandmother was an actress in Hanoi. Maybe I inherited some of her talent."

She told me all about it. She'd gone to the

Strand, and she was able to see that there was no key in the pigeonhole for 514, so it was probably occupied. She took a chair in the lobby, and watched as a well-dressed man picked up his key at the desk and headed for the elevators.

Smiling, she fell into step beside him, chatting like an old friend. Wasn't it a hot day? But an exciting city all the same, no?

In the elevator, he pushed 4 and she pushed 5. As the car rose, he said, "You're not getting off at the fourth floor, are you." She agreed that she wasn't. "Then I don't suppose you're coming to my room." Alas, she said, she was not. "That's probably just as well," he said, "because I was wondering how I could possibly explain you to my wife. Still, I have to say I'm disappointed."

He got off at 4. She ascended to 5 and found Room 514. If no one was there she would have to find a chambermaid and talk her into opening the door with her passkey, and she didn't know how hard that might be. A bribe might work, but it might not.

She knocked, and a man opened the door. He was in shirtsleeves, his tie loosened. Please, she said, could she come in? There was a man following her, and she was afraid he was going to kill her.

He let her in and she sagged with relief. The man was her husband, she explained. Two days ago in Mandalay she had finally got up the courage to leave him. And now he was here in Rangoon! She had ducked into the Strand

205

when she realized he was following her, and she didn't know if she'd shaken him, and she was afraid to look. Could he possibly check the lobby and see if her swinish husband was there? She described the mythical husband— tall, fat, balding, with a scar on one cheek, even told how he was dressed. Could he be an angel and see if he was downstairs, or even lurking on the street outside? And could she wait in his room while he looked?

When he hesitated, she said, "But you do not know me. I could be a thief! Please, take with you anything that is valuable. Do not worry that you will hurt my feelings! And please, take this with you." And she twisted the ring off her finger and insisted that he take it in pawn.

Once he was out the door, she swung into action. With the chain belt securing the door against a sudden return, she stripped his bed and felt along the top seam at the end of the mattress until she found where I'd cut it open, my knife making a foot-long slash running alongside the seam. She reached in and felt around and drew out the brick wrapped in foil and the smaller parcel done up in oilskin.

They went in her purse, and no harm if he asked for a look through her bag when he returned, as they were nothing he'd ever seen before. But of course he did no such thing. There was plenty of time to get the bed back as it was, plenty of time to catch her breath before he returned to tell her the coast was clear; there was no sign of her future ex-husband, not in the lobby, not in the wood-paneled bar, not in the street outside. And, speaking of that bar, it was the best place in town for a cool drink, and did she have a minute to spare?

"So I let him buy me a drink," she said. "That was all right, wasn't it, Evan?"

"It was only gracious of you."

"That is what I thought. It was very elegant. There was a piano, with a Chinese man playing Cole Porter songs. He bought me a large gin and tonic and asked me to join him for dinner."

"You must have been tempted."

"No," she said. "It could have been a pleasant evening, with good food and plenty to drink. And he was an attractive man, Evan. He was English."

"With black hair," I said, as a sinking feeling came over me. "Except at the temples, where it had turned as white as snow."

"Why do you say that, Evan?"

"It's true, isn't it?"

"Not at all," she said. "His hair was blond like mine, only a little darker. Receding in front, and thin on top."

"Oh."

"What made you think—"

"Never mind," I said. "Anyway, you found him attractive."

"Moderately so. I could have spent a pleasant evening with him. But when I woke up I would still be in Burma."

"You'll still be in Burma tomorrow no matter what," I said. "And for quite a few mornings after that."

207

"But you will take me with you, my little Vanya?"

"I'll try."

"And these will help us, this treasure from inside the mattress? What is inside these?"

"I don't know," I said. "I'm afraid I can guess what's in the brick. I don't know about the other."

"Aren't you going to open them?"

I opened the brick first, and I can't say I was surprised by what I found. It was indeed a brick, white in color, with the slightest yellowish tint to it. I scratched it with my fingernail, raising a bit of white powder. I put a few grains on my tongue.

"Bitter," I said. "Must be Lariam."

"You are joking."

"I'm afraid so," I said. "Although I may be closer to the truth than you would think. I have to assume this is heroin, but I have no idea how pure it is. Somebody may have stepped on it."

"Stepped on it?"

"With or without shoes," I said. "Stepping on it means cutting it. They process a lot of opium into heroin in the Golden Triangle, part of which is in northeast Burma. And they don't cut it there because it's simpler to ship it in pure form. But they're not shipping it through Rangoon, so who knows what the source of this particular brick is, or how close to pure it is?"

"What does that have to do with Lariam?"

"If they cut it," I said, "they might have used milk sugar. That's a popular staple in the drug trade. I wonder what effect it has on a junkie who happens to be lactose-intolerant?" I shrugged. "Probably the least of his problems. The point is, they also commonly add some quinine, which is a component of Lariam. In fact, for all I know, this brick could be all milk sugar and quinine, because why waste good heroin just to frame me for drug trafficking?"

"So you don't think it's heroin after all?"

"No," I said. "I think it must be. And it wouldn't have cost anybody anything. It was probably confiscated in the first place, and they expected to get it back when they arrested me. That's why they were so upset when they searched the room and came up empty. They weren't getting their heroin back, and someone up above was going to want to know what happened to it."

"You hid it well."

"I didn't have much time," I said, "and I couldn't flush it down the toilet, and I didn't know what would happen if I threw it out the window. If nothing else, it would mean I'd never see it again. I was going to stick it under the mattress, but I figured they'd look there, and in fact they did. They stripped the bed and lifted the mattress. But they didn't look *in* the mattress. I had my Swiss Army knife, and I used it, and it worked." I frowned. "I wish I still had it. I wish I'd stuck it in the mattress, too, and I could have tucked in my cash and passport while I was at it. But there just wasn't time. As a matter of fact, there wasn't even time to think of it."

"What are you going to do with the heroin?"

"I don't know," I said. "Before we're done, I'll probably want to use it. For now it's an asset, and we don't have too many of those."

"And this?" She pointed at the oilskin packet I'd taken off the dead man. "Another asset?"

"Could be," I said. "Let's see."

The parcel was mostly wrapping. Bubble wrap under the oilskin, and cotton wool under that. And, huddled together within the cotton wool, three perfect carvings.

"Ivory," Katya said.

They were indeed ivory, the rich cream color slightly yellowed with age. They stood just under four inches tall, each depicting an Oriental gentleman of a certain age. One held a bird on the back of his hand, one leaned on a cane, one had his hands clasped and his head bowed. Each was exquisitely detailed and impeccably executed.

"Good luck," Katya said.

"Cheers," I agreed absently. "What's the significance of these, do you suppose?"

"But I am just telling you, Evan! This one is good luck, this one is long life, and the last is good health."

"They're good-luck charms?"

"Oh, how do you say it?" She switched to Russian. "They are not charms, like an amulet or a lucky ring. It is more that they are the personification of the three aspects of good fortune. It is a Chinese custom to have such carvings in one's home, perhaps in a shrine devoted to one's ancestors." She picked up Long Life and turned him over in her hands. "But this is not Chinese."

"How can you tell?"

"The facial features. The dress. See? He is wearing a longyi. No Chinese man would dress this way."

"Maybe it's a Chinese woman."

"With a long flowing beard?"

"Maybe a Chinese drag queen," I suggested. "A *bad* Chinese drag queen."

"Evan—"

"Just a joke," I said, and picked up Good Health for a closer look. "I see what you mean. Burmese, not Chinese."

"But showing the Chinese influence. And very old, I think."

"Valuable?"

"I would think so. There is a man I know, he has a stall at the large indoor market. Every few months I sell him a ruby."

"Where do you get the rubies?"

"I did not tell you about the rubies? It seems to me we drank the ayet piu and I told you the story of my life."

"Not all of it. You got as far as India, and the deputy governor-general of Goa."

"The former deputy governor-general. I never told you of my marriage? I married an Indian gem trader based in Jaipur. He made frequent trips to Burma, and he always wanted me to go with him. Are you sure I didn't tell you this?"

"I would remember."

"I was always unwilling to go with him, because he was smuggling stones, and I was afraid he would get caught. And finally I said yes, and we stole into Burma illegally, and one day he gave me a packet of rubies to hold because he feared his partners would betray him and rob him. And then he disappeared, and days later I heard his body had been found floating in the Irriwaddy. His throat was cut."

"Jesus," I said.

"I had no papers, I had no money, I had no way to get out of Burma. I went to the Indian consulate and waited for hours to see an awful little man, and he listened and nodded and made notes, and I never heard from him again. When I went back he would not even see me. I went to other consulates and they laughed at me. Evan, I am a citizen of nowhere in the world! I have lived in so many countries but belong to none of them. I have no passport. How could I have a passport? I have no nationality. I feel myself more Russian than anything else, but my family fled Russia seventy years ago. They picked the wrong side and they left."

"You know," I said, "this is going to sound far-fetched, but there's a decent chance of a Romanov restoration in Russia. The country's very unstable, and there seems to be a groundswell of monarchist sentiment."

212

"You think it is truly possible?"

"I think anything's possible," I said. "As a matter of fact, I'm associated with people who are working hard to make it happen. Our candidate for tsar is a grand duke with first-rate credentials, and I think his popular support base is growing nicely. Oh, I wouldn't rush out and put my money in tsarist bonds, not just yet. But I think we've got a chance."

"And if your grand duke becomes the tsar? Then will I be able to get a Russian passport?"

"You could probably get more than that," I said. "You're probably in line for a title. Your grandfather was a count or something, wasn't he?"

"My great-grandfather," she said. "My grandfather was a general in the Kuomintang."

"The point is you're descended from the Russian nobility. You can't expect a restoration of lands and privileges, but you might wind up with a title."

"A title," she said. "I would be happy with a passport and a plane ticket. Any sort of passport, and a ticket to any place but Burma. I can't stay here much longer, Evan. I am down to my last ruby."

"The ring?"

She nodded, and rubbed the tip of her forefinger against the dark red stone. "I had a little packet of them," she said. "I know nothing about rubies. I was afraid a dealer would try to cheat me. And I knew the stones would be more valuable outside of Burma. In

213

Amsterdam, say, or London or Paris. But even in India they would bring a higher price than here. That is why Nizam was able to make money buying rubies here and smuggling them back to Jaipur."

"So you didn't want to sell them all."

"And get worthless kyat for them? No, of course not. I found a dealer who seemed to be honest, or at least more honest than the rest of them. And I sold him a stone and used the money to live on, and when it was gone I went back and sold him another stone. I thought the rubies would last forever, but nothing lasts forever. I have rent to pay and I have to feed myself, and I spend far too much money on bad whiskey. But I have nothing else, Evan, and so I buy ayet piu and drink it."

"Isn't there any kind of work you can do?"

"I tried giving English lessons. But so many Burmese speak English, especially the older people who remember when the British were here. And my English is not so good, anyway. There is no other work for me." She fingered the ring. "The last ruby. I have money enough for a few more weeks, maybe a month. And then I sell the ring, and in a few months that money is gone. It is no good, Evan. I must get out of Burma."

"It's good the Englishman in Room 514 didn't run off with your ring."

"It is funny. I thought he might. And I almost hoped he would, because that would mean I would not have to sell it." She held out her hand so I could look at the stone. "It was not in the packet," she said. "Those were all unset stones. This was a gift, Nizam gave it to me. It is all I have left from my marriage."

"Maybe you won't have to sell it," I said. "Speaking of selling, what do you suppose these are worth?"

"The carvings? I don't know. They are Burmese, which makes them much rarer than the Chinese. And they are old, and very finely done. A few hundred each, certainly."

"Dollars?"

"Of course. Perhaps much more than that. They could be valuable rarities, museum pieces, even. But you cannot take them out of Burma because they are antiques."

"And you couldn't bring them into the U.S."

"Because they are old?"

"Because they are ivory. The importation of ivory is prohibited in order to discourage poachers from killing elephants."

"But this elephant was killed hundreds of years ago."

"The law doesn't distinguish between old and new ivory."

"And does it work? Does it stop the slaughter of elephants?"

"Maybe it slows it down a little. Anyway, we can't take these guys out of Burma or into the United States. Maybe the best thing to do is sell them here. Except—"

"Yes?"

"Well, the man who got killed didn't just stick

these in his pocket. He had them taped to the small of his back. He went to a lot of trouble to safeguard them."

"Yes. I think perhaps they are stolen."

"I was thinking the same thing."

"From an important collection," she said. "Perhaps from the National Museum."

"So they might be extremely valuable."

"Yes."

"And completely unsalable. We can't take them out of Burma or into the U.S., and we can't sell them here. In fact, if they're important pieces and they've been stolen recently, it's probably dangerous to have them in our possession."

"That is possible," she agreed.

"Well, I'm really glad I took them off the corpse," I said, "and even happier that I sent you chasing after them. When they're done hanging us for the kilo of heroin, they can string us up all over again for stealing national relics." I shook my head. "I never should have sent you to the Strand, Katya."

"But it was an adventure," she said. "And a gentleman bought me a drink, and I listened to a Chinese man play Cole Porter. He played well, Evan. The music did not sound Chinese at all."

"That's remarkable."

She put her hand on mine. "And I did what you asked me to do. So now it is your turn, my Vanya. Take me out of this country."

"Heroin, ivory, and thou," I said. "Three things I can't take out of Burma."

"But you will."

"I've been thinking," I said, "and there might be a way. Do you have any money at all?"

"Just kyat, and not very much. A few thousand."

"Let me have a couple hundred."

"All right."

"And have a look across the street every once in a while, in case I can't slip past the clerk when I come back."

"All right."

"And hide those things, the dope and the carvings."

"Where?"

Where indeed? "Lock the door," I said, "and if the cops come, throw them out the window."

"All right."

"The statue and the carvings, I mean. Not the cops."

"I knew what you meant, Evan. This carving is Good Luck. Touch him before you go."

"And his buddies are Good Health and Long Life? I'll tell you what," I said. "I'll touch them all."

Chapter Fifteen

"Change money," the fellow murmured. "Change money."
He was tall and thin, with an infection leaking pus in the corner of one eye. He wore

a navy blue longyi and a Reebok T-shirt and carried a canvas shoulder bag, presumably chockful of kyat to be exchanged for dollars.

"I'm looking for a money changer," I said.

"This is good," he said, "for I am a money changer, the best in Rangoon. Let us have a cup of tea and we shall do some business."

"The money changer I am looking for," I said, "is named Ku Min."

"You do not want to do business with this man. I will give you a much better rate."

"I already changed all my money," I said. "I have other business with him."

"He is a money changer. What other business could you have with him?"

"It is personal business," I said.

"Personal."

"Yes."

"I am the man for this personal business," he said, taking my arm. "I can get you a much better girl than Ku Min can. More younger, more cleaner." He cupped his hands and held them to his chest. "Bigger tits," he said. "You American, right?"

"Right."

"So you like big tits. I get you girl with great tits."

"I don't want a girl," I said, "or a boy or a chicken."

"A chicken?"

"Never mind."

"Wait," he said. I had started to walk away, and he was walking with me. "You sure you want Ku Min? He is Shan, you know."

"I know."

"You are more better off," he said, "doing personal business with me."

"I have to see Ku Min," I said. "Later, you and I can do some real business."

"Why wait? We do business now."

"First Ku Min, then business."

"But he is not here! Men like me work day and night. Shan people like Ku Min stop when sun goes down. Go watch men punch each other." He shadow-boxed, grinned. "Boom boom! Just like Rocky!"

"Boxing," I said.

"Boxing match, yes."

"But that was last night."

"Last night, tonight, tomorrow night. All week long, boxing match every night."

"How do I get there?"

"You not like it."

"You're probably right," I said. "They probably stand on opposite sides of the ring and punch the air. But if Ku Min's there, that's where I want to go. Can you tell me how to get there?"

"You really not like it, mister."

"That's not the point. Look, I'll give you a hundred kyat if you tell me how to get there."

He looked shocked. "I show you the way," he said. "No charge. I am businessman, not guide. Show you because we are friends."

"That's very decent of you."

"But," he said, "you not like it."

A forty-five-kyat note got me into the arena. It was a good-sized room, with around fifteen rows of folding chairs and backless benches on all four sides of the square ring. Most of the seats were taken, and a lot of men were on their feet, smoking cheroots and cigarettes, drinking beer from the bottle, and chattering away. I didn't see another Westerner, nor did I see any women.

Would I be able to spot Ku Min in this mob? Could I even remember what he looked like?

I was scanning the room, hoping to catch sight of him, when two fighters climbed through the ring ropes and bowed, first to various sections of the audience, then to the referee, and finally to each other. They were small and wiry—bantamweights, I suppose—and they wore shiny black pajama bottoms that stopped at mid-calf. They were bare from the waist up, and, surprisingly, they were not wearing gloves.

There was an announcement, but it was offered without a public-address system, so I couldn't hear it, let alone understand it. Then there was a bell, and then the fight started.

It was the damnedest thing I ever saw.

They rushed at each other, throwing punches. Then one kicked the other in the stomach, and knocked him down with an elbow smash to the face.

There was no mandatory eight-count. The floored boxer jumped to his feet, sidestepped his opponent's charge, and somehow grabbed hold of him by the ears and butted him three times in the face. The recipient of the butts fell back, blood streaming from his nose and mouth. The bell sounded, and the bleeding fighter went to his corner, where his trainer, looking only mildly agitated, wiped at the blood with a wet towel. Then he gave his fighter a shove, and the bell sounded again, and the two of them went at it some more.

It was hard to figure out what they were trying to do—aside from their obvious clear intention to kill one another. But as far as what was or wasn't allowed, I was very much in the dark. Knockdowns signaled only a momentary halt in the action. Evidently you didn't hit or kick your opponent while he was on the canvas, but once he was up again there seemed no limit to what you were allowed to do to him. Kicks, elbows, holding and hitting, butts, slaps—just about everything that was against the rules in the West was all part of the deal here in this gentle Buddhist land.

Marquess of Queensbury, eat your heart out....

Blood seemed to slow things down, and after one of the fighters had evidently reached the stage where he was going to need a transfusion, the referee stopped the proceedings and raised the bleeder's opponent's hand in victory. There was no little dance of triumph, nor did the two men hug each other. They bowed—

to each other, to the ref, and to all of us—and they climbed on out of the ring.

"Evan!"

I turned at the sound of my name, startled. I had not managed to find Ku Min, I had been too absorbed in the bloodletting to look for him, but somehow he had found me. He hadn't even been looking for me, which made his accomplishment an impressive one. On the other hand, his was the easier task. He looked, to my untrained American eye, an awful lot like everybody else in the hall. I, on the other hand, was as hard to miss as a black satin sheet at a Klan rally.

"Is great sport," he said. "Yes?"

"No," I said.

"No? You do not like?"

"I'm just not sure it's a sport," I said. "Why not let them bring machetes into the ring with them? Or chainsaws, that would be sporting."

He shook his head. "Is boxing," he said. "No weapons allowed."

"Well, then that's the only place they draw the line," I said. "I'm not sure I understand why they bother to stick a third man in the ring. The referee doesn't have anything to do. Because there aren't any rules for him to enforce."

"There are rules."

"But what are they? There doesn't seem to be anything you can't do. If there are rules, they must be about as effective here as the Geneva Convention is in Bosnia."

"I do not know Geneva Convention."

"Neither do the Serbs, apparently. Never mind. Look, Ku Min, I have to talk to you."

"We talk."

"I need your help."

"I help."

"Can we go someplace?"

"After," he said firmly. "Plenty matches to go. After last match we go somewhere, we talk, I help. But first we watch boxing."

"Well—"

"And I explain rules," he said. "So you understand."

There were rules, after all. And the participants observed them scrupulously. All in all, what I saw gave force to the argument the Libertarians have been advancing for years—i.e., the fewer rules you have, the less inclined people are to break them.

Biting was against the rules. So was kicking or striking a floored opponent. Kicks to the groin were not allowed, or punches either. Eye gouging was out, and strangulation was also against the rules.

Just about everything else was fine.

In essence, you could use just about any part of your own anatomy to belabor just about any part of your opponent's. You could kick him above the waist, as you are allowed to do in Thai boxing and karate, and you could also kick him below the waist, as long as you took care to avoid the groin. You could use your elbows and your knees, and it was entirely kosher to employ your head as a battering ram.

You could grab with your hands to facilitate any of these other stratagems. You could clutch your opponent's ears prefatory to butting him in the face, as I'd seen in the first bout, and you could also cup his head in your clasped hand and bring his face down into his upraised knee, which I saw done to spectacular effect toward the end of the evening

Knockdowns didn't mean much, but blood did. The object was to draw blood, and a fighter could wipe away the blood twice, but the third time it flowed the bout was over. There were other ways a fight could end. If one fighter was unable to go on, the ref could end the bout even if no blood had been drawn. If a fighter was knocked out cold, that too meant the bout was over. And any fighter could call it quits on his own initiative, but I never saw that happen. My guess was that, if you had a well-developed instinct of self-preservation, you wouldn't have gotten in the ring in the first place. Once there, you just stayed at it until they made you stop.

I think I must have watched seven or eight bouts. Some of them lasted a good long time, while others were over in hardly any time at all. Early on I just wanted the whole thing to be over. Watching the fights was something I had to do to win Ku Min's cooperation later, and it was a small enough price to pay, and he was the only game in town. The so-called sport we were watching was a scant notch up the evolutionary ladder from the Christians-versus-lions stuff that diverted the Romans way back when, but at least these guys were in the ring of their own volition, which was more than you could say for the Christians—or, come to think of it, for the lions, either.

It was bloody, and it was brutal, but it wasn't my blood that was flowing, so what did it hurt me to watch it? And watch it I did, and after three or four bouts something curious happened.

I started to get into it.

Ku Min was a help, not only explaining the rules but filling me in on the fine points. And, because he was betting avidly on each bout—everybody in the place, as far as I could tell, was gambling feverishly—I had at least a vicarious stake in the outcome. He would let me know which combatant he was supporting, and I would root ardently for our guy, and groan when he took a fierce elbow to the ribs, and exult when he planted a knee in the pit of his opponent's stomach.

It didn't hurt, either, that we were on the winning side in all but one bout. It's always more satisfying when your man wins, of course, but this meant that Ku Min was making a small fortune for himself. That would put him in a good mood, and I wanted him in a good mood.

The final bout ended with a bang, when our guy launched a roundhouse kick that caught the other fighter flush in the mouth, spraying blood and teeth over the ringside spectators.

Ku Min collected his bets, clapped me hard on the shoulder, and steered me toward the exit.

It was my bad shoulder that he walloped, but I barely felt it.

～

"All you must do," Ku Min said, "is get to Shan state. There the Shan people will help you."

"And from there I can get to Thailand."

"With ease," he said. "Shan forces control the roads."

"I thought they made peace with SLORC."

"Peace," he said, and spat, and grinned. We were in a tea shop, drinking Tiger beer, and spitting on the floor beside one's table was probably not recommended by the Burmese equivalent of Miss Manners, but no one took any notice. "There is no fighting since the peace was made," he said, "or not too much, but our Shan rebel army is still in control of the territory. They leave us alone, and we leave them alone. Someday there will be war again, but for now there is peace."

"It's that way everywhere."

"Yes," he said. "The great army of the SLORC patriots"—he paused and spat —"is still strong in the western part of the Shan state. But when you cross the Salween River you will be among friends."

"That's great," I said.

"But from here to the other side of the Salween," he said, "is a great distance."

"I know," I said.

"You must go north and east. There is a boat that could take you north from Rangoon to Mandalay. But I think you will not ride all the way to Mandalay. I think you will leave the boat at Bagan."

"The old city," I said, "with all the ruined pagodas."

"Yes. I could get you on the boat. It is a cargo boat, you understand. The passenger boats on the Irriwaddy are forbidden to tourists."

"Why?"

"No one knows. They just tell you that you would not like it."

"Ah," I said. "An-ah-deh."

"Yes, an-ah-deh. But you will be on a cargo boat, hidden in a load of goods bound for Mandalay. But when you leave the boat at Bagan, how will you make your way eastward?"

"It's a long way to the Salween."

"You would need to get to Kalaw," he said, "or to Taunggyi, the capital of the province. People there would help you. But from Bagan to Taunggyi—"

"How far is that?"

"Perhaps two hundred and fifty kilometers."

Say a hundred and fifty miles. It would take a week to walk it. Longer if the terrain was rough and the weather adverse. Longer still if I got lost along the way.

"But to walk the road without papers, a foreigner in Myanmar—"

"And a wanted man," I said. "A fugitive."

"Yes. Government troops patrol those roads, Evan. They would insist on seeing your papers."

I drank some beer straight from the bottle. I pointed to a man passing in front of the tea shop window. It may have been bad manners to point, but at least I used my hand. I didn't point with my foot. I knew better.

I said, "I bet the patriotic government forces"— I spat— "would not ask him for papers."

"But he is not a Westerner, Evan!"

"How do you know?"

"But look at him! He is—"

"I know what he is," I said. "At least I know what he looks like."

Ku Min looked at me.

"Clothes make the man," I said. "Do they have that expression over here? Probably not, in the land of the longyi. But you see what I'm driving at, don't you?"

Chapter Sixteen

"You are truly determined to leave Burma."

"Vanya, I would do anything to get out!"

"It will be dangerous."

"I do not care."

"And there will be hardships. It will not be an easy journey, or a comfortable one."

"It does not matter."

"And we will have to travel light."

"That is the best way, Evan."

"Very light," I said. "You will have to leave everything behind."

"So? You know my family history. Every generation has left everything behind and fled one country to start anew in another."

And every generation, I thought, has managed to choose the wrong side.

"Besides," she said, "look around you, Evan. What is there that I would regret losing? I have nothing. You think it will sadden me to leave these four walls? Or these ragged clothes? Or anything else in my possession?"

"We'll really be traveling light," I said. "You'll have to leave more than that."

"But I have nothing else! Evan, tell me what else I have to leave. I will be delighted to leave it, but there is nothing else that I own."

I looked at that beautiful face, that rich and exotic blend of East and West. Kipling was proven wrong; East was East and West was West, but the twain met spectacularly in those high cheekbones, that arch of brow, those almond-shaped eyes, that luxurious curtain of straight blond hair.

"This," I said, reaching to touch her hair. "I'm afraid it has to go."

"You think" she said, wielding the scissors savagely, "that because I am a woman I am overly concerned with my appearance."

Snip! Snip! "But I do not care about super-
ficial things." Snip! Snip! "Hair is just hair.
You cut it off and it grows back." Snip! Snip!
Snip! "It is true I like my hair"— Snip! —"and
perhaps I take some pride in it"— Snip!
Snip!—"but it is a small sacrifice if it will
get me out of this godforsaken country"—
Snip! —"and give me a chance at a new life!"
Snip!

"That's great," I said.

"Yes."

"Because I was a little worried. I know
hair's a big deal for women."

"And not for men?"

"Not in the same way. We worry about
losing it, but we don't care what it looks like.
We don't even mind cutting it all off so long
as we know it'll grow back."

"And you will not mind shaving off all of
yours now?"

"No, of course not."

"Then neither will I." Snip! "There, Evan.
I think that is as much as I can get off with the
scissors." She ran her hand through the mound
of hair on the floor in front of her. "Well? You
are the one who will have to look at me. How
does it look?"

All she needed was a safety pin through
her cheek and she could pass for a punk rock
star. "It looks unfinished," I said, "and it'll
be better when I've shaved it all off. But it's
not so bad." I nodded at the mirror. "Have a
look for yourself."

"Why not? It is just hair. It is not important,

it will surely grow back." Then she fell silent as she looked in the mirror.

Then she burst into tears.

Her hair was fine and soft, and offered little resistance to the razor. When I'd finished, she looked again into the mirror, and for a long moment she was silent.

Then she said, "Do I look like a man? I don't think so, Evan. I don't look like a woman, but neither do I look like a man. I look like some sexless creature from another planet."

"It just takes getting used to," I said. I picked up the scissors, then turned to her. "I don't know," I said. "Maybe this is a bad idea. Suppose I just turn myself in. What can they do to me?"

"Evan—"

"I mean, they're not going to hang me. So they'll slap me around a little and kick me out of the country. Hell, I've been thrown out of better places than this."

"Evan, please—"

"So maybe that's what I'll do," I said. "How about you? You'll be all right, won't you?" I held up a hand. "Hey, I'm just kidding. Honest."

"I know you are kidding," she said. "That is why the scissors are still in your hand. Otherwise they would be in your heart."

"Uh," I said.

"My ears are large," she said. "I never realized this before. I have large ears."

"Your ears are beautiful."

"They were better when one did not see so much of them. Suddenly I have ears like a bat. And look at the shape of my head."

"What's wrong with the shape of your head?"

"I don't know. I was never so aware of it before, the shape of my head. Now I am suddenly aware of nothing else." She patted at her skull, framing and reframing it with her hands. "It is small," she said. "I have a small head. With big ears."

"It just looks that way because you're used to it with hair."

"Of course I am. Evan, we should have made love before I did this. When I was still beautiful."

"You're beautiful now."

"You don't have to say that. I will get over this, Evan. I am in shock, that is all, but I am adjusting to it. This is just part of the process of adjustment."

"I understand."

"Anyway," she said, "we will travel light, yes? No mirrors."

I took her place in front of the mirror, looking at my own closecropped skull. If a barber had done this to me, I thought, I'd kill him. It would be better once I shaved it, I told myself. And then I remembered that I'd told Katya the same thing.

"No mirrors," I said. "Count on it."

With our hair scissored off we'd looked like victims, and a tad demented in the bargain. With our heads shaved, we just looked weird.

In our new robes, we looked like monks.

Or did we? It was hard to tell, even as it was hard to wrap oneself properly in the dark red cloth. It was probably the first thing you learned at monk school, how to wrap the set of three cloths so that they covered everything they were supposed to cover and wouldn't fall open at an inopportune moment. They all seemed to know how to do it, even the small boys, but there had to be a trick to it, because we didn't seem to have gotten the hang of it.

"Don't wrap the outer robe too tight across your chest," I advised Katya. "It makes you look, uh—"

"Like a woman," she said, and adjusted the drape of the robe. "All my life," she said, "I felt that my breasts were too small, and now I find out they are too large. Should I bind them, Evan?"

"It's too late now," I said. "They're already grown."

"To flatten them," she said.

"Oh, I was thinking of Chinese women, you know, binding their feet."

"I don't think they do that anymore, Evan."

"No, of course not. But should you try to flatten them? I don't know. Let me see."

She opened the robe.

"I just meant let me look at you in profile, Katya. I didn't mean let me look at your breasts."

"I'm sorry. I thought you wanted to see them."

"Well, I suppose I did," I said. "But that's not what I meant. My God."

"What is the matter?"

"You're beautiful," I said.

"Even with my head shaved?"

"Even if you wore a Richard Nixon Halloween mask," I said. "Your breasts are—"

"Too small."

"No."

"Too large."

"No," I said. "Just right." I took a deep breath. "You'd better close the robe. Now let's see how it looks."

"And how does it look, Evan?"

"It looks fine to me," I said. "But to tell you the truth, I liked it better open."

I looked hopelessly white.

Part of that, I knew, was attitudinal, and would change of its own accord. An actor's face changes slightly when he gets into character, and the same thing happens when a traveler in another country speaks and thinks in another language. Speak French, or even speak English with a strong French accent, and one begins to shrug in a characteristic French fashion, and in a short time one's features take on a Gallic cast.

But that wouldn't help me from a distance, and my freshly shaven head would be a positive beacon of whiteness. I said as much to Katya and she produced an answer, working on my head with cosmetics. Her supply was limited, as was my patience for this sort of thing, but I have to say it made a difference. I still looked white enough to join a neo-Nazi group—and God knows I had the right hairdo for it—but at least I didn't gleam.

"Besides," she said, "there are white monks."

"Sure," I said. "Franciscans, Carthusians, Dominicans, Benedictines—"

"White Buddhist monks."

"In Burma?"

"In Burma," she said. "I have seen them. They come here to study Theravada Buddhism. That is the same branch as in Sri Lanka."

"And in Thailand," I said. "And Laos and Cambodia."

"They come to live in one of the meditation centers. I have seen them on the street in the morning, Evan, dressed in robes like ours and carrying their begging bowls."

"Maybe they're just hippies," I said, "looking for a free meal."

"They are monks."

"I'm sure you're right," I said. "It's just that I haven't seen any."

"Well, there are so many monks."

"No kidding."

"Every Buddhist is expected to pass some time as a monk. For a week or two as a young boy—"

"Shit," I said, remembering the kid with the bird.

"I beg your pardon?"

"Never mind."

"The boys serve for a week or two," she said. "They are novices. There is a word for it."

"Samanera," I said.

"You know all this?"

"Ku Min gave me a crash course," I said, "along with the robes and begging bowls. He's a Buddhist, and he was a samanera and also a pyongyi. That's when you're a grown man and you spend three months at a monastery as a fully ordained monk. Not everybody stays the whole three months, some figure three days is enough, but Ku Min went the distance. He thought of spending the rest of his life there."

"But instead he became a money changer."

"And threw himself out of the temple," I said. "But he's still a good Buddhist. I think it bothered him a little, the idea that I'd be pretending to be a monk. Sacrilege and all that. But he gave me a quick course in the religion so that I'd know what kind of behavior will be expected of me."

"You'd better tell me, too."

"Monks have to live by ten precepts," I remembered. "There are the five rules that all Buddhists are expected to follow—no killing, no stealing, no unchastity, no lying, and no intoxicating substances."

"The last three, Vanya, may be a problem."

"I've broken two of them already today," I said, "and I stole some guy's shoes. I'm chaste, though, and I haven't killed anybody lately. Anyway, those are the standard ones. There are five more for monks."

"What else can't we do?"

"No eating after noon," I said. "No listening to music or dancing."

"What if there is music playing? How do you keep from hearing it?"

"I guess you just think of something else. Just so you don't break into a fast fox trot." I scratched my head. "There's three more. No wearing jewelry or perfume. No sleeping on high beds. And no accepting money for personal use."

"We cannot eat after noon?"

"Not when people are watching."

"And I cannot wear my ring, but I already thought of that. A ruby ring would look out of place on the hand of a monk."

"Oh, I don't know. The color's a good match for the robe."

"No high beds. To remain humble, I suppose. The difficult one will be not to eat after noon."

"All it means," I said, "is we have to avoid being *seen* eating after noon. Look, the monks probably rise and shine around two in the morning and go to sleep by sunset, so abstaining from meals after noon probably isn't that much of a stretch for them. We'll manage to stow some food and eat it when nobody's looking. Remember, most of the time we'll be walking along the road, with nobody anywhere near us. We can eat all we want then. Hell, we can even talk."

"Can't we talk the rest of the time?"

"I don't think it would be a good idea. We'd call attention to ourselves by speaking in Russian or English. And your voice is a little higher than the average monk's."

"Of course. If they hear me—"

"The jig is up," I said, "and I don't know what they'd do if they found out a woman was pretending to be a monk, but I think it might involve a violation of the First Precept."

"The one against unchastity?"

"Uh-uh," I said. "The one against killing."

We each had a cloth shoulder bag. They were both the same, and both matched our robes. Each contained a black lacquer begging bowl, a cup, and a razor. (I thought the razors would be of the old-fashioned cut-throat variety, but Ku Min had furnished a couple of disposable Gillettes. That was going to make shaving easier, but it substantially reduced the razor's potential value as a defensive weapon. "Watch it, you son of a bitch, or I'll slice you open with my plastic safety razor." No, I don't think so.)

We each had a small strainer of woven bamboo, for removing insects from our drinking water. That didn't bear thinking about. A pair of wandering monks wouldn't be buying bottled water, not that we'd be likely to find it on sale in the little village markets along the way. That meant we'd be drinking tap water or well water or ditch water, whatever the locals drank, without having built up the immunity that the locals had.

That being the case, I figured it would be a good sign to find insects swimming around in our drinking water—it meant the stuff would support life. And the insects, if we chewed them up and swallowed them, might be all the protein we got that day. Of course it would mean violating the precept against killing—and, depending on the time of day, the one against eating after twelve noon.

The few kyat we had left went in my bag, since I'd be more able to speak up safely if we needed to buy something. The three ivory carvings, wrapped up again in their bubble wrap and oilskin, went in Katya's shoulder bag. I didn't know how or to whom we could peddle them, but their value was high in proportion to their weight.

Besides, I wasn't going to leave them behind. A man had died giving them to me (although he probably hadn't planned on giving them to me any more than he'd planned on dying). I figured I ought to hang on to them. And, as Katya pointed out, Good Luck and Good Health and Long Life were much to be desired, and by no means to be taken for granted in the adventure we had in store for ourselves.

Katya's eyes widened when I put the brick

of heroin in my bag. Was it not dangerous to be carrying it? And would it not add unnecessary weight? And, at the risk of being picky, was it not somehow a violation of one of the precepts? Surely it was an intoxicating substance, was it not?

"We're not going to ingest it," I said. "As a matter of fact we're not even going to take it with us. At daybreak Ku Min's coming to take us to the boat."

"That is very nice of him."

"Well, he's a nice fellow, and the two of us really hit it off."

"And he bought these sets of robes, and the begging bowls, and the shoulder bags."

"And the Gillette razors, too," I said. "And in return we're going to give him a kilo of heroin."

"It is for him?"

"Why not? Have you got any use for it? Because I don't."

"No, but—"

"I told him I wasn't even certain what it was. I said it's probably heroin, but it might be milk sugar and quinine, for all I knew. He seemed to think it was worth the gamble."

"Evan, if it is heroin, how much is it worth?"

"You got me," I said. "If the DEA seized it in a drug raid in Miami, the newspapers would tell you it had a street value of a quarter of a million dollars. But that would be what it would wind up retailing for after it had been stepped on three or four times and parceled out into twenty-dollar bags and sold to desperate junkies. That's a lot different from what it's worth to a wholesale buyer in the States, let alone to someone in Rangoon."

"Even so—"

"Even so," I said, "it's worth a lot more than a couple of red schmattes and a pair of black bowls. Is that what you were going to say?"

"I guess so. What is a schmatte?"

"A rag," I said. "Or in the present instance a robe. If Ku Min finds a buyer for the stuff, I guess he'll make out handsomely. But he's making more of an investment than the robes and the rest of our gear. He got us the sandals, don't forget."

She picked up one and studied its bottom. "It doesn't say Ferragamo," she said. "In fact it was cut from an automobile tire."

"That means it'll probably outlast anything Ferragamo makes. He also set things up with the guys on the boat, and he'll let people in Shan country know that we're coming. Katya, I was planning on leaving the heroin behind and trying to think of a way to get rid of it that wouldn't get it traced back to us. If you think I made a mistake—"

"I did not say that, Evan."

"I'm not sure any of this is a good idea," I said. "All we can do is roll the dice and take our best shot."

"It would be safer for you to travel alone."

"I'm not even sure of that. Maybe a monk knocking around on his own is cause for suspicion. Maybe they're like nuns, always traveling in pairs."

"But they do not travel with women, Evan."

"Well, no," I said. "They don't."

"I think I will go to sleep now," she said after a moment. "We have only a few hours before daybreak. Will you come to sleep, Evan? It may be your last chance to sleep in a high bed."

"I think I'll sit up for a while," I said.

"Are you sure?"

"I'm too tense to sleep."

"There must be a way to get rid of tension."

"I don't think that would be a great idea, Katya."

"I do not blame you," she said. "Who could make love to someone who looks like this?"

"That's not it."

"It is," she said, "but it is all right. I am too tired, and you're right, it is not such a good idea. Good night, Evan."

"Good night, Katya."

She was silent for a while. Then she said, "Vanya, could you just lie with me and hold me for a little while? I will be strong once our journey begins, but right now I am frightened."

I got in bed with her. She had shucked her outer robe and one of the others, leaving only the third, a sort of glorified loin cloth. She came into my arms and burrowed close, and her fear was a palpable thing. I could feel her trembling, and I held her gently but firmly in my arms until the trembling ceased.

She murmured something. I could tell it was in Russian, but it was too soft for me to make it out. I went on holding her and breathed in her scent, and even as her own breathing deepened with the onset of sleep, I felt myself stirring in response.

Easy enough to open my own robes, easy too to take the last bit of cloth from around her loins. Easy to part her thighs, easy to ease between them....

I don't know what stopped me. Not fear of disapproval, God knows. If anything, she'd welcome it. But it just didn't seem appropriate, not hours before our entry into monastic life. And it struck me as strategically unwise. The role we would be playing was a sexless one, and how sexless an energy would we project if we had just squeezed in a quickie?

My mind knew this, even if my body had a will of its own. I clenched my teeth and breathed deeply, and my resolve stiffened. It wasn't the only thing that did, but it proved the stronger, and after a few minutes I got out of bed without disturbing Katya and sat cross-legged in a corner of the room, waiting for the dawn.

I felt, by turns, virtuous and stupid. And after a while I realized it was possible to feel both those things at once.

Chapter Seventeen

Sunrise and sunset are increasingly abrupt as you approach the Equator. It was still dark when Ku Min met us in front of the shuttered teahouse across from the Char Win. By the time we boarded the flat-bottomed boat that would take us upriver to Bagan, the sun had cleared the horizon and the sky was bright.

I moved to follow Katya on board, but Ku Min caught my arm. "Evan," he said, "your companion is very quiet."

"He doesn't say much," I agreed. "He only speaks one language."

"Ah. And what is that?"

"Norwegian."

"And you speak Norwegian also?"

"Yes."

"But you are from America."

"Yes."

"And your friend, he is from Norwegia?"

"Norway."

"Yes, Norway. He is from Norway?"

"He is."

"It would probably be best," he said, "if he does not speak at all."

"That's what I thought, Ku Min."

"He is tall," he said. "That is a point in his favor. But, Evan, my friend, if one looks closely—"

"I hope nobody looks too closely."

"His hands are small, you know."

"Well," I said. The nails were clipped short, and there was no polish on them, but we hadn't been able to do anything about the size of Katya's hands.

"And his aura," he said.

"His aura?"

"Some people can see auras," he said.

"Especially monks trained in meditation. I cannot. But anyone can sense the energy of another human being, is it not so?"

"And your sense is...."

"That you and your male companion must be very careful, Evan. You should be all right on the boat. The captain is my friend, and the crew members know to take no interest in the passengers. Still, they could talk afterward, and word travels quickly."

"I'll try not to give them anything to talk about."

"Yes. And when you leave the ship at Bagan—"

"We'll be careful."

"Yes. You will see other monks, Evan. There are monks everywhere. Be especially careful around them."

"We will."

"If I had known...."

"You'd have helped us just the same."

"Yes," he said. "But I would not have slept well. Good luck, my friend."

I shook his hand, boarded the boat, and found the place in the hold where they'd made room for us. We'd be out of the crew's way there, and out of sight of the people on the banks and the passing river traffic. I settled in next to Katya, my back braced against a burlap sack of rice. The boat started its engines, and I closed my eyes and breathed deeply, inhaling the rich smell of foodstuffs and other goods bound for Mandalay.

The cargo included a load of dried fish and

a pile of hides, and their smells predominated, but there were other top notes to be detected, a whiff of this and a sniff of that. A hound dog would have had the time of his life.

We got underway. Katya was quiet for half an hour or so, and I thought she might be sleeping. Then her hand caught mine and she gave a squeeze.

"He knows," she said. "Doesn't he?"

"Who, Ku Min? Knows what?"

"You know. About me."

"Doesn't suspect a thing," I said. "We fooled him completely."

I'm not sure she believed me, but she relaxed, and the next thing I knew she was sleeping, curled up on one burlap sack and using another for a pillow. I closed my own eyes and tuned in to the motion of the boat and the thrum of its engines. I snacked on one of the cakes of sticky rice we'd brought along, and when Katya stirred I fed her one.

The ship sailed lazily upstream, stopping at little river ports to load and unload cargo. After one such stop around noon a crew member brought down lunch for us, twin paper cones of rice and vegetables. The food was greasy and salty enough to sink the spirits of a cardiologist, but it was tasty and we were both hungry. He didn't seem to expect to be paid for it, either, or for the two bottles of beer he brought us.

Just like the airlines, I thought. Except the food on the boat was better.

After he was out of earshot, Katya held her bottle aloft and raised her eyebrows. "Beer," she said. "And it is past noon, is it not?"

"You'd have to ask the little uniformed prick who took my watch," I said. "I'd say it's pretty close to noon."

"The men on the boats, Evan. Do they know we are not true monks?"

"They know there's something dodgy about us," I said, "or they wouldn't be smuggling us with the dried fish. As far as the beer is concerned, that may be a gray area for monks. I'm not completely sure. They may distinguish between distilled spirits and beer. The idea is to avoid intoxication. The beer in these countries is a whole lot safer than the water, and maybe they take that into consideration."

"There's no label on the bottle."

"Well, I can see why. It's not very good beer."

"And there's only one bottle for each of us."

"It's the standard complaint," I said. "'The food is terrible and the portions are small.' I'm not sure if monks can drink beer or not. My guess is, nobody's going to put it in our begging bowls."

"Will we really go begging?"

"It's what monks do. It has a different connotation when a monk does it; it's not like being hit on by a child in Calcutta who's been maimed by her parents so she'll look more pathetic. A begging monk makes it possible for people to earn merit by putting some rice in his bowl. He's performing a useful function."

"I should look forward to it," she said. "It has been a long time since I performed a useful function."

The sun was just setting when we docked in Bagan. The captain came for us and helped us ashore. He said some parting words that I couldn't make out, so I just nodded and pressed his hand in reply.

We were on our own now.

And I'd have to say the first few hundred yards were the hardest. It was a little early for tourist season—December and January would be the peak months—but Bagan was a town for tourists, and there were plenty of them in evidence, large hearty fair-haired Europeans with cameras.

It seemed to me that they were staring at us, and of course they were—not because we didn't look like true monks but because we did. A few of them pointed their cameras at us, and I decided they must be very recent arrivals. If they took pictures of every monk they saw, their film wouldn't last long.

We lowered our eyes and walked past them, and it turned out to be easy to ignore them once we got the hang of it.

It was a little harder to ignore Bagan.

It was all pagodas. There were literally thousands of them, ranging in all directions for as far as the eye could see. There were big ones and small ones, ornate ones and simple ones, pagodas in good repair after UNESCO's restoration efforts and crumbling pagodas badly in need of attention. Most of them were the work of a Burmese king who'd converted to Theravada Buddhism with a vengeance a thousand years ago. He'd built pagoda after pagoda, and so had his successors, and the result, all these centuries later, was dazzling, if incomprehensible.

Why?

I could understand why UNESCO was engaged in restoration, mending the gradual damage of centuries of neglect and the more dramatic effects of the 1975 earthquake. The town's archaeological value was enormous, and undeniable. And I could understand why the tourists came, and wouldn't have been surprised if there had been far more of them. The sight of all those gold and silver stupas glowing in the setting sun was as impossible to prepare for as a first glimpse of the Grand Canyon.

But why build the damn things in the first place? That's what I couldn't figure out. What on earth made old King Anawrahta think it was a good idea?

We spent the night in a ruined pagoda.

I wasn't sure of the propriety of that, but I figured it would be reasonably safe. Tourists climb some of the pagodas before dawn in order to watch the sunrise, even as they climb others in late afternoon to watch the sun go down over the Irriwaddy. But the pagoda I picked for us was a rundown dun-colored wreck, not tall enough to attract climbers or remarkable enough in any other way to draw anyone else. In a place like Bagan, the unquestioned pagoda capital of the world, it wouldn't make anybody's must-see list, especially at night.

We sat together in one of its darkened corners and polished off the last of the sticky rice. A beer would have been nice, Katya said. Or a slug of ayet piu.

"We may be able to have beer," I said, "once we get off the beaten track. But I think we can forget ayet piu."

"I know."

"They get their drinking water from the river," I said, "and I guess it doesn't kill them. And you've had a few years to acclimate to the water in Rangoon, so you'll be all right. I guess I'll come down with a case of Burma belly, but it won't kill me. And I can't buy bottled water. They might accept a monk drinking beer, but not paying for water."

"Maybe the water won't be so bad."

"Maybe not," I said. "I'm more worried about the mosquitoes."

"I have had a couple of bites."

"I just nailed one of the little suckers. But I don't think he was the last mosquito in Bagan."

"If you killed him, you violated the First Precept."

"Nobody's perfect. I just wonder what kind of mosquitoes they are."

"Females," she said. "The males don't bite."

"I mean the species. In other words, are they the kind that carry malaria? I still have Lariam working in my system, but I'm supposed to take a pill once a week, and the week's up tomorrow. So the mosquitoes will have one or two Lariam-free weeks to bite me, maybe more."

"And you are worried?"

"Well, yes," I said. "I suppose it's a more romantic disease than, say, the heartbreak of psoriasis, but I don't imagine it's a lot of fun. Come to think of it, what do you do?"

"What do I do?"

"You've been living here for years, and I gather you don't take Lariam or anything else. How do you keep from getting malaria?"

"I don't worry about it."

"The malarial mosquitoes only bite at night," I said. "At least that's what the book says, though who knows if the mosquitoes have read it. I suppose a person could stay inside from dusk to dawn, but I know you don't live that way. And there were no screens on the windows of the Char Win, anyway."

"No."

"Some people never get bitten. It's their body chemistry, mosquitoes just don't like the taste of them. But you said you've already been bitten a couple of times tonight, so that can't be it."

"No."

"I suppose some people are naturally immune. The parasites can't thrive in their bloodstream, so even if they get bitten they aren't infected." She was shaking her head. "Then I give up," I said. "How come you don't have malaria?"

"I do have it."

"You do?"

She nodded. "For years, before I ever got to Burma. You never get over it, you know."

"That's what I heard. I think there's a new treatment, but—"

"Perhaps there is. But they told me the parasites stay in your system forever. The body adjusts to them, and most of the time you are fine. Unless the immune system is badly stressed, and then you get an attack."

"And that happens to you, Katya?"

"Not so often. Only twice since I have been in Burma. It is not so bad. Chills and fever, and a terrible aching in the bones."

"That sounds pretty bad to me."

"Well, it is not good. But when you recover you cannot remember it too clearly. Because of the fever, I guess. So it is not so bad."

"Oh," I said. "You're not naturally immune, then—"

"Obviously not."

"—but it's possible that some people are, isn't it?"

"I suppose it is possible."

"And it's possible I am one of those people."

"That is possible, too."

"But not terribly likely," I said, and slapped

another of the bloodsucking little bastards.

Shortly after that she curled up in a corner and went to sleep, leaving me with nothing to do but think and hours to do it in. After a while I slipped out of the pagoda and looked up through the clear desert air at a sky full of stars. I watched them for an hour or so, hoping they'd make me turn philosophical, but my thoughts stayed on a worldly plane, switching back and forth from the probable consequences of malarial infection to those of being exposed as a mock monk, and in the company of a woman.

What would they do to us?

Precepts or no precepts, I somehow didn't think they would be inclined to shrug it off. I hate to generalize, but I think you can say that no religion is terribly good at taking a joke. The Ayatollah Khomeini hadn't been able to have a good laugh over *The Satanic Verses*, and even those faiths that place great stock in turning the other cheek are apt to lose it in the face of sacrilege and heresy.

Great thoughts to wile away the hours of darkness. I'll tell you, it was a relief when dawn came up (not quite like thunder, but impressively all the same) and we could go out and start begging.

It was easier than I'd thought it would be.

I had seen how it was done, but I'd watched a man fly a jet fighter plane, too, and that hadn't made me feel qualified to replace him at the controls. Begging, however, wasn't like that, nor was it one with brain surgery or rocket science. You walked along the street, and you held out your bowl, and people put something in it. Rice mostly, but sometimes it had bits of vegetable in it, and sometimes they gave you a little cake of sweet sticky rice.

And they liked doing it. It was something the average Burmese got a chance to do every day, so they didn't make a big deal out of it, but they genuinely seemed to welcome the chance to earn merit for the price of a handful of rice.

For our part, we would wait until no one was looking, then scoop the contents of our bowls into the plastic bags in our shoulder bags. I gathered monks generally quit begging when their bowls were full, but we had to net enough calories in a morning's scrounging to carry us for the rest of the day. We wouldn't be sitting around meditating, either. We'd be walking east across Burma.

So we filled our bowls and stowed our take and kept going, holding our newly empty bowls in front of us and smiling benevolently on everyone in our path. We repeated the process, and the third time around the donations got a little more interesting. No one thought to toss in a Big Mac or a pint of Johnny Walker, but we were showered with nuts (almonds and cashews), dried fruit (raisins and apricots), and little fried dumplings, contents unknown.

Time to sit on our haunches somewhere and chow down, I thought. And up pops a pair of young soldiers, with holstered pistols on their hips and rifles slung across their backs. Where had they come from?

Well, we wouldn't have to worry about malaria, I thought. Or dysentery, or whether Social Security would still be intact when we were old enough to collect it.

One of them said something in rapid-fire Burmese. I didn't catch any of it, but replied with an all-purpose smile and a finger to my own lips, the latter accompanied by a shake of the head. I'd tried out that routine earlier, hoping it would convey the notion that we couldn't speak, and most people had gotten the message.

It was hard to tell what the soldiers made of it. The one who'd spoken now turned to Katya and either repeated his first question or asked her something else. She did as I had done—a smile, a finger to her lips, a shake of her shaven head.

Jesus, could he stand this close to her and not notice she hadn't needed to shave her face? But maybe not. He was wearing a uniform and carrying enough weaponry to wipe out a small village, and it didn't look as though *he* had had to shave yet himself.

He barked out a command that was as incomprehensible to me as everything else he'd said, turned on his heel and trotted off. I smiled stupidly at the other soldier, inclined my head in a slight bow, and took a step away from him. He moved quickly, extending an arm to block my path, and said something. I didn't need a Burmese-English dictionary to get the message. He wanted us to stay right where we were.

The rifle was slung across his back, I noticed, and the pistol's holster was snapped shut. How hard would it be to jump him and knock him senseless? If I took him by surprise I could probably bring it off, and I'd have his automatic rifle in hand by the time his buddy came back with their commanding officer.

Good thing I didn't try it. It probably would have worked—the kid's guard was down, and the last thing he expected was a sudden attack by a red-robed monk. But I'd have felt like an awful fool when the other kid came back alone, carrying a couple of bananas and two cakes of sticky rice.

"We're not going to starve," I told Katya. "We may get hanged as spies or burned at the stake for sacrilege, and we may die of malaria or sunstroke, but we're not going to starve."

We were on the road, heading eastward from Bagan, and there was nobody near us to see us or hear us, a line that came readily to mind just then because we'd recently had tea for two.

We'd eaten, stuffing ourselves without depleting the hoard in our shoulder bags. There was plenty left to carry us through to nightfall. I was thirsty, and mentioned as much to Katya. I didn't really want beer just yet, nor did I want to chance buying it in Bagan, where word of two odd-looking beer-drinking monks could all too easily filter back to Rangoon. The water might do a number on my stomach, but so would the food, and I couldn't worry about that now. I'd take my chances.

But how did you go about getting water? The locals fetched jugs of it from the river, and the tourists bought the pure stuff in bottles at their hotels, but what was a poor but honest monk to do?

"Nobody poured water in our bowls," I said. And she gave me a look and got her cup from her shoulder bag and marched into a teahouse, smiling warmly and holding out her cup with both hands.

The proprietor didn't even get a chance. A customer leapt to his feet, snatched up his teapot, and filled her cup. I got out my own cup, and another man earned himself six ounces of merit. We hit three teahouses and drank three cups of tea apiece, and I have to say it hit the spot.

"We won't starve," I said again. "We might even get out of this alive."

Chapter Eighteen

Day by day, we settled into a routine. Up at daybreak, beg for food, eat breakfast, beg for tea, and hit the street. Stop at a village around midday, get something to drink, wait in the shade until the sun had dropped a few degrees from its zenith, then walk to the next village, or as close to it as we could get. Then eat the final meal of the day where no one could see us, polishing off whatever was still stowed in our shoulder bags. (An evening meal might violate a monastic precept, but cross-country trekkers have precepts of their own, and "Don't go to bed hungry" is one of them.)

By the time the sun went down, we would find a place for Katya to sleep. Within a few days, she had noticed that I never seemed to be sleeping myself, and I wound up telling her about the sleep center, and how I didn't have one anymore. (I didn't tell her I'd been like this since before she was born, or that I'd spent the past quarter-century in cold storage. That, I felt, was more information than she needed to contend with.)

We'd usually make our camp at the edge of a village, though one night we dossed down in the middle of nowhere rather than try to walk with only starshine to guide us. It would have been great to use those evening hours, when the sun was down and the air cooled off and the roads were empty, but not when the trade-off was an inability to see where we were going. I lamented my little flashlight, along with my Swiss Army knife and so many other indispensable articles I was now forced to dispense with, and I wished all kinds of ill fortune upon the head of the little SLORCist martinet who'd taken them away from me.

As far as that goes, I'd have liked my sneakers back. The Formerly Firestone sandals, staple footwear throughout the Third World, were not so bad once you got used to them, but Michael Jordan was never going to want to swap his Nikes for them.

Of course I couldn't have worn my sneakers even if I had them. They would have looked out of place peeping out from under a red robe. The sandals slowed us down, and gave us sore calf muscles the first few days, and God knows they never provided much in the way of cushioning. But they were a better fit than those wing tips I had filched, and one did tend to get used to them.

"This isn't so bad," I told Katya one morning. "Plenty to eat, loads of fresh air, and not a lot of decisions to make about what clothes to put on in the morning. I can see why a good percentage of the men who try it decide to make it their life work."

"Of course," she said, "that means a lifetime of the ten precepts. Never to sleep in a high bed might not be so bad, but always to sleep alone?"

"There's a downside to everything," I admitted. "And it's not just ten precepts when you're a lifer. On that level you've got two hundred and twenty-seven precepts to contend with."

"So many! How could a person even learn what they all are, let alone follow them?"

"That's why the short-timers make do with ten."

"Two hundred and twenty-seven of them! Evan, there are not that many things that I do to begin with. How could I give them all up?"

"Think of the poor nuns," I said. "They've got three hundred and eleven precepts."

"Nuns?"

"Right."

"You mean Carmelites and Poor Clares? Catholic nuns?"

"Buddhist nuns."

"There is such a thing?"

"I saw some in Rangoon," I said. "Their robes are pink. You've lived here for years. Didn't you ever see any?"

"I thought they were monks," she said. "With robes of a different color, to signify that they were novices, perhaps. Or monks of a different order."

"Well, they're monks of a different gender," I said. "In other words, nuns."

"Evan!"

"What's the matter?"

"I could have been a nun!"

"This is an odd time to discover a vocation," I said. "I thought you were hellbent on getting out of this country, but if you really want to spend your life in a convent in Rangoon—"

"I mean I could have *pretended* to be a nun," she said, "the way I am pretending to be a monk. Ku Min could have brought me pink robes instead of red, and I would not have had to shave off all my hair—"

"Buddhist nuns shave their heads," I reminded her. "That's why you didn't know they were women. Remember?"

"So I would have shaved my head. That is the least of it. It is every moment pretending to be what I am not that is such a strain on me."

"You'd still be pretending," I said. "You'd be pretending to be a nun instead of a monk, that's all."

She'd goofed earlier that day, automatically heading for the women's lavatory at a village teahouse. A man had caught her arm in time and pointed her toward the men's instead, and he and his companions had all had a good laugh at the unworldly monk who'd almost dishonored himself by squatting over the wrong hole in the ground.

"I don't know why they laughed," she said now. "What was so funny about it?"

"The irony of it," I said. "As a monk, you're not even supposed to look at women, and here you came that close to using a woman's toilet."

"And what would that do? Shrink my precious penis? Cause my balls to fall off?"

"It's a violation of a precept, that's all."

"If I had a pink robe," she said, "I would

261

not have to concern myself with such nonsense."

"If you had a pink robe," I said, "I wouldn't be able to have anything to do with you. Nuns are women, even if they don't look like it. I'm not supposed to look at you, and I'm definitely not allowed to touch you or speak to you, so it would raise a few eyebrows if the two of us set out to walk across Burma together."

"Of course," she said. "I forgot."

"But if you wanted to spend your life wearing a pink robe in Rangoon—"

"Evan."

"Or in some rural convent, where there are no men for miles around."

"Evan, please." She was silent for a few minutes, and then she said, "Why do they hate women so much? Didn't Buddha have a mother?"

"Sure he did, and so did Jesus. A lot of people can simultaneously revere the Virgin Mary and insist that women can't be priests. It may look contradictory to you, but it makes sense to the pope."

"But to think it defiles a monk to be touched by a woman—"

"Not defiled exactly," I said. "I don't think that's quite it. I think it all grew out of the chastity precept. Maybe it's a way of playing it safe. If a man never lays eyes on a woman, let alone touches her, he's not in much danger of losing control and jumping her bones."

"Perhaps that is the justification for it, Evan. But that is not what it says to me. To me it says women are dirty, women are immoral, women exist to lure men into sinful behavior. It is cloaked in religion, but it is not religion because it is to be found in one form or another in all religions."

"You're right about that part," I said.

"It is men," she said. "They despise women, so they make a religion out of it. But it is not religious. It is just men being disgusting."

"Men are swine," I agreed. "Are you sure you don't want to look for a nunnery along the way? It would shake them up a little when you walked in the door, but as soon as you got rid of your robes and stood naked before them they'd recognize you as a soul sister."

"Oh, shut up," she said.

A while later, she said, "I am sorry, Evan."

"For what?"

"For telling you to shut up. For saying nasty things about men."

"I'm the one who said men are swine," I said, "and we probably are, all things considered."

"Nevertheless, I apologize. It is the sun, I think. It is so strong."

"Why don't we take a break? There's a shady spot coming up."

"If I sit down I won't want to get up again."

"Are you feeling all right, Katya?"

"Yes, I think so," she said. "I think it is just the sun."

A couple of hours later the sun was lower in the sky, and we had eaten and rested a little, and shared a large bottle of orange soda from a roadside stand. This didn't go in the begging bowl; the vendor expected to be paid for it. But it was only twenty kyat. That was hardly any money, but we had started out with hardly any money, so I was doing what I could do to make our remaining kyat last.

The orange soda tasted of sugar and chemicals, but I found I didn't mind. The sugar was welcome after all the exercise we'd had, and the chemicals were reassuring; I knew the stuff was safe to drink, because no known pathogens could possibly survive in it.

We got back on the road, and I was wondering where we would spend the night. There was another village down the road ahead of us—there always is, sooner or later—but it was hard for me to gauge just how far it was, or if we could expect to reach it before it was too dark to walk.

We were walking more slowly today, it seemed to me. I kept having to ease my pace to accommodate Katya. And we were making more frequent stops.

I looked at her now, and she caught me looking and asked me what was the matter.

"You look a little tired," I said.

"I am a little tired."

"Yes, but you look different. Stressed out."

"There is nothing wrong with me, Evan."

"I didn't say there was. I just—"

"I am perfectly fine."

"Whatever you say," I said.

Traffic was generally pretty light. A couple of times a day a bus would pass, each time reminding me that a bus would have conveyed us from Bagan to Taunggyi in a day instead of the week or more it was taking us. But I had not seen how we could have spent that much time in such close quarters without having our deception exposed by the other passengers. We'd be in Taunggyi in a matter of hours, all right, and as soon as we got there we'd be placed under arrest.

There were other public conveyances, too, for those citizens who couldn't afford the luxury of a broken-down bus. For even fewer kyat one could ride in a van, with everybody's luggage tied to the roof and everybody's children hanging out the windows. The van passengers stood up throughout the journey, pressed together like upright sardines. I didn't imagine monks ever rode those things. A monk could be deaf and blind, and he'd still break the chastity precept before the van had gone ten miles.

There was some military traffic, too, and the first time a truck full of soldiers passed us I got a little nervous. But we got used to it.

This afternoon a whole convoy passed us, every driver sounding his horn, young men in fatigues leaning out of the troop carriers to wave to us as they went by.

"So many soldiers," she said. "Where do you think they are going, Evan?"

"To the Shan state," I said.

"The same as us."

"Yes."

"But why?"

"Probably to kill the very people who are supposed to help us get out of the country."

"There is fighting there? I thought there was peace."

"There was," I said, "the last I heard. But they've been waging this war off and on for close to forty years. All a peace treaty does is give both sides a chance to catch their breath."

"I wish I could," she said.

"You wish you could what?"

"Catch my breath. We have to stop for a minute, Evan."

"There's some good shade just up ahead on the left."

"I don't think I can wait that long," she said, and dropped her shoulder bag to the ground, and dropped down next to it herself.

I squatted beside her. "Katya," I said, "you don't look well."

"I don't feel well."

"It must be something we ate this morning. It hasn't hit me yet, but—"

"It is not something we ate, Evan." She took my hand, put it to her forehead.

"My God, you're burning up!"

"Yes," she said. "And I feel dizzy and light-headed. And I have been seeing things out of the corners of my eyes. Flashing lights, bolts of lightning. And my muscles are sore, but not from walking so much. A different kind of soreness. And there is a pain deep in my bones."

"It sounds terrible," I said. I put my hand on her forehead again and tried to estimate how much fever she had. "You're very calm about it," I said. "Has this happened before?"

"Many times," she said. "Evan, this is malaria."

Chapter Nineteen

It was not that bad, she assured me. She had had it before and she knew what to expect. When this happened in Rangoon she had a way of dealing with it. She would take a lot of aspirin and quinine, drink a pint of whiskey, and get in bed underneath a lot of blankets. And she would feel much better in the morning.

The only problem lay in the fact that we didn't have any aspirin or quinine. Or any whiskey. Or any blankets. Or even a bed for her to get into.

"I'll stop a car," I said. "We'll get you to a hospital. There has to be some kind of clinic somewhere. In Taunggyi, or back in Bagan."

"I do not want to go back to Bagan, Evan. And I do not need to go to a hospital."

"Are you sure?"

"I am positive. We will find a place for me to sleep, and the fever will break during the night. And I will feel better in the morning."

And we did, and it did, and she did. We bedded down in an orchard a few dozen yards from the side of the road. The trees were laden with a fruit I couldn't recognize, the size of a peach but shaped like a pear, with a glossy yellow skin. It would have been nice if they'd turned out to be durian, but when I broke the skin of one, the odor was closer to that of an apple. Whatever they were, they were a long way from ripe, and I let them stay on the trees.

When she was comfortable—or as comfortable as she was likely to get, lying out in the open wracked with malaria—I went out foraging. I found the farmhouse where the keeper of the orchard presumably lived, and I skirted it carefully, hoping my scent wouldn't set off a canine burglar alarm. But my luck held. Either the family dog wasn't paying attention or the family had eaten him. Whatever it was, nobody barked at me.

There were several outbuildings, and I slipped in and out of each of them. I found a heavy canvas jacket with a fleece lining, and I found a couple of reasonably clean towels, and that was all I could turn up that looked at all useful. Back in the orchard, I wrapped

Katya's feet in the towels and laid the coat over her for a blanket.

It seemed to me there ought to be something more I could do, but I couldn't think what. There would be a village within a few miles, but it might be an hour's walk there and an hour's walk back, and I didn't want to leave Katya alone that long. Suppose she woke up in a panic? Suppose the coat's owner decided to check his fruit trees in the middle of the night? Suppose the last man-eating leopard of Burma ran into her while making his midnight rounds?

I ate some of my leftover food but made sure I saved most of it for the morning. Then I lay down at her side and did my relaxation exercises, and then I sat up and tried meditating. I suppose an accomplished monk could have meditated until the cows came home, or at least until the sun rose, but a half hour was about my limit.

I wished I had a book and a flashlight. I wished I had a Billie Holliday record and something to play it on. I wished I had a bathtub full of gin. I wished I had any sort of bathtub—that bath in the Strand had worked wonders, but the best bath in the world can only deal with the dirt of the moment. Once you dry off and go back out into the world, you get dirty all over again. I had dried off a long time ago, and I'd shared a jail cell with an unrepentant durian eater and a boat with a load of dried fish, and I'd sweated my way down the hot and humid and dusty roads of central

Burma. My red robes were pretty filthy, and so was I.

—~—

She was a lot better in the morning. Her fever had broken during the night, and her robes were wet with perspiration. I spread them out in the sun to dry while she wore the farmer's canvas coat. When I brought her the robes—drier, and somewhat aired out—she wrinkled her nose at them. But she got dressed, and we ate our breakfast and got on our way.

"So that's what it's like," I said.

"Malaria? That is what it is like."

"It can't be much fun."

"It is always bad in the evening and not so bad in the morning. It may be different for different people, and with different strains of the disease. The good thing is that I know it will not kill me. When I first came down with it I did not know that, because it does kill some people, you know, so how could I be sure I was not to be one of them? I had never felt so bad in my life, Evan, and I was afraid I was dying, and the fear made it all so much worse."

"Fear does that."

"Yes. But I did not die the first time, and I feared it less from then on. And it was not so bad. When you know you will be all right, then it is not so bad." She smiled. "If it does not kill you early on, then it will probably never kill you. Unless, you know, you develop other problems. If your heart is bad, or you are weakened with age. But I think my heart is good, and I am not so old, am I?"

"Not old at all."

"But it is still not eating outdoors." That threw me, until we worked it out—she was saying it was no picnic, and I couldn't argue the point.

The next village turned out to be a scant half hour from our orchard, and if I'd known that I'd probably have chanced walking there while Katya was sleeping off a malaria attack. It would have been something to do, but I don't know that it would have been worth the trip. It wasn't much of a village, really, just the Burmese equivalent of a wide place in the road.

We managed to fill our begging bowls a few times, hit up the local teahouse for a couple of cups each, and snacked on cakes of sticky rice as we resumed our walk. I'd noticed over the past several days that we were doing more uphill than downhill walking, which suggested that we were gradually gaining altitude. This morning was the first time I actually felt the difference, in that I noticed the air was a little cooler and drier, and the vegetation less tropical. We were beginning to reach the hills.

I told Katya, and she was relieved to hear it. "I know it was harder for me to walk. We seemed to be walking uphill all the time."

"Well, we are."

"I was afraid it might be the malaria. It makes me weaker. I'm better now, Evan, but I am still not strong. I cannot go too fast."

"We'll take it easy," I said, "and we'll stop and rest more than usual."

"I am slowing you down, Evan, I am sorry."

"You're not slowing me down."

"But of course I am! You would not have to go so slow or rest so much. And you could walk at night."

"I'd fall on my face. I wouldn't be able to see where I was going."

"You could walk longer and cover more miles each day. And you would not have to pretend you had taken a vow of silence, because you would not worry that a word from me would disclose that your companion was a woman. It is much more difficult for you to be with me, Evan, and more dangerous. I am sorry I made you take me with you."

"I'm not."

"You must be."

"No," I said. "Not at all. The dumb act I put on with other people isn't just because I've got you with me. I'd probably do it anyway, to cover up the fact that I can't speak the language and I don't know a lot about being a monk. If I opened my mouth, I'd just put my foot in it.

"And I'd go nuts without you to talk to. We can't talk when we're around other people, and that's one reason I'm always in a hurry to get away from the villages and get back on the road. It doesn't matter whether we're speaking Russian or English."

"Because I am not so good in either one of them, Vanya."

"You're fine in both. I'm glad I have you with me. And I'm very happy you're feeling better."

"Yes, I feel much better. But it is not over, you know. The attack."

"I was going to ask you about that."

"The first night is over. And the third night is not so bad, and that is usually the end of it. After that there is some weakness and soreness, but the worst of it is over."

"The third night's not so bad," I echoed. "Today's the second day, isn't it? What's the second night like?"

"The second night is bad," she said.

It hit her late in the afternoon. I had hoped we'd get to the next village before the fever caught up with her. It was the most substantial way station between Bagan and Taunggyi, and I thought I might be able to find aspirin there, and possibly quinine as well. Maybe I could get her indoors; failing that, I could at least scare up something a little better in the way of blankets than an old coat and a few towels.

"We can keep walking," she insisted. "It's not too bad yet, Evan."

"Promise you'll tell me when it is."

"I won't have to," she said. "I'll fall down."

It was hard to know what pace to set. I wanted to walk faster, in order to beat the fever to our destination, but a faster pace meant a greater strain on Katya. She needed rest breaks, but they cost us precious time. I kept second-guessing myself until I just gave up trying to figure it out, and we found our own pace and just tried to keep moving.

The sun was lower and the air noticeably cooler when she stumbled, and I reached to steady her before she could fall. Her eyes were glassy, her cheeks bright with fever.

"We'll stop here," I said.

"No, Evan. I can go on."

"It's hopeless," I said, but then I thought I saw something, and we walked another fifty yards and I could see smoke rising, drifting skyward from the cooking fires of the village that lay ahead of us.

The place was big enough to have outskirts, and I was tempted to stop at the first teahouse we saw. But if we stopped I wasn't sure we could get started again. We kept going, aiming at the town center, and before we got there a couple of guys with shaved heads and red robes turned up to greet us with big smiles. The smiles faded to looks of concern when they got a look at Katya's flushed cheeks and glazed stare.

One of them, the taller and older of the two—the alpha monk, I suppose—asked a question in Burmese. I caught a word or two and guessed that he was asking if my companion was all right, but I'd have figured that out even if he'd been speaking Martian. I did my little forefinger-to-the-lips routine, and I guess I wasn't the only monk who'd sworn vows of silence, because he nodded as if this was quite normal. He nodded his head toward Katya, eyebrows raised, and for reply I took his hand and placed it on her forehead.

If I hadn't recently touched her forehead myself, I'd have known her fever was high from the alarm that registered on his face. He looked at me and his eyes searched my face, registering my otherness.

He said, "European?"

That was close enough, and I nodded.

"Speak English? Français? Deutsch?"

Since German was his third choice, I nodded enthusiastically when he got to it. If rumors were going to drift back toward SLORC headquarters, let them be a couple of German monks. And let our communication take place in the tongue of which he was least confident.

"Come with us," he said, in German that was a whole lot better than my Burmese. "We will help you."

I put an arm around Katya's waist. The other monk, the one who hadn't said anything, took her shoulder bag, slung it over his own shoulder, and gripped her arm in his. And off we all walked, with the alpha monk leading the way.

I guess I didn't want to think about how ill

she was, or about our fate if the masquerade fell through. So all I could think about as we paraded through town was that she had just been touched by two men who'd have recoiled in horror if they'd known what she was.

How bad was it? I wondered. The contact was voluntary, at least in the case of the fellow who had taken hold of her arm. But it was done in ignorance.

Suppose a Catholic, in the days before Vatican II, ate meat on a Friday while thinking it was Thursday. Was it still a sin? Suppose he knew it was Friday but thought it was shad roe? Or suppose a Jew ate a ham sandwich under the impression that *it* was shad roe. Or suppose—

That was different, I decided. Eating meat on Friday was sinful, or used to be. Eating ham was unclean and a betrayal of one's heritage. Touching a woman was something else, but I wasn't sure what.

I was still pondering the point when we all kicked off our sandals and entered the monastery.

That's what it was. It consisted of a walled compound of a couple of acres right smack in the middle of East Jesus, Burma, or whatever the hell they called the town. There were trees, including the sort under one of which Buddha was sitting when he attained enlightenment. (There's something illuminating, evidently, about sitting under trees. A bodhi tree for Buddha, an apple tree for Sir Isaac Newton. The only thing I ever got sitting under a tree was shat on by starlings.)

There were three wooden buildings. We made our way past the largest one in the center to a smaller structure off to the right. We entered, climbed a flight of stairs, and walked along a floor of smooth polished planks. The room he led us to was small, unfurnished except for a narrow sleeping pallet on the floor.

"You will want to stay here with your friend," the leader said. "Nicht wahr?"

I nodded, and he turned and said something to *his* friend, who went out and came back with a second pallet. He rolled it out on the floor next to the first. I eased Katya down on one of these and felt her forehead, and the alarm must have shown in my face.

He said, "It is malaria, ja?"

I opened my mouth, caught myself in time, and nodded.

"We have some medicine. And water. He should drink a good deal of water."

And they brought medicine. I didn't know what it was. There were tablets that were probably aspirin and capsules that might have been quinine, and there was a pot of herbal tea with a taste and bouquet that was new to me. I fed it all to Katya. She was in bad shape, shivering violently, heaving, her eyes rolling wildly in her head. I was afraid she might let out a stream of curses in high-pitched Russian.

When the others left us at last, closing the door to our little room after them, I became less anxious that she would give the game away with a word.

I crouched beside her, put my lips to her ear. "Try to rest," I urged her. "We're alone now, but the walls are thin. You can whisper if you want."

"Where are we, Vanya?"

"We have our own room," I said. "In a sort of dormitory, from the looks of it."

"Monks," she said.

"Yes."

"All monks, Vanya?"

"Yes."

"I need something to drink."

"More water? Or more of the herbal tea?"

"Is that what it was? It tasted like boiled grass."

"You may have guessed the recipe. Which do you want?"

"I will take some water," she said, "because it is good for me, but that is not what I want. Can you get me whiskey?"

"Jesus," I said. "I don't see how."

"Something with alcohol. Ayet piu, they must have it for sale in this town."

"Are you sure it's a good idea, Katya?"

"It is the best idea there is," she said. "I have had this many times, Evan. Nothing helps like alcohol. I don't care what it says in the books. I know what my experience tells me, and...God, I'm burning up!"

She threw aside the blankets they'd given

me to cover her with, then began trembling violently and reached again for the blankets.

"I swear it helps," she said. "Please, Vanya? Can you get me some?"

——〜——

The market was small—a couple dozen stalls, each taking up just a few square feet. I looked them over, and their proprietors looked me over, evidently surprised to see a monk shopping, and in the evening, too.

"Ayet piu," I said to one of them, hoping I was pronouncing it correctly. He gaped at me, and it was hard to tell if he didn't understand what I wanted or couldn't believe a monk would want it.

"Ayet piu," I said again, and mimed guzzling from a bottle, my head thrown back.

He shook his head. "Shwe le maw," he said.

What on earth did that mean? I said "Ayet piu" again, because I couldn't think of anything else to say.

"Shwe le maw," he said again, and reached into a crate and produced a pint bottle, the glass a cobalt blue. It didn't have a label. "Shwe le maw," he said, and brandished the bottle. I reached for the bottle, and he smiled, drew the cork, and poured an ounce or so into an earthenware teacup. They never give out samples at liquor stores in New York, so the gesture took me by surprise, but I accepted the cup and inhaled the smell of ripe oranges. I took a taste, then tossed off the drink. It had a full-bodied burnt orange taste, and a reasonable kick to it. It was neither as raw nor as potent as ayet piu, but there was definitely alcohol in it.

I asked the price—Beh laut the?—but couldn't make out the response, so I took out my supply of kyat and let him help himself. He took twenty-five kyat and seemed happy, and I couldn't believe this stuff was cheaper than beer.

Maybe it wasn't much stronger than beer. Maybe she'd need a gallon of it to get any benefit from it.

Better safe than sorry, I thought. Especially at these prices.

And so when I shucked my shoes at the gateway to the monastery, I had three flasks of shwe le maw in my shoulder bag.

It was stronger than beer.

She was curled up in a ball when I got back, her hands clutching her shoulders, her knees drawn up to her chest. She was moaning and rocking, and at first she didn't even know I was there. Then she opened her eyes and looked at me, and I got out a flask and poured her a cup of the stuff.

"I smell oranges," she said. "Is it orange juice? No. I also smell alcohol." She drank. "Oh, it is good," she said. "Not as strong as ayet piu, but better tasting."

She reached for the bottle. I held on to it for a moment, then let her have it. She tipped her head back and took a long swallow, then looked at me.

I don't read minds, but just then her thoughts couldn't have been more evident if they'd been written on her forehead. She knew she should offer me some, but then there would be less for her.

I didn't wait to see how she'd resolve the dilemma. "There's another bottle," I told her, and saw her jaw go slack with relief. She gave me the bottle and I drank deeply and gave it back to her. I wasn't running a fever myself, and the mosquito bites I'd sustained over the past week hadn't done anything worse than itch, but you can't be too careful, can you?

So she took a drink and I took a drink, and she took another and I took another, and lo and behold, the bottle was empty. I capped and traded it for one of the full ones in my shoulder bag, and uncapped that and took a sizable swig without thinking about it. And I passed the bottle to Katya and watched her tip it up and drink deep.

Her Adam's apple didn't go up and down when she swallowed, I noticed. That was because she didn't have one, it not being part of the standard equipment for females. The presence of an Adam's apple was one of the tip-offs to male-to-female transsexuals, although I'd read that some of them went so far as to have their Adam's apples shaved surgically. That sounded a little extreme to

281

me—I found it enough of a nuisance to have to shave the outside of my Adam's apple—but it set me wondering. Had anybody thought about Adam's-apple implants for female-to-male transsexuals? An interesting new frontier for Medicare, though the HMOs would never cover it.

An even better opportunity, it seemed to me, lay in importing shwe le maw into the States. In taste it ran somewhere between Grand Marnier and Curaçao, although it wouldn't make the bottles of either turn pale and reach for the Valium. Still, at twenty-five kyat a pint, you were getting a lot of bang for the buck.

No question. It was stronger than beer.

And it was working. As we made our way through the second bottle, I could see that it was the best thing for malaria since bug spray. Katya had stopped shaking and her color was better. She was still running a considerable fever, but the wild stare was gone from her eyes and the desperate agitation had passed. She took a last long drink that left Bottle Number Two as empty as its predecessor, pulled all the blankets over her, buried her face in the crook of her arm, and left the land of the conscious for a better world by far.

I sat beside her, looking down at her. Her breathing, easier and less ragged now, was the only sound I could hear in all the monastery's severe stillness.

I thought about where we were, and what we had done, and what the future might hold. And I did something that may seem questionable in retrospect, but which made perfect sense at the time.

I opened the third bottle of shwe le maw.

I didn't put that much of a dent in Bottle Number Three. I just nipped at it from time to time, and there was no more than a third of it gone when Katya stirred at my side. I capped the bottle and turned to her.

"I am better, Evan," she whispered.

And indeed she was. The fever hadn't merely broken. It had shattered into bits. The blankets were soaked, as were her red robes and the pallet she lay on. She cast the blankets aside and stood up, peeling off her wet red wrapping, and I turned the pallet over so she would have its dry side to lie on.

And she giggled and plopped herself down on it.

"Vanya," she said. "My little Vanya. My Vanushka."

And she giggled again.

Well, every medicine has a side effect. What lowers your blood pressure calcifies your liver, and what clears up your acne makes you break out in hives. Shwe le maw had knocked malaria down for the count, and now she wasn't feverish or delirious or twisted in pain. She had slept and rested, and she felt much better.

But she was stoned out of her mind.

And, see, she wasn't the only one. We were both of us pretty well oiled. If she'd had a little more than I—the lioness's share, say—it had been offset by the fact that the booze she drank used up a good part of its fury on the malaria. The stuff I poured into me all went to the end of getting me drunk.

And drunk is what I was. Not falling-down drunk, because you can't fall down if you haven't stood up in the first place. Not roaring drunk, either, because a Buddhist monastery in Burma was no place for anything louder than a whisper.

What I was, all the same, was Very Fucking Drunk.

Which may explain what happened next.

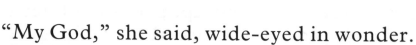

"My God," she said, wide-eyed in wonder. "What happened?"

"Nothing," I said. "It was a malarial dream."

"It was better than a dream. It was wonderful."

"Well," I said.

"I don't know how you could bear to touch me," she said. "I was sweating like a pig before. I must smell foul."

"You probably do," I said, "and so do I, in all likelihood. If we bathed in the Irriwaddy we'd leave a ring. But evidently not bathing knocks out the sense of smell, because I didn't notice."

"Neither did I." She yawned, stretched. I reached out a hand and stroked her breast. She purred.

"I hope I didn't make noise."

"Just a little," I said.

"Maybe they'll think it was the malaria."

"Let's hope so."

"I was drunk, Evan. Were you drunk?"

"Very."

"But now I think I am sober."

"It feels that way to me, too."

"That I am sober? Or that you are sober?"

"Both."

"We screwed ourselves sober," she said, and giggled.

"Well, maybe not a hundred percent sober. Not what you might call stone cold sober."

She sighed. "It has been so long, Evan. I have not been with anyone in a very long time."

With all the new diseases that had popped up while I chilled out in Union City, this had to come under the heading of Good News. "Neither have I," I said. "It's been a long time."

"Longer for me, I bet."

"Save your money."

"Oh? How long?"

She'd never believe me, so why tell her? "So long," I said, "that I almost forgot how to do it."

"But you remembered."

"Well, there are certain things you never forget how to do. Like falling off a bicycle."

"Or drowning," she said.

"Exactly. Once mastered, those skills are with you forever."

"So it has really been a long time, Evan?"

"Ages."

"Perhaps you are a true monk after all. It sounds as though you have been living like one."

"Until tonight."

"Yes, until tonight. But you should not keep him cloistered, Vanya."

"Him?"

"Your little man," she said, and reached out and took, uh, him in hand. "He is cute," she announced. "He is a good little man. A standing-up man. Yes?"

"Upstanding, I think you mean."

"And also I mean standing up. You see?"

"Oh."

"So it is not right to keep him under lock and key. You should let him out more."

"I see what you mean."

"And I should let him in. Vanya?"

"God," I said, reaching for her. "We have to be very quiet this time."

"I know."

"Extremely quiet."

"Like mice, Vanya. Oh, yes. Oh, that is nice, my darling. That is so good."

Perhaps, I thought, perhaps we were not absolutely sober....

Chapter Twenty

It struck me as less than good manners to sneak off without a word to the fellow I could only think of as the alpha monk, the one who'd given us shelter and provided the medicine and the blankets. On the other hand, I'd gotten through all that without a word, so why alter a successful formula?

And why worry about good manners at this late date? I'd already snookered him into touching a woman and bringing her into his sacred precincts, where she and I had engaged in two acts of drunken sex (and, I blush to admit, one act of hungover sex when she woke up the morning after). The sooner we were out of there, and the less ceremony attending our departure, the better for all concerned.

And so we wrapped ourselves up in those reeking red robes (and who knew any longer which robes were mine and which were hers, and what difference did it make, anyway?) and slipped out of there as unobtrusively as possible. I'd put one of the empty blue bottles in Katya's bag and tried to arrange the other two so that there'd be as little telltale clinking as possible, and we slipped out of the room and walked softly but swiftly along the hall and down the stairs and out the door.

The great open courtyard of the central building was full of novice monks—boys, really—each sitting on a little rug and studying a lesson. We hurried on past them, trying to move as quickly as possible without looking as though that was what we were doing. At the compound entrance we were confronted by a great row of slippers and sandals, and spotting ours among all those others was like trying to pick out one's own son from among those dozens of lads sitting on their rugs and doing their lessons. No, the boys were not identical, and neither were the sandals, but it took more time to tell them apart than one really cared to spend.

I found a pair that might have been mine, and Katya took a pair that suited her, and off we went. And we took ten or a dozen steps and ran into the alpha monk.

He smiled—beamed might be a better word for it—and asked if he could have a word with me. *"Bitte,"* he said to Katya, still beaming, and held up a hand to indicate that she should stay where she was.

He led me around the corner and stood with his hands clasped in front of his waist. It was easy, I realized, to pick him out in a crowd. He was somehow recognizable, although I would be hard put to say just how. I could say that he didn't look Burmese, but I wasn't sure exactly what I meant by that, or even if it was accurate. It struck me that he looked Tibetan, in that something about him put me in mind of photos I'd seen of the Dalai Lama. But I don't know if I was responding to a genuine resemblance or something about his energy.

In German he said, "I see your friend is better."

I nodded.

"The fever broke during the night?"

Another nod.

"My German is not so good," he said,

switching smoothly to English. "I express myself better in English. Will you be able to follow me?"

I nodded again.

"Good. I am glad your friend feels better. It seems to me that she looks better, too. Her color is healthier and her eyes are clearer."

He'd used the pronoun three times. Just to make sure I wouldn't miss it.

"I am ashamed," I said.

"Why?"

"For deceiving you."

"You did not deceive me."

"When did you know?"

"The moment I touched her brow. Perhaps before then. Her energy is a woman's energy."

"But you allowed me to place your hand on her forehead."

"Yes."

"I don't understand," I said.

He was silent for a moment. Then he said, "As soon as I saw the two of you I knew you were not monks."

"How did you know?"

"Your energy."

"Oh."

"One acquires certain strengths through years of meditation. You were dressed as monks, you behaved as monks, but you did not have the energy of monks. It is difficult to explain more precisely than that."

"I think I understand."

"And you are Western, and your companion

is part Western. There are monks from the West who come here to study meditation. But they do not walk across the interior. They do not keep vows of silence."

"But you did not expose us."

"No."

"In fact, you helped us. Instead of punishing us for sacrilege—"

"But where is the sacrilege?" He smiled. "It is clear you did not come to mock us. And you have not broken my precepts, because you are not a monk and so are not bound by them. Surely you have reasons for posing as monks."

"Yes."

"You are heading east? Deeper into Shan state?"

"Yes."

"So perhaps you are avoiding the eyes of the authorities, and for such a purpose your disguise is not a bad one. The authorities are not aware of such subtle matters as energy. When they see a red robe they assume a monk."

"But you saw something else."

"I saw a man and woman, and I saw that the woman was ill and in need of attention. And, yes, I touched her. That is a profanation, and I will have to go through a sanctification ritual, and that will be a nuisance, but that is all it will be. A nuisance and an inconvenience."

"I see."

"And the room where you stayed will be cleansed, and some herbs burned in it. Again, a small inconvenience."

"Yes."

"Our little rules are important," he said. "The major precepts and the minor ones as well. But they exist to guide our feet on the Buddha's eightfold path, and the object of that path is right living.

"And your friend was ill and needed assistance." He thought for a moment. "There is a story, a very old story. Perhaps it is a parable, perhaps it happened. Or both, eh?

"Once two monks were walking through a forest. And they came to a rushing stream where there stood a woman who was afraid to cross. She begged them for help. And one of the monks, true to his vows, shrank away from the woman and diverted his eyes from her. Deaf to her pleas, he waded across the stream and went on his way.

"His companion had taken the same vows. Nonetheless, without hesitation he picked the woman up in his arms, carried her across the stream, set her down on the opposite bank, and then hurried onward to rejoin his fellow monk.

"For several hours they continued onward in absolute silence. Finally the first monk could stand it no longer. He turned on his companion, seething. 'How could you do such a thing?' he demanded. 'You know we are not to look upon a woman, let alone touch her. Yet you actually picked her up in your arms and carried her across that stream!'

"The other monk shrugged. 'I carried that woman for twenty paces,' he said softly. 'You have been carrying her for ten miles.'"

291

"That's a great story," I said.

"Well, it is just a story. Who knows if it ever happened?"

"I think it happens all the time."

"I think so, too." He touched my arm. "Good luck on your journey. You should get the nats to bless your venture. You know about our nats?"

"They're animist spirits, aren't they?"

"Yes. They are not a part of Buddhism at all, but many of our pagodas contain nat shrines as well. We have a saying in Burma: 'Revere the Buddha but fear the nats.'"

"In America we say, 'Trust God but keep your powder dry.'"

"Powder? Oh, gunpowder, of course. Yes, it is much the same, isn't it? There is a pagoda you will pass, just on your right as you leave town. There are lions flanking the entrance. You will be able to recognize it. It contains a large nat shrine. There is one nat with a form similar to Ganesh. You know Ganesh?"

"From Hindu mythology? The elephant-headed god?"

"Yes. You will see his statue. Perhaps you will give him an offering."

"What would I give him?"

"He is said to be very fond of liquor," he said. "Perhaps you might sprinkle a few drops into his offering dish. If you have any left, that is."

"He knows," Katya said. "Doesn't he?"

I nodded.

"How much does he know, Evan?"

"He knows everything."

"It is my fault," she said. "He heard me cry out when we were—"

"Profaning the sanctuary," I finished for her. "But no, that's not it, and nothing's your fault. He knew all along. He knew before he even touched you."

"And he touched me anyway? And took us into the monastery? I do not understand."

"Well, maybe this will help," I said. "It seems there were these two monks, and they were walking through this forest, and they came to a stream...."

We stopped at the pagoda on the edge of town, the one with the golden lions guarding its entrance. We let them guard our sandals while they were at it and found the nat shrine to the left of the central altar. One of the nat statues did have a distinctly elephantine countenance, and I uncapped our blue flask and poured him a couple drops of shwe le maw.

What could it hurt?

Chapter Twenty-one

Four days after we poured out a libation at the feet of the elephant-headed nat, we walked into the city of Taunggyi. It took another hour to find the market stall of Sai Thein Lwin. I asked for him by name, and the young man who'd been portioning out rice into two-pound sacks nodded thoughtfully and went away, returning a few minutes later with an older man in tow.

"I am Thein Lwin," he said. Sai, I knew, was an honorific, the Shan equivalent of the Burmese *U*.

"I am Evan Tanner," I said. "Ku Min told me you could help me."

"Ku Min."

"In Rangoon."

"You know Ku Min?"

"Yes."

"And you are Evan Tanner?"

"Yes."

He looked searchingly at me. At length he said, "You are alive."

"Well, yes."

"And this is—"

"Katya," I said.

He repeated the name, not without difficulty. It was evidently not a name that flowed trippingly off a Shan tongue. Then he said my name again. "Ku Min sent word that you were

294

coming," he said. "And then I received word that you were dead."

"Well," I said, "I'm not."

"No."

"Never have been, actually. Not in this lifetime, anyway."

"No," he said, and thought about it, then exchanged some rapid-fire words with the youth. "This is my son," he said to us. "You go with him. He has a car. He will drive you."

"Where?"

"To where they were waiting for you," he said. "Until they learned of your death."

I don't know what did it, the nat blessing or the herbal tea or the shwe le maw, but the stretch from the monastery to Taunggyi had been smooth sailing compared to what we'd been through earlier. Katya's malaria had one more night to run, as she'd predicted, but the third night was relatively mild, as she'd also predicted, and we got through it with ease.

The days were cooler, too, as we moved into the Shan highlands. The nights were cooler as well, and we spent them outside. We'd have been cold if we hadn't huddled together for warmth, but that did the trick, along with the shwe le maw, two bottles of which I managed to buy every afternoon along the way.

I knew what to ask for now, and became pretty good at spotting the market stalls that were likely to have it on hand. It continued to take people aback—a monk in his red robes was not expected to buy intoxicating spirits—but I decided I didn't really give a damn if the locals regarded me as the Buddhist equivalent of a whiskey priest. The nights were chilly and my companion had a taste for the burnt-orange brandy and, truth to tell, so did I.

We had a taste for each other, too, which led to our huddling together for more than mere warmth. And, tossing the ten precepts to the four winds, we drank and screwed our way to Taunggyi.

I don't know that my friend the alpha monk would have been proud of me. But I was having a good time.

Thein Lwin's son drove us eastward in a Toyota Corolla that needed springs and shocks and, for all I know, a quadruple bypass. But it was amazing to me how much faster it was than walking. In twenty minutes it would cover as much ground as we could manage in the better part of a day. We'd been walking for so long that a walker's pace had become our frame of reference.

The drive was pleasant, and the only time it got the least bit dicey was when we stopped for a roadblock manned by government troops. A snotty little functionary took a long hard look at our driver's papers while troops kept automatic weapons trained on our car. The Corolla had been backfiring periodically the whole trip, and I had visions of it doing so now, and sounding like gunfire to the smooth-cheeked kids pointing guns at us. I could imagine how that scene would play out. We'd wind up looking like the last frame of *Bonnie and Clyde*.

But the car maintained a respectful silence, and the self-important little shit who took such a keen interest in the driver's papers didn't spare more than a glance at the two monks dozing in the back seat. He stepped back and waved us through, and the next roadblock was manned by Shan insurgent forces who recognized the car, greeted the driver by name, and didn't care who or what he had by way of cargo.

Our next stop was a Shan camp perhaps a dozen miles past the checkpoint. We drove through an opening in a stockade fence and entered a large open area. A two-story frame house was flanked by half a dozen low concrete-block buildings that looked like barracks. We wound up on the large front porch of the frame house, where men in fatigues were drinking Tsing Tao beer out of long-necked bottles. Someone handed bottles to each of us, and to the driver.

One, with gray hair and a salt-and-pepper mustache, seemed to be in charge. He asked which of us was Evan Tanner. I said I was.

"And your friend?"

"Katya Singh."

"Singh? That is an Indian name."

"My husband was Indian," she said.

"You are a woman," he said. He seemed a little dismayed not to have noticed this himself. "A woman dressed as a monk," he said, and repeated the line in his own language, whereupon all of his fellows had a good laugh.

"Ku Min said two monks," he told me. "He said nothing about a woman."

"Well, you know Ku Min," I said.

He laughed, and translated for the others, and everybody laughed.

"You are a woman," he said to Katya. "And you are alive," he said to me.

"Actually," I said, "we're both alive."

"Yes, but we were told you were dead."

"Me?"

"Evan Tanner."

"That's me," I said. "Who told you?"

"It was on the radio. It was also in the newspaper. Do we still have that newspaper?" He turned and barked an order, and one of the younger men ran off to check. "He will look for it," he said. "But you want to bathe, yes?"

"God, yes," I said.

"And perhaps you are tired of dressing as monks, eh? You have other clothes?"

"I'm afraid this is it," I said.

"We have clothes that will fit you." And he said something else I didn't understand, and one of the youths indicated that we should follow him.

An hour later we were back on the porch. We'd had showers, and I would have liked to stay under the stream of hot water until my

298

fingerprints washed off. It wasn't as luxurious as the loo at the Strand, but it was at least as welcome. We dried off and dressed in khaki fatigues, the same as the others were wearing. My shirt was a little tight across the shoulders, and the pants ended an inch or two prematurely, but otherwise it was a good fit.

Katya told me, admiringly, that I looked very military. Her own affect, clad in khaki, was hard to sum up. She looked at once waiflike and combat-ready, and the ruby ring was back on her finger.

Back on the porch, there were handshakes all around, and drinks poured, and toasts offered. We went from there to dinner, where we sat around two long tables and passed around platters of rice and vegetables and several kinds of meat. There was goat and chicken, and there was something I wasn't sure of, but I'm fairly certain it hadn't spent its time on earth barking, or turning around in a circle three times before lying down.

Our after-dinner drinks were that orange brandy Katya and I had come to know and love. I don't suppose it had aphrodisiacal properties—I don't suppose anything does, really—but we seemed to wind up making love every time we drank it, and that sort of thing establishes an association in your mind. I looked at her and she looked at me, and I sensed we were two minds with but a single thought, and a prurient one at that. Time to make our excuses, I thought. All that walking out in the hot sun, and such a fine and substantial meal, and it was really time we got to bed, wasn't it?

But instead I heard myself asking the fellow in command if he'd had any luck finding that newspaper.

"The newspaper! Yes, we still have it. Now where did he put it?" He called out something to someone. "I will show it to you," he said, "but will you even know what you are looking at? Do you read Burmese?"

"No."

"Then it will look like nothing to you."

That wasn't quite true. I'd glanced uncomprehending at Burmese newspapers in Rangoon, and the articles didn't look like nothing. Generally they looked like a staph infection reaching epidemic proportions.

"Here. 'Evan Tanner, American soldier of fortune.' That is you, is it not?"

"Soldier of misfortune," I said.

"Also a terrorist and an agent provocateur, it says here. Apprehended after an intensive police investigation and subjected to intensive interrogation—you know what that means?"

"Torture?"

"Of course. After all that, you admitted your role in the terrorist bombing of Shwe Dagon Pagoda and—"

"What bombing?"

"The great pagoda. Do you not know it?"

"I was there my first day in Rangoon. It didn't look as though it had been bombed."

"It happened more recently. Ten, twelve days ago."

After we'd left the boat and struck out on foot from Bagan. We hadn't had a drop of news since, from Rangoon or anywhere else on earth.

"But it's such a beautiful structure," I said. "Was the damage very great?"

"There was very little damage to the pagoda. A shrine disturbed, some Buddha images injured. But lives were lost. Three tourists, two French schoolteachers and a retired Austrian businessman. And four Burmese school-children."

"And they say I placed the bomb?"

He shook his head. "A local man placed the bomb. He was set upon by citizens on the scene and torn apart."

"That must have slowed down the investigation."

"They gave his name," he said, "and it is a Shan name, but no one knows him. And then, several days later, there was this story, telling how you were the terrorist mastermind behind the outrage."

"And I was dead?"

"You broke down under questioning, you admitted everything, and you were tried and convicted and sentenced to death by hanging."

"And they hanged me on the spot?"

"No. They waited until the following morning."

"Decent of them," I said.

"And they published your picture," he said, "but I do not think it looks very much like you."

"They probably got it off my passport," I

said, "and they never look like the person."

"This does not look like you at all," he said.

"Remember," I said. "I had hair then. I didn't shave it off until it was time to put on red robes."

"Still," he said. "It says American terrorist Evan Tanner, but it does not look like you in any respect."

"Let's see," I said.

He handed me the paper. I looked, and a face looked back at me.

"Stone the crows," I said.

Chapter Twenty-two

"His name was Stuart," I said. "If he told me his last name I've forgotten it, and it seems to me he didn't. We started out on a first-name basis. I guess that's natural enough for two people who are sharing a cell."

"You met this man in prison?"

"It wasn't exactly a prison. It was a cell, all right, a cage of steel bars, and there was a guard and he had a gun. But it was more of an out-of-the-way holding cell than part of an official prison. They parked me there while they were figuring out what to do with me."

"And this Stuart was there as well?"

I nodded. "The guard left the door unlocked and went for a walk. I didn't know if he was following orders or if someone had bribed him, but one way or another I was being offered the opportunity to escape."

"And you took it?"

"In a hot second. Stuart was afraid it was a trap. But we were already in jail. Why bother to trap us at that stage of the game? He couldn't make up his mind whether to stay or to go, and I didn't hang around waiting for him to decide. I just got out of there."

"Perhaps he was a terrorist."

"He wasn't."

"But if he was, and if he did organize the explosion at Shwe Dagon, and they captured him again, they could have made a mistake with the name. He was one of two men who escaped from this cell, yes? So there is a mix-up, and they call him by the wrong name."

I shook my head. "He was no terrorist," I said. "He was just this sweet Australian kid who came over on a holiday to drink beer and look at the pagodas. Do you know how he wound up in jail? He ate durian."

"But it is not against the law to eat durian."

"In his hotel room."

"Oh," he said. "That is another story."

"Still," I said, "it is not a hanging offense."

"Of course not."

"They would have hanged me," I said in wonder. "I never took it seriously. I thought it was going to be a nuisance, getting thrown out of the country, being kept from completing my mission, whatever it was. But they were just locking me up until they figured out just how to get the most mileage out of me for propaganda purposes. Then it would have been a long drop and a short rope."

My face was flushed, my heart pounding. I had this vivid image of Stuart, baffled, protesting, being half led and half dragged to the scaffold. They'd taken his cigarettes away. Did they give him a last smoke before they put the rope around his neck and the hood over his face? Did they even use a hood?

The poor son of a bitch.

I was burning up with rage, chilled with an icy fury. "They planted the bomb themselves," I said. I was standing on top of the table, not sure how I got there, livid, impassioned. "They damaged the pagoda themselves! They did it, the oppressors who call themselves SLORC. They duped some poor innocent into placing the bomb and saw that he was killed on the spot before anybody could ask him any embarrassing questions. Children died in that explosion! Shrines and Buddha images were damaged! And by the same fiends who stand square in the way of Shan independence!"

I don't remember everything I said. I don't really know what got into me, aside from the better part of a quart of shwe le maw. But I was utterly caught up in what I was saying, entirely provoked by the outrage of Shwe Dagon and the unwarranted execution of my durian-eating chum.

"To think we have made peace with this government!" I cried. "To think we allow them to maintain a roadblock and an armed garrison minutes from here, on land that is the historic heritage of the Shan people! Are we men? Or are we vassals of SLORC, minions of the government in Rangoon, a cabal of devils and degenerates who oppress their own people even as they stifle the flames of the Shan spirit?"

It's funny what happens when you get into something like that. I guess it's the same with preachers when the message takes them over. They're in the grip of the spirit, and so was I. I hadn't planned on saying any of this—I hadn't actually planned on saying anything at all—but I was going on and on, with a dramatic cadence to my speech. I found myself pausing at the end of each rhythmic burst, and the leader filled in each pause by translating what I'd just said. And damned if they weren't all hanging on every word.

"Evan, are you all right?"

"I guess I got carried away," I said. We were back in our room, and I could barely remember leaving the table. My head was throbbing, and my whole body felt as though I'd been thoroughly and systematically worked over by a crew of bully boys from SLORC. "All caught up in the sound of my own words," I told Katya.

"How do you feel?"

"Not so good. I've got a killer headache and I can't catch my breath. I don't know what got into me."

"I think you should get undressed," she said. "I think you should get under the blankets."

"Maybe that's not a bad idea," I admitted, peeling off my clothes. "I'm hot and cold all at once. Just the body mirroring the emotions, I guess. Burning with rage over what those bastards did to that poor Australian kid, and chilled at the idea that it could have happened to me."

"You were very effective, Evan. They were all moved by what you had to say."

"Maybe it gained a little in the translation," I said.

"You stirred their passions, Evan."

"Well, that's what passions are for," I said. "To get stirred now and then. They'll be calm by morning."

"In the morning," she said, "they will attack."

"How's that? They'll attack what?"

"But he told you," she said. "You do not remember?"

"I got a little vague there at the end, Katya. I was ranting away, and the next thing I knew I was back here in the room with you. I may have had a little too much of that orange stuff."

"No, I think—"

"Tell me about this attack," I said. "Tell me what's going on."

"We are all to arise at daybreak, Evan. And overrun the government checkpoint, and then attack the encampment."

"You're kidding."

"No, Evan. You do not remember? You suggested it."

"I did?"

"You said they must do it or they would not be real men, or true Shan."

"I said that?" It had a familiar ring to it, now that she mentioned it. "And they bought it?"

"Some of them did not want to wait until morning. Ku Min sent a shipment of new weapons with the money from the heroin, and they are anxious to try them out. They would have gone tonight, but the head man insisted they wait for daylight."

"The voice of reason," I said. "Jesus, Katya, I must have been out of my mind. And they must have been twice as crazy to listen to me."

"Tell me how you feel, Evan."

"Lousy," I said. "My headache's worse and my muscles are sore. And I'm hot and cold all at once, and I swear my bones ache. It must be the shwe le maw. I think the damn stuff's toxic."

"No, Evan. In fact I brought a bottle to the room. You should have some more."

"You're kidding."

"No," she said. "I am not. It will help you, Vanya. And there is some quinine and aspirin that they gave me for you. I wish we had the herbal tea they gave us at the monastery, but we will get along without it. Vanya, my darling, it is not the food or drink or even the excitement that makes you hot and cold and gives you a pain in your muscles and bones. Don't you see?"

307

I did, but I let her say it.

"Vanushka, you have malaria."

Chapter Twenty-three

We were rolling by sunup. I was in the lead car, the same beat-up Toyota that had brought us from Taunggyi. This time, though, I was dressed in fatigues, as were the driver and the two men in the back seat.

Two jeeps rolled out behind us, and a pair of canvas-topped troop carriers followed in their wake.

We rode past the Shan checkpoint and pulled up a mile or so from the government roadblock. Half a dozen men dismounted from one of the troop carriers and disappeared into the brush on either side of the road. The commander—his name, I'd finally learned, was Ne Win—passed out cheroots, and checked his watch as the men lit up and smoked.

Waiting, Ne Win asked me how I felt. I was much better, I told him. I'd been in a bad way the night before, I added, and I hadn't even recognized the symptoms as malaria.

"Ah," he said. "You have never had it before?"

"No."

"Well," he said, "you will have it again."

He checked his watch from time to time, and after twenty minutes or so he gave an order and our Toyota headed on down the road, with the other vehicles staying put for the time being. It took us only a couple of minutes to reach the government checkpoint. As before, young men in uniforms trained guns on us, and the same officious martinet strutted over and demanded to see the driver's papers.

I had a blanket over my lap, and under it I held the machine pistol Ne Win had issued me. It was Czech-made, and I wondered what hands it had passed through before it got all the way to an outpost of Shan insurgents. What kind of tale would it tell if it could talk?

I wondered if our advance party was in position and ready. I wondered how long we'd last if they'd been delayed.

And then I lifted the Skoda a little, aiming across the body of the driver and through the open window at his side. And then, just as the little captain was making some sort of bureaucratic fuss over the driver's papers, I triggered a burst into his chest.

And all hell broke loose.

Our sharpshooters had managed to get themselves into position, and my gunfire was their signal to open up on the troops who had their guns trained on the Toyota. We took them completely by surprise, and all the shooting was done by our side. Then our men were emerging from the brush at the side of the road, cheering, flushed with success. They piled up the bullet-ridden corpses of the government troops while Ne Win pointed his pistol in the air and fired three spaced shots, a signal to the rest of our forces. By the time they reached us, the jeeps and the troops carriers, the roadblock was dismantled and the weapons and ammunition of the dead enemy soldiers stowed in the trunk of the Toyota.

And we rolled on to attack their camp.

That took a little more doing. The government outpost had numerical superiority—around a hundred and fifty men to our forty—and enjoyed an advantage over us in weaponry. They were in a fortified compound, and had the edge of defending while we had to attack. All things being equal, they would have swamped us.

Fortunately, all things weren't equal. We had the great advantage of surprise, and they had every reason to be surprised, having had not the slightest intimation of unrest among us. And how could they? There hadn't been any unrest until my fevered speech—and fevered it was—had turned a quiet group of men into impassioned killers.

So they weren't expecting us, and indeed a good many of them were still in their beds when we hit them. They responded quickly, I have to give them that, and they fought well, but they were outclassed. Along with everything else, we were better motivated. We were fighting to avenge an Australian durian-eater, and to bring glory to the Shan people, and to hasten the day when the Shan would take their place among the free and independent nations of the world.

They, on the other hand, were just fighting for their lives. They didn't stand a chance.

We hit them fast and we hit them hard, and it was at once awful and wonderful, as warfare generally is. It catches you up and carries you away, as it has always done since the Israelites went up against the Midianites. I ran around just like all my comrades, firing my gun, dodging bullets that whined overhead, shooting men and seeing them die.

It's a little embarrassing to admit what a thrill it was. But if combat weren't exciting, if men didn't love it, how could it have lasted for all these millennia? The pleasure's diminished, of course, if you get wounded, and it stops altogether if you get killed. But if you emerge without a scratch, and if your team wins, I swear there's nothing like it.

When it was over we piled our vehicles with their weapons, along with the sacks of rice and cases of canned goods and cartons of medical supplies we confiscated. Then, when the last of the prisoners had been shot, we placed our explosive charges, blew up the buildings, and headed back to camp.

I had just enough time to eat a meal and drink a pot of tea and tell Katya about the morning's action. And then the malaria hit me.

It was worse the second day. I couldn't lie still and it was torture to move. Everything hurt, and I was freezing and burning up all at once, and the fever had me out of my mind, hearing colors and seeing odors and tasting music. I had impassioned conversations with people I'd never met—Pyotr Kropotkin and Lajos Kossuth and Emilio Zapata, to name three who paid visits to my fever-wracked side. I had occasional moments of clarity, and I was just as glad when they were over, because my mind was such that I was better off out of it. Some of the time I was afraid I was going to die, and the rest of the time I was afraid I wasn't.

I don't know if the aspirin helped, or the quinine, but I took them when Katya gave them to me. I don't know if the shwe le maw helped, either, but I drank deep when Katya held a cup to my lips. Sometimes it was boiled water and sometimes it was the orange brandy. Maybe it helped. It certainly didn't hurt.

And sometime during the night the fever broke. Foul perspiration poured out of me in a flood, soaking the mattress under me and the covers piled on top of me. My pulse slowed and the pains in my limbs receded and I not only knew I was going to live, but I was even glad of it.

"Vanya?"

I looked up at her. "I think I saw angels," I said, "and you were one of them."

"You saw many people, Vanya. You had many conversations."

"I remember the one with Kropotkin," I said.

"I was asking him about some points that always bothered me in his pamphlet, *On Mutual Aid*. And he answered my questions, but I can't remember what he said."

"He was not really here, Vanya."

"Well, I know that," I said. "Still, if his arguments were valid, it would be useful if I could remember them. Whether he was here or not."

"You are here," she said. "That is what is important."

And damned if she didn't slip under the covers with me, with predictable (but still surprising) results.

Afterward she curled up beside me and slept, her breath warm against my shoulder. I thought about the events of the day, and the horrible joys of war. The only part I hadn't liked was when my Shan brothers had shot the handful of men who had tried to surrender. It was fairly standard—an insurgent army can't be expected to care for prisoners, and the troops who'd thrown up their hands had done so with no real hope of survival. Ne Win's men, never having signed the Geneva Convention, were not bound by it. They didn't torture their prisoners, or mock them, or make cruel sport of them. They simply gunned them down.

I understood it, but I didn't like it much. Aside from that, I had a distressingly good time. I shot some people before they could shoot me, I stood shoulder to shoulder with other like-minded men, and I had the good fortune to be on the winning side. When it was all over, we brought home six dead and four wounded, which had to rank as remarkably light casualties in a battle that had cost upward of a hundred and fifty government lives, plus the ten troops we'd gunned down at the roadblock checkpoint.

A famous victory, I thought. It wasn't the Battle of Blenheim, and it didn't have Robert Southey to write a poem about it, but when the Shan state achieved independence, it might rate a mention in the high school history books.

So I thought about it, and about the relationship of war and testosterone, and the previously unnoted aphrodisiacal effects of malaria. And about Stuart, in whose memory the day's slaughter had been undertaken.

And other things, things to think about while I waited for the dawn.

~

While Katya and I breakfasted on duck eggs and sticky rice, the rest of the camp was a beehive of activity. It was only a question of time until army headquarters in Rangoon sent a brigade to avenge yesterday's action, and Ne Win wanted to be prepared.

Katya wanted to know what would happen. I wondered myself. Would Ne Win try to defend the little compound? Or would his troops slip away into the hills, pausing now and then to ambush the SLORC regulars, then disappearing before the army could exact retribution?

There was something to be said for either approach, but we weren't going to be around for it. Because, as soon as we'd finished our meal, he put us in a car, assigned us a driver, and sent us off to Thailand.

"Evan Turner," he said, "you are a true Shan brother." He placed a hand on my head, where, were I still a monk, I'd be well advised to shave. "You were a splendid monk," he assured me, "but an even better soldier. A safe journey, my friend."

By nightfall we were at the border. We had to cross a river via a rope bridge, a passage I found scarier than the firefight the previous day. The third night of malarial fever was on me by then, which didn't make it easier. But we got across, and they found me a safe place to sweat out the fever, and I was better in the morning.

The following day we reached Chiang Mai, where we caught an overnight train to Bangkok. And by nightfall I was back where I'd started, in the little teahouse across the street from the Swan Hotel.

Mr. Sukhumvit wasn't there. I ordered a Kloster and a basket of prawn chips. I was on my third beer and my second basket of chips when he came in. He walked toward his usual table, then spotted me out of the corner of his eye. I looked different—my hair gone, my skin darkened by the sun and yellowed by malaria—but something clicked and he rec-

315

ognized me. He looked my way, and I nodded, and he came to the table.

"So," he said. "I heard you were dead."

"You can't believe everything you hear."

"You are quite right. I also heard you planted a bomb at Shwe Dagon Pagoda."

"That is not true either. Soon you will no doubt hear that I was involved in a massacre of a Burmese army post by an insurgent Shan force."

"The Shan are at peace with the government."

I smiled.

"Ah," he said. "I think you bring me valuable information. Tell me more, and then we will go eat some dog."

"To tell you the truth," I said, "I'm sick of dog."

"You must have eaten your fill of it in Burma."

"Day and night," I said. "It's hard for me to pass a fire hydrant."

"I do not understand."

"Never mind," I said. "There was some difficulty in Rangoon, as you may imagine. I find myself in need of a passport."

"Ah," he said.

"I thought you might be able to help."

"You need a passport."

"Two passports, actually." I took an envelope from my breast pocket, removed two pairs of inch-square photographs, one showing a man with his head shaved, the other a woman with long black hair. We'd had them

316

taken at a drugstore in Chiang Mai, right next door to the shop where Katya bought the wig.

"And here is the data for the passports," I said, and handed him a slip of paper.

"Evan Michael Tanner. And Katerina Romanoff. A Russian woman?"

"In part."

"The problem with American passports—"

"Is the scanner. I know. I thought perhaps passports of another country."

He nodded thoughtfully and named several countries. Some of them, like Vanuatu, had not even existed before I took my little trip to Union City. Then he mentioned Ireland, and I stopped him.

"As a matter of fact," I said, "I think I'm entitled to an Irish passport. They let you claim dual citizenship if you have an Irish grand-parent."

"And one of your grandparents came from Ireland?"

"My great-grandmother," I said. "That's not the same as a grandparent, but it ought to be close enough to qualify me for a forged pass-port."

"And your friend? She does not look Irish."

I squinted at the photo. "She could be Irish," I said. "In dim light."

"Romanoff is not an Irish name, is it?"

I reached for a pencil.

"Katherine O'Shea?" Katya said. "What kind of a name is Katherine O'Shea?"

"Well, it's Irish," I said.

"But—"

"As a matter of fact," I said, "it's a name with a lot of resonance to it. Kitty O'Shea was Parnell's girlfriend, and her jerk of a husband caused a scandal that ruined the man's career. It's a name with a real history to it."

"So is Romanoff, Evan."

"You can be Katya Romanoff as soon as we clear Immigration," I assured her. "You can be Katya Romanoff or Katya Singh or Katya Kovalshevsky, whatever you want. But first we have to get you into the country."

"When will we have the passports?"

"The day after tomorrow. And the day after that we fly from Bangkok to New York via Los Angeles."

"They gave you tickets?"

"They didn't really want to," I said. "But I had a return ticket in business class, and it was in my name even if I had lost it. I'll have to show them a passport to prove I'm really me, so I won't have the tickets in hand until I do, but once Sukhumvit comes through with the passports it won't be a problem. One ticket in business class more than covers two tickets in economy."

"Poor Evan. If you didn't have me along you could sit in the front of the plane."

"That's all right. Even the luggage compartment would feel luxurious to me after the past couple of weeks."

"What's the matter, Vanya?"

"Well, I'm sure I'll figure it out."

"What?"

"A way to pay for our passports. I showed Sukhumvit the ivory statues, and he all but laughed in my face. They may be worth something, they may even be museum quality, but this is no place to sell them. He's giving me a pretty good deal on the passports, but I don't know where I'm going to find the money."

"My poor little Vanya," she said. "Maybe it is not so bad after all that you have me with you."

And she twisted the ruby ring from her finger and dropped it in my palm.

Chapter Twenty-four

I thought you were dead," the Chief said. "There were these stories out of Burma. Great work, setting off a bomb at one of their sacred sites. Nothing quite gets a headline like blowing up the Holiest of Holies, eh?"

I'd been back for less than a week when the call came, and we were meeting in a bare-to-the-crumbling-walls apartment on the top floor of a tenement in Alphabet City. The building was abandoned, and I could see why. Squatters had nested in some of the other apartments, but only the Chief had wanted to climb five flights of stairs to this one.

How he finds these meeting places, or why he thinks they're suitable, is just one of the mysteries that hover about him.

"But then they arrested you and hanged you," he went on, "and I found that disturbing in the extreme. That's not like Tanner, I told myself. It's never happened before."

"Once is generally plenty," I said.

"And the irony of it," he said. "Here I'd just got you back after having lost you for what, twenty-five years?"

"Something like that."

He put his fingertips together, looking almost as though he were praying, which I somehow knew he was not. "One sends men out," he said, "knowing that there's a chance one will not see them again. Of all the burdens of command, that is by far the heaviest. Yet in this instance I had no real concern that you might be lost. I felt confident that you'd execute your assignment and return in good time, and in all likelihood net yourself a tidy profit in the bargain."

Some tidy profit, I thought. I'd lost everything I brought with me, including my flashlight and my Swiss Army knife, and I'd still be stuck in Bangkok but for Katya's ruby ring.

"The shock," he said, "when I learned you were dead. But of course, that was your doing, wasn't it? Covering your tracks by having someone else carry your name to the scaffold."

"This Rufus Crombie," I said. "Your...what? Employer?"

"Patron, you might say."

"How sure are you of him?"

He gave me a long look. "Why?" he said at length.

"I didn't arrange the bombing at Shwe Dagon Pagoda. It's about the last thing I would have done. Well, the second last, actually. The last thing would be harming Aung San Suu Kyi."

"That woman."

"Yes."

"But your assignment—"

"Was to destabilize the SLORC regime," I said, "and that would have been the worst way to do it. And bombing Shwe Dagon runs a close second. They framed me for it, and if they'd had the chance, they'd have hanged me for it. As it was, they did the next best thing. They hanged an Australian kid and said he was me." I drew a breath. "It was a setup from the jump. That's what I was there for. To be framed. And caught. And hanged."

He was sitting up straight now, a frown creasing his brow. All the years seemed to drop away, and he was his old self again, the man I'd known back when the Cold War was red hot. Of course he hadn't been all that sharp back then, but it was still comforting to see him as I remembered him.

"Report," he said.

When I'd finished he went to the window and spent a few minutes staring out. Then he said, "It's all very confusing."

"Yes."

"And unsettling as well. Disturbing, even."

"That too."

"You were set up, as you said. You also seem to have been protected. Someone arranged your escape from jail, for example."

"Unless I was supposed to be recaptured. But you're right, I had a guardian angel hovering around somewhere. The warning I got at Shwe Dagon was well sent."

"And someone killed the man who planted heroin in your luggage."

"But how did that work? I think that was all part of the frame, the heroin and the dead body, so that I could be charged with drug trafficking and murder at the same time. Who was the dead man in my bed at the guest house? And why had they chalked his temples so he would look like Harry Spurgeon?"

"Harry Spurgeon," the Chief said. "He's everywhere in this, isn't he?"

"But what's his job? Was he pulling my chestnuts out of the fire or poking them in deeper? I think he must have tipped off the cops that I was holed up in the Strand. If he knew the phones were out, he'd have been able to figure out that I could only have called from within the Strand. Then a simple inquiry at the front desk would have told him what room I was in. But who was he working for? Crombie?"

He sighed. "I'm not sure of Mr. Crombie," he said. "At first I found his idealism quite plausible. His wealth is literally beyond measurement. The desire for profit could hardly continue to motivate him. Having so much, how could he want more?"

"They always want more," I said.

"That's what I failed to grasp, my boy. That's how they get that rich in the first place. By never being satisfied with what they have. By always wanting more. Oh, I'll give Crombie the benefit of the doubt. I think he was sincere enough at the beginning, wanting to do some good in the world. But how could he avoid wanting to do himself some good at the same time?"

"And in Burma?"

"Trade concessions," he said. "Development rights. The Chinese have the inside track, and a main competitor of Crombie is hooked in tight with the Singapore Chinese. And Crombie's hand in glove with a consortium of Dutch and Belgians out of Jakarta."

He went into more detail than I needed to hear. Crombie, he felt sure, had not sent me to Burma in the hope that I'd fail, purposely sabotaging my mission in the bargain. But the Singapore faction could have had a spy in his organization, and Harry Spurgeon was very likely their man on the scene.

"They want SLORC in power," he said,

"and hanging an American and tying him to Jakarta would help reinforce their position enormously. Crombie can't really hope to get SLORC out of there, but anything that loosens their hold helps pressure them into opening up the country to other interests, not just handing it to the Chinks. Well, there are all sorts of ramifications, aren't there?"

We discussed some of them in some detail. Then he said, "I'll tell you this much, Tanner. Mr. Crombie is well pleased with your efforts."

"He is?"

"He likes results," he said, "and you've produced some, or at least it looks that way. There seems to be a full-blown insurrection in the Shan state, and some of the other hill tribes are said to be joining in. Now you and I know it for sheer coincidence, but if Rufus Crombie thinks otherwise, why don't we let ourselves take the credit?"

"Why not?"

"SLORC put a lot of effort into making peace with the ethnic minorities. The last thing they wanted was for the Shan and the other hill dwellers to make common cause with that woman and her pro-democracy faction, but that's what seems to be happening. And SLORC is making concessions on reforms. They've restored journalists' access to that woman, and she's giving interviews left and right. And they've allowed other trade interests to come in and compete with the fellows from Singapore."

"So it all worked out," I said.

"And there ought to be a bonus for you," he said, "seeing as you're alive after all, and came out of the affair empty-handed. I'll see that you get it, Tanner. And I suppose you'll need a new passport as well."

"The one I have is Irish," I said, "and I'm afraid it's not authentic."

"You might as well have a fraudulent American one to go with it. I've found an absolute wizard who can fabricate passports that pass the scanner. Build a better mousetrap, eh?"

"While he's at it," I said, "how is he on whipping up phony green cards?"

"Child's play for him, I should think. But what on earth do you need with a green card?"

"It's not for me," I said.

"My Vanya," Katya said, the green card in hand. "Now I am legal? I can stay in this country?"

"You're as close to legal as you can get," I told her. "The government didn't issue that particular green card, but it's every bit as good as the real one. No INS agent could find anything wrong with it."

"Katarina Romanoff. That is a good name, yes?"

"It should guarantee you a good table in any restaurant in Brighton Beach."

And that was where she lived now, in the Russian neighborhood at the end of the subway line in Brooklyn. She'd stayed on 107th Street at first, but neither she nor Minna was entirely at ease with the arrangement, and after a week it was clear to all of us that she needed a place of her own. When I took her to Brighton Beach for dinner and a walk around the neighborhood, she felt instantly at home.

Our own romance had been very much a creature of circumstance, fueled by shwe le maw and malaria, and we were both ready for her to take a small apartment in a good Russian neighborhood and make a life for herself. Lately she'd been keeping company with a Russian Jewish gangster who was, she assured me, very proud of her heritage. That her forebears had very likely launched pogroms against his forebears evidently didn't distress him.

Minna was relieved when Katya moved out, and so was I, truth to tell. It was good to have the apartment to ourselves again. I got busy with my correspondence, catching up via letters and faxes and e-mail with some very good people all over the world. I got to work studying Burmese in earnest, and the Shan language too, while I was at it. I didn't expect to go back to Burma, but I hadn't expected to go there the first time, either, and if I did return I'd be prepared.

I relaxed, I settled in. I got a job writing a thesis—on Prince Kropotkin, coincidentally enough, and it infuriated me that I couldn't remember the confidences he'd shared with me while I writhed in the throes of malaria.

Speaking of malaria, I found a doctor who thought he could knock it out permanently.

So far I haven't had any more attacks, but it's too early to say whether or not the cure is permanent. Maybe it will hang on, making its unholy presence known every once in a while.

Like Harry Spurgeon.

"Hello?"

"Evan Tanner," a voice said. "Can you believe it? I heard you were dead."

"But it turned out I was only sleeping."

"So it would appear, yes. You never did come to tea that afternoon, old boy. I waited and waited."

"I hope you ate all the sticky buns."

He laughed. The connection was clear as a bell, but that didn't mean he was down the block. He could be anyplace with decent phone service, so all that ruled out was Burma.

"I just wanted to pay my respects," he said, "and to say I'm just as glad it wasn't your neck that got stretched by a Burmese rope."

"Just as glad, are you?"

"Indeed. You're a worthy adversary, Tanner. If that indeed is what we were this time around. Sometimes it's hard to be sure."

"I suppose it is."

"Do you want to know something? I have the certain feeling that we'll meet again. Have you ever had that sort of feeling about someone?"

"Once or twice."

"I have it now. Perhaps we will be on the same

side next time around. That would be inter-esting, wouldn't it? You and I, working together."

"Interesting."

"Or we might come up against one another, and that would be interesting, too. In another way, of course."

"Of course."

"Well," he said. "I guess that's all I have to say, Tanner. That and to wish you good luck."

I looked over at the shelf above the fireplace, where the three ivory figures stood in Oriental— sorry, Asian—splendor. Good Luck, Good Health, and Long Life.

"Thanks," I said.

"I'll be seeing you, Tanner."

"Yes," I said. "You probably will."